AYALA'S ANGEL

BY

ANTHONY TROLLOPE,

AUTHOR OF " DOCTOR THORNE," " THE PRIME MINISTER," " ORLEY FARM,"
&c., &c.

IN THREE VOLUMES.

VOL. I.

LONDON :

CHAPMAN AND HALL (LIMITED),

11, HENRIETTA STREET, COVENT GARDEN.

1881.

CONTENTS OF VOL. I.

CONTENTS.

AYALA'S ANGEL.

CHAPTER I.

THE TWO SISTERS.

When Egbert Dormer died he left his two daughters utterly penniless upon the world, and it must be said of Egbert Dormer that nothing else could have been expected of him. The two girls were both pretty, but Lucy, who was twenty-one, was supposed to be simple and comparatively unattractive, whereas Ayala was credited,—as her somewhat romantic name might show,—with poetic charm and a taste for romance. Ayala when her father died was nineteen.

We must begin yet a little earlier and say that there had been,—and had died many years before the death of Egbert Dormer, a clerk in the Admiralty, by name Reginald Dosett, who, and whose wife, had been conspicuous for personal beauty. Their charms were gone, but the records of them had been left in various grandchildren. There had been a son born to Mr. Dosett, who was also a Reginald and a clerk in the Admiralty, and who also, in his turn, had been a handsome man. With him,

VOL. I. B

in his decadence, the reader will become acquainted. There were also two daughters, whose reputation for perfect feminine beauty had never been contested. The elder had married a city man of wealth,—of wealth when ho married her, but who had become enormously wealthy by the time of our story. He had when he married been simply Mister, but was now Sir Thomas Tringle, Baronet and was senior partner in the great firm of Travers and Treason. Of Traverses and Treasons there were none left in these days, and Mr. Tringle was supposed to manipulate all the millions with which the great firm in Lombard Street was concerned. He had married old Mr. Dosett's eldest daughter, Emmeline, who was now Lady Tringle, with a house at the top of Queen's Gate, rented at £1,500 a year, with a palatial moor in Scotland, with a seat in Sussex, and as many carriages and horses as would suit an archduchess. Lady Tringle had everything in the world ; a son, two daughters, and an open-handed stout husband, who was said to have told her that money was a matter of no consideration.

The second Miss Dosett, Adelaide Dosett, who had been considerably younger than her sister, had insisted upon giving herself to Egbert Dormer, the artist, whose death we commemorated in our first line. But she had died before her husband. Tliey who remembered the two Miss Dosetts as girls were wont to declare that, though Lady Tringle might, perhaps, have had the advantage in perfection of feature and in unequalled symmetry, Adelaide had been the more attractive from expression and bril-

liancy. To her Lord Sizes Lad offered his hand and coronet, promising to abandon for her sake all the haunts of his matured life. To her Mr. Tringle had knelt before he had taken the elder sister. For her Mr. Progrum, the popular preacher of the day, for a time so totally lost himself that he v/as nearly minded to go over to Rome. ' She was said to have had oflPers from a widowed Lord Chancellor and from a Russian prince. Her triumphs would have quite obliterated that of her sister had she not insisted on marrying Egbert Dormer.

Then there had been, and still was, Reginald Dosett, the son of old Dosett, and the eldest of the family. He too had married, and was now living with his wife; but to them had no children been born, luckily, as he was a poor man. Alas, to a beautiful son it is not often that beauty can be a fortune as to a daughter. Young Reginald Dosett,—he is anything now but young,—had "done but iittle for himself with his beauty, having simply married the estimable daughter of a brother clerk. Kow, at the age of fifty, he had his £900 a year from his office, and might have lived in fair comfort had he not allowed a small millstone of debt to hang round his neck from his earlier years. But still he lived creditably in a small but very genteel house at Netting Hill, and would have undergone any want rather than have declared himself to be a poor man to his rich relations the Tringles.

Such were now the remaining two children of old Mr. Dosett,— Lady Tringle, namely, and Reginald Dosett, the clerk in the Admiralty. Adelaide, the beauty in chief of

b2

AY ALAS ANGEL.

the family, was gone; and now also her husband, the improvident artist, had followed his wife. Dormer had been by no means a failing artist. He had achieved great honour,—had at an early age been accepted into the Royal Academy,—had sold pictures to illustrious princes and more illustrious dealers, had been engraved and had lived to see his own works resold at five times their original prices. Egbert Dormer might also have been a rich man. But he had a taste for other beautiful things besides a wife. The sweetest little phaeton that was to cost nothing, the most perfect bijou of a little house at South Kensington,—he had boasted that it might have been packed without trouble in his brother-in-law Tringle's dining-room,—the simplest little gem for his wife, just a blue set of china for his dinner table, just a painted cornice for his studio, just satin hangings for his drawing-room,— and a few simple ornaments for his little girls; these with a few rings for himself, and velvet suits of clothing in which to do his painting; these, with a few little dinner parties to show off his blue china, were the first and last of his extravagances. But when he went, and when his pretty things were sold, there was not enough to cover his debts. There was, however, a sweet savour about his name. When he died it was said of him that his wife's death had killed him. He had dropped his pallette, refused to finish the ordered portrait of a princess, and had simply turned himself round and died.

Then there were the two daughters, Lucy and Ayala. It should be explained that though a proper family inter-

course had always been maintained between the three families, the Tringles, the Dormers, and the Dosetts, there had never been cordiality between the first and the two latter. The wealth of the Tringles had seemed to convey with it a fetid odour. Egbert Dormer, with every luxury around him which money could purchase, had affected to despise the heavy magnificence of the Tringles. It may be that he affected a fashion higher than that which the Tringles really attained. Reginald Dosett, who was neither brilliant nor fashionable, was in truth independent, and, perhaps, a little thin-skinned. He would submit to no touch of arrogance from Sir Thomas; and Sir Thomas seemed to carry arrogance in his brow and in his paunch. It was there rather, perhaps, than in his heart; but there are men to whom a knack of fumbling their money in their pockets and of looking out from under penthouse brows over an expanse of waistcoat, gives an air of overweening pride which their true idiosyncracies may not justify. To Dosett had, perhaps, been spoken a word or two which on some occasion he had inwardly resented, and from thenceforward he had ever been ready to league with Dormer against the " bullionaire," as they agreed to call Sir Thomas. Lady Tringle had even said a word to her sister, Mrs. Dormer, as to expenses, and that had never been forgiven by the artist. So things were when Mrs. Dormer died first; and so they remained when her husband followed her.

Then there arose a sudden necessity for action, which, for a while, brought Reginald Dosett into connexion with Sir Thomas and Lady Tringle. Something must be done

G AY ALA'S ANGEL.

for the poor girls. That the something should come out of the pocket of Sir Thomas would have seemed to be natural. Money with him was no object,—not at alb Another girl or two would be nothing to him,—as regarded simple expenditure. But the care of a human being is an important matter, and so Sir Thomas knew. Dosett had not a child at all, and would be the better for such a windfall. Dosett he supposed to be,—in his, Dosett's way,—fairly well off. So he made this proposition. He would take one girl and let Dosett take the other. To this Lady Tringle added her proviso, that she should have the choice. To her nerves affairs of taste were of such paramount importance ! To this Dosett yielded. The matter was decided in Lady Tringle's back drawing-room. Mrs. Dosett was not even consulted in that matter of choice, having already acknowledged the duty of mothering a motherless child. Dosett had thought that the buUionaire should have said a word as to some future provision for the penniless girl, for whom he would be able to do so little. But Sir Thomas had said no such word, and Dosett, himself, lacked both the courage and the coarseness to allude to the matter. Then Lady Tringle declared that she must have Ayala^ and so the matter was settled. Ayala the romantic; Ayala the poetic I It was a matter of course that Ayala should be chosen. Ayala had already been made intimate with the magnificent saloons of the Tringles, and had been felt by Lady Tringle to be an attraction. Her long dark black locks, which had never hitherto been tucked up, which were never curled, which were never so long as to be awkward;

were already known as being the loveliest locks in London. She sang as though Nature had intended her to be a singing-bird,—requiring no education, no labour. She had been once for three months in Paris, and French had come naturally to her. Her father had taught her something of his art, and flatterers had already begun to say that she was born to be the one great female artist of the world. Her hands, her feet, her figure were perfect. Though she was as yet but nineteen, London had already begun to talk about Ayala Dormer. Of course Lady Tringle chose Ayak, not remembering at the moment that her own daughters might probably be superseded by their cousin.

And, therefore, as Lady Tringle said herself to Lucy with her sweetest smile—Mrs. Dosett had chosen Lucy. The two girls were old enough to know something of the meaning of such a choice. Ayala, the younger, was to be adopted into immense wealth, and Lucy was to be given up to comparative poverty. She knew nothing of her uncle Dosett's circumstances, but the genteel house at Netting Hill,—No. 3, Kingsbury Crescent,—was known to her, and was but a poor affair as compared even with the bijou in which she had hitherto lived. Her aunt Dosett never rose to any vehicle beyond a four-wheeler, and was careful even in thinking of that accommodation. Ayala would be whirled about the park by a wire-wig and a pair of brown horses which they had heard it said were not to be matched in London. Ayala would be carried with her aunt and her cousin to the show-room of Madame

Tonsonville, the great French milliner of Bond Street^ whereas she, Lucy, might too probably be called on to make her own gowns. All the fashion of Queen's Gate, something, perhajDs, of the fashion of Eaton Square, would be open to Ayala. Lucy understood enough to know that Ayala's own charms might probably cause still more august gates to be opened to her, whereas Aunt Dosett entered no gates. It was quite natural that Ayala should be chosen. Lucy acknowledged as much to herself. But they were sisters, and had been so near! By what a chasm would they be dissevered, now so far asunder!

Lucy herself was a lovely girl, and knew her own loveliness. She was fairer than Ayala, somewhat taller, and much more quiet in her demeanour. She was also clever, but her cleverness did not show itself so quickly. She was a musician, whereas her sister could only sing. She could really draw, whereas her sister would rush away into effects in which the drawing was not always very excellent. Lucy was doing the best she could for herself, knowing something of French and German, though as yet not very fluent with her tongue. The two girls were, in truth, both greatly gifted ; but Ayala had the gift of showing her talent without thought of showing it. Lucy saw it all, and knew that she was outshone ; but how great had been the price of the outshining !

The artist's house had been badly ordered, and the two girls were of better disposition and better conduct than might have been expected from such fitful training. Ayala had been the father's pet, and Lucy the mother's.

Parents Jo ill in making pets, and here they had done ill. Ajala had been taught to think herself the favourite, because the artist, himself, had been more prominent before the world than his wife. But the evil had not been lasting enough to have made bad feeling between the sisters.

Lucy knew that her sister had been preferred to her, but she had been self-denying enough to be aware that some such preference was due to Ayala. She, too, admired Ayala, and loved her with her whole heart. And Ayala was always good to her,—had tried to divide everything,—had assumed no preference as a right. The two were true sisters. But when it was decided that Lucy was to go to Kingsbury Crescent the diflPerence was very great. The two girls, on their father's death, had been taken to the great red brick house in Queen's Gate, and from thence, three or four days after the funeral, Lucy was to be transferred to her Aunt Dosett. Hitherto there had been little between them but weeping for their father. Now had come the hour of pai'ting.

The tidings had been communicated to Lucy, and to Lucy alone, by Aunt Tringle,—" As you are the eldest, dear, we think that you will be best able to be a comfort to your aunt," said Lady Tringle.

I will do the best I can. Aunt Emmeline," said Lucy, declaring to herself that, in giving such a reason, her aunt was lying basely.

" I am sure you will. Poor dear Ayala is younger than her cousins, and will be more subject to them." So in truth was Lucy younger than her cousins, but of that

she said nothing. " I am sure you will agree with me that it is best that we should have the youngest."

'^ Perhaps it is, Aunt Emmeline."

" Sir Thomas would not have had it any other way," said Lady Tringle, with a little severity, feeling that Lucy's accord had hardly been as generous as it should be. But she recovered herself quickly, remembering hov,^ much it was that Ayala was to get, how much that Lucy was to lose. " But, my dear, we shall see you very often, you know. It is not so far across the park; and when we do have a few parties again "

" Oh, aunt, 1 am not thinking of that."

" Of course not. We can none of us think of it just now. But when the time does come of course we shall always have you, just as if you were one of us." Then her aunt gave her a roll of bank-notes, a little present of twenty-five pounds, to begin the world with, and told her that the carriage should take her to Kingsbury Crescent on the following morning. On the whole Lucy behaved well and left a pleasant impression on her aunt's mind. The difference between Queen's Gate and Kingsbury Crescent,—between Queen's Gate and Kingsbury Crescent for life,—was indeed great I

" I wish it were you, with all my heart," said Ayala, clinging to her sister.

" It could not have been me."

" Why not I"

" Because you are so pretty and you are so clever."

"No I"

" Yes ! If we were to be separated of course it would be so. Do not suppose, dear, that I am disappointed."

"Iam."

"If I can only like Aunt Margaret,"—Aunt Margaret was Mrs. Dosett, with whom neither of the girls had hitherto become intimate, and who was known to be quiet, domestic, and economical, but who had also been spoken of as having a will of her own,—" I shall do better with her than you would, Ayala."

" I don't see why."

" Because I can remain quiet longer than you. It will be very quiet. I wonder how we shall see each other I I cannot walk across the park alone."

" Uncle Eeg will bring you."

" Not often, I fear. Uncle Keg has enough to do with his office."

" You can come in a cab."

" Cabs cost money, Ayey dear.

" But Uncle Thomas "

" We had better understand one or two things, Ayala. Uncle Thomas will pay everything for you, and as he is very rich things will come as they are wanted. There will be cabs, and if not cabs, carriages. Uncle Heg must pay for me, and he is very very kind to do so. But as he is not rich, there will be no carriages, and not a great many cabs. It is best to understand it all."

" But they will send for you."

" That's as they please. I don't think they will very often. I would not for the world put you against Uncle

Thomas, but I have a feeling that I shall never get on with him. But you will never separate yourself from me, Ayala!"

" Separate myself!"

'You will not—not be my sister because you will be one of these rich ones ? "

" Oh, I wish,—I wish that I were to be the poor one. I'm sure I should like it best. I never cared about being rich. Oh, Lucy, can't we make them change ? "

" No, Ayey, my own, we can't make them change. And if we could, we wouldn't. It is altogether best that you should be a rich Tringle and that I should be a poor Dosett."

" I will always be a Dormer," said Ayala, proudly.

" And I will always be so too, my pet. But you should be a bright Dormer among the Tringles, and I will be a dull Dormer among the Dosetts. I shall begrudge nothing, if only we can see each other."

So the two girls were parted, the elder being taken away to Kingsbury Crescent and the latter remaining with her rich relations at Queen's Gate. Ayala had not pro-babl\'7d' realized the great diiference of their future positions. To her the attractions of wealth and the privations of comparative poverty had not made themselves as yet palpably plain. They do not become so manifest to those to whom the wealth falls,—at any rate, not in early life,— as to the opposite party. If the other lot had fallen to Ayala she might have felt it more keenly.

Lucy felt it keenly enough. Without any longing after

the magnificence of tlie Tringle mansion she knew how great was the fall from her father's well-assorted luxuries and prettinesses down to the plain walls, tables, and chairs of her Uncle Dosett's house. Her aunt did not subscribe to Mudie's. The old piano had not been tuned for the last ten years. The parlour-maid was a cross old woman. Her aunt always sat in the dining-room through the greater part of the day, and of all rooms the dining-room in Kingsbury Crescent was the dingiest. Lucy understood very well to what she was going. Her father and mother were gone. Her sister was divided from her. Her life offered for the future nothing to her. But with it all she carried a good courage. There was present to her an idea of great misfortune; but present to her at the same time an idea also that she would do her duty.

CHAPTER II.

LUCY WITH HER AUNT DOSETT.

For some days Lucy found herself to be absolutely crushed,—in the first place, by a strong resolution to do some disagreeable duty, and then by a feeling that there was no duty the doing of which was within her reach. It seemed to her that her whole life was a blank. Her father's house had been a small affair and considered to be poor when compared with the Tringle mansion, but she now became aware that everything there had in truth abounded. In one little room there had been two or three hundred beautifully bound books. That Mudie's unnumbered volumes should come into the house as they were wanted had almost been as much a provision of nature as water, gas, and hot rolls for breakfast. A piano of the best kind, and always in order, had been a first necessary of life, and, like other necessaries, of course, forthcoming. There had been the little room in which the girls painted, joining their father's studio and sharing its light, surrounded by every pretty female appliance. Then there had always been visitors. The artists from Kensington had been wont to gather there, and the artists' daughters, and perhaps the artists' sons. Every day had had its round of delights,—its round of occupations, as the girls would call them. There had been some reading, some painting, sonie music,—perhaps a little needlework and a great deal of talking.

How little do we know how other people live in the houses close to us! We see the houses looking like our own, and we see the people come out of them looking like ourselves. But a Chinaman is not more different from the English John Bull than is No. 10 from No. 11. Here there are books, paintings, music, wine, a little dilettanti getting-up of subjects of the day, a little dilettanti thinking on great affairs, perhaps a little dilettanti religion; few domestic laws, and those easily broken ; few domestic duties, and those easily evaded; breakfast when you will, with dinner almost as little binding, with much company and acknowledged aptitude for idle luxury. That is life at No. 10. At No. 11 everything is cased in iron. Tliere shall be equal plenty, but at No. 11 even plenty is a bondage. Duty rules everything, and it has come to be acknowledged that duty is to be hard. So many hours of needlework, so many hours of books, so many hours of prayer ! That all the household shall shiver before daylight, is a law, the breach of which by any member either augurs sickness or requires condign punishment. To be comfortable is a sin ; to laugh is almost equal to bad language. Such and so various is life at No. 10 and at No. 11.

From one extremity, as far removed, to another poor Lucy had been conveyed; though all the laws were not exactly carried out in Kingsbury Crescent as they have been described at No. 11. The enforced prayers were not there, nor the early hours. It was simply necessary that Lucy should be down to breakfast at nine, and had she not appeared nothing violent would have been said. But it was required of her that she should endure a life which was altogether without adornment Uncle Dosett himself, as a clerk in the Admiralty, had a certain position in the world which was sufficiently maintained by decent apparel, a well-kept, slight, grey whisker, and an umbrella which seemed never to have been violated by use. Dosett was was popular at his office, and was regarded by his brother clerks as a friend. But no one was acquainted with his house and home. They did not dine with him, nor he with them. There are such men in all public offices,—not the less respected because of the quiescence of their lives. It was known of him that he had burdens, though it was not known what his burdens were. His friends, therefore, were intimate with him as far as the entrance into Somerset House,—where his duties lay,—and not beyond it. Lucy was destined to know the other side of his affairs, the domestic side, which was as quiet as the official side. The link between them, which consisted of a journey by the Underground Kailway to the Temple Station, and a walk home along the Embankment and across the parks and Kensington Gardens, was the pleasantest part of Dosett's life.

Mr. Dosett's salary has been said to be £900 per annum. What a fund of comfort there is in the word I When the youth of nineteen enters an office how far beyond want would he think himself should he ever reach the pecuniary-paradise of £900 a-year I How he would see all his friends, and in return be seen of them I But when the income has been achieved its capabilities are found to be by no means endless. And Dosett in the earlier spheres of his married life had unfortunately anticipated something of such comforts. For a year or two he had spent a little money imprudently. Something which he had expected had not come to him ; and, as a result, he had been forced to borrow, and to insure his life for the amount borrowed. Then, too, when that misfortune as to the money came,—came from the non-realization of certain claims which his wife had been supposed to possess,—provision had also to be made for her. In this way an assurance office eat up a large fraction of his income, and left him with means which in truth were very straitened. Dosett at once gave up all glories of social life, settled himself in Kingsbury Crescent, and resolved to satisfy himself with his walk across the park and his frugal dinner afterwards. He never complained to any one, nor did his wife. He was a man small o nough to be contented with a thin existence, but far too great to ask any one to help him to widen it. Sir Thomas Tringle never heard of that £175 paid annually to the assurance office, nor had Lady Tringle, Dosett's sister, even heard of it. When it was suggested to him that he should take one of the Dormer girls, he consented to take her and said nothing of the assurance office.

Mrs. Dosett had had her great blow in life, and had suffered more perhaps than her husband. This money had

VOL. I. c

been expected. There had been no doubt of the money,— at any rate on her part. It did not depend on an old gentleman with or without good intentions, but simply on his death. There was to be ever so much of it, four or five hundred a-year, which would last for ever. When the old gentleman died, which took place some ten years after Dosett's marriage, it was found that the money, tied tight as it had been by half-a-dozen lawyers, had in some fashion vanished. Whither it had gone is little to our purpose, but it had gone. Then there came a great crash upon the Dosetts, which she for a while had been hardly able to endure.

But when she had collected herself together after the crash, and had made up her mind, as had Dosett also, to the nature of the life which they must in future lead, she became more stringent in it even than he. He could bear and say nothing; but she, in bearing, found herself compelled to say much. It had been her fault,—the fault of people on her side,—and she would fain have fed her husband with the full flowery potato while she ate only the rind. She told him, unnecessarily, over and over again, that she had ruined him by her marriage. No such idea was ever in his head. The thing had come, and so it must be. There was food to eat, potatoes enough for both, and a genteel house in which to live. He could still be hapj^y if she would not groan. A certain amount of groaning she did postpone while in his presence. The sewing of seams, and the darning of household linen, which in his eyes amounted to groaning, was done in his absence.

After their genteel dinner he would sleep a little, and she would knit. He would have his glass of wine, but would make his bottle of port last almost for a week. This was the house to which Lucy Dormer was brought when Mr. Dosett had consented to share with Sir Thomas the burden left by the death of the improvident artist.

When a month passed by Lucy began to think that time itself would almost drive her mad. Her father had died early in September. The Tringles had then, of course, been out of town, but Sir Thomas and his wife had found themselves compelled to come up on such an Oiccasion. Something they knew must be done about the girls, and they had not chosen that that something should be done in their absence. Mr. Dosett was also enjoying his official leave of absence for the year, but was enjoying it within the economical precincts of Kingsbury Crescent. There was but seldom now an excursion for him or his wife to the joys of the country. Once, some years ago, they had paid a visit to the palatial luxuries of Glenbogie, but the delights of the place had not paid for the expense of the long journey. They, therefore, had been at hand to undertake their duties. Dosett and Tringle, with a score of artists, had followed poor Dormer to his grave in Kensal Green, and then Dosett and Tringle had parted again, probably not to see each other for another term of years.

" My dear, what do you like to do with your time ?" Mrs. Dosett said to her niece, after the first week. At this time Lucy's wardrobe was not yet of a nature to need

c 2

much work over its ravages. The Dormer girls had hardly known where their frocks had come from when they wanted frocks,—hardly with more precision than the Tringle girls. Frocks had come—dark, gloomy frocks, lately, alas ! And these, too, had now ccme a second time. Let creditors be ever so unsatisfied, new raiment will always be found for mourning families. Everything about Lucy was nearly new. The need of repairing would come upon her by degrees, but it had not come as yet. Therefore there had seemed, to the anxious aunt, to be a necessity for some such question as the above.

" I'll do anything you like, aunt," said Lucy.

" It is not for me, my dear. I get through a deal of work, and am obliged to do so." She was, at this time, sitting with a sheet in her lap, which she was turning. Lucy had, indeed, once offered to assist, but her assistance had been rejected. This had been two days since, and she had not renewed the proposal as she should have done. This had been mainly from bashfulness. Though the work would certainly be distasteful to her, she would do it. But she had not liked to seem to interfere, not having as yet fallen into ways of intimacy with her aunt. " I don't want to burden you with my task-work," continued Mrs. Dosett, " but I am afraid you seem to be listless."

" I was reading till just before you spoke," said Lucy, again turning her eyes to the little volume of poetry, which was one of the few treasures which she had brought away with her from her old home.

'^ Reading is very well, but I do not like it as an excuse,

Lucy." Lucy's anger boiled within her when she was told of an excuse, and she declared to herself that she could never like her aunt. '^ I am quite sure that for young girls, as well as for old women, there must be a great deal of waste time unless there be needle and thread always about. And I know, too, unless ladies are well off, they cannot afford to waste time any more than gentlemen."

In the whole course of her life nothing so much like scolding as this had ever been addressed to her. So at least thought Lucy at that moment. Mrs. Dosett had intended the remarks all in good part, thinking them to be simply fitting from an aunt to a niece. It was her duty to give advice, and for the giving of such advice some day must be taken as the beginning. She had purposely allowed a week to run by, and now she had spoken her word,—as she thought in good season.

To Lucy it was a new and most bitter experience. Though she was reading the " Idylls of the King," or pretending to read them, she was, in truth, thinking of all that had gone from her. Her mind had, at that moment, been intent upon her mother, who, in all respects, had been so different from this careful, sheet-darning housewife of a woman. And in thinking of her mother there had no doubt been regrets for many things of which she would not have ventured to speak as sharing her thoughts with the memory of her mother, but which were nevertheless there to add darkness to the retrospective. Everything behind had been so bright, and everything behind had gone away from her! Everything before was so gloomy, and everything before must last for so long! After her aunt's lecture about wasted time Lucy sat silent for a few minutes, and then burst into uncontrolled tears.

" I did not mean to vex you," said her aunt.

" I was thinking of my—darling, darling mamma," sobbed Lucy.

" Of course, Lucy, you will think of her. How should you not ? And of your father. Those are sorrows which must be borne. But sorrows such as those are much lighter to the busy than to the idle. I sometimes think that the labourers grieve less for those they love than we do just because they have not time to grieve."

" I wish I were a labourer then," said Lucy, through her tears.

" You may be if you will. The sooner you begin to be a labourer the better for yourself and for those about you."

That Aunt Dosett's voice was harsh was not her fault,— nor that in the obduracy of her daily life she had lost much of her original softness. She had simply meant to be useful, and to do her duty ; but in telling Lucy that it would be better that the labouring should be commenced at once for the sake of '^ those about you,"—who could only be Aunt Dosett herself,—she had seemed to the girl to be harsh, selfish, and almost unnatural. The volume of poetry fell from her hand, and she jumped up from the chair quickly. " Give it me at once," she said, taking

hold of the sheet,—which was not itself a pleasant object; Lucy had never seen such a thing at the bijou. " Give it me at once," she said, and clawed the long folds of linen nearly out of her aunt's lap.

" I did not mean anything of the kind," said Aunt Dosett. ^^ You should not take me up in that way. I am speaking only for your good, because I know that you should not dawdle away your existence. Leave the sheet."

Lucy did leave the sheet, and then, sobbing violently, ran out of the room up to her own chamber. Mrs. Dosett determined that she would not follow her. She partly forgave the girl because of her sorrows, partly reminded herself that she was not soft and facile as had been her sister-in-law, Lucy's mother; and then, as she continued her work, she assured herself that it w^ould be best to let her niece have her cry out upstairs. Lucy's violence had astonished her for a moment, but she had taught herself to think it best to allow such little ebullitions to pass off by themselves.

Lucy, when she was alone, flung herself upon her bed in absolute agony. She thought that she had misbehaved, and yet how cruel,—how harsh had been her aunt's words ! If she, the quiet one, had misbehaved, what would Ayala have done ? And how was she to find strength with which to look forward to the future ? She struggled hard with herself for a resolution. Should she detei'mine that she would henceforward darn sheets morning, noon, and night till she worked her fingers to the bone ? Perhaps there had been something of truth in that assertion of her aunt's

that the labourers have no time to grieve. As everything else was shut out from her, it might be well for her to darn sheets. Should she rush down penitent and beg her aunt to allow her to commence at once ?

She would have done it as far as the sheets were concerned, but she could not do it as regarded her aunt. She could put herself into unison with the crumpled soiled linen, but not with the hard woman.

Oh, how terrible was the change! Her father and \uv mother who had been so o^entle to her! All the sweet prettinesses of her life ! All her occupations, all her friends, all her delights ! Even Ayala was gone from her ! How was she to bear it? She begrudged Ayala nothing,—no, nothing. But yet it was hard! Ayala was to have everything. Aunt Emmeline,—though they had not hitherto been very fond of Aunt Emmeline,—was sweetness itself as compared with this woman. " The sooner you begin to labour the better for yourself and those about you." Would it not have been fitter that she should have been sent at once to some actual poor-house in which there would have been no mistake as to her position ?

That it should all have been decided for her, for her and Ayala, not by any will of their own, not by any concert between themselves, but simply by the fantasy of another I Why should she thus be made a slave to the fantasy of any one I Let Ayala have her uncle's wealth and her aunt's palaces at her command, and she would walk out simply a pauper into the world,—into some workhouse, so that at least she need not be obedient to the harsh voice

and the odious common sense of her Aunt Dosett! But how should she take herself to some workhouse ? In what wa\'7d^ could she prove her right to be admitted even then ? It seemed to her that the same decree which had admitted Ayala into the golden halls of the fairies had doomed her not only to poverty, but to slavery. There was no escape for her from her aunt and her aunt's sermons. Oh, Ayala, my darling,—my own one; oh, Ayala, if you did but know !" she said to herself. What would Ayala think, how would Ayala bear it, could she but guess by what a gulf was her heaven divided from her sister's hell! "I will never tell her," she said to herself. " I will die, and she shall never know."

As she lay there sobbing all the gilded things of the world were beautiful in her eyes. Alas, yes, it was true. The magnificence of the mansion at Queen's Gate, the glories of Glenbogie, the closely studied comforts of Merle Park, as the place in Sussex was called, all the carriages and horses, Madame Tonsonville and all the draperies, the seats at the Albert Hall into which she had been accustomed to go with as much ease as into her bed-room, the box at the opera, the pretty furniture, the frequent gems, even the raiment which would make her pleasing to the eyes of men whom she would like to please-—all these things grew in her eyes and became beautiful. No. 3, Kingsbury Crescent, was surely, of all places on the earth's surface, the most ugly. And yet,—yet she had endeavoured to do her duty. *^ If it had been the workhouse I could have borne it," she said to herself; " but not to be

the slave of my Aunt Dosett!" Again she appealed to her sister, " Oh, Ayala, if you did but know it!" Then she remembered herself, declaring that it might have been worse to Ayala than even to her, " If one had to bear it, it was better for me," she said, as she struggled to prepare herself for her uncle's dinner.

CHAPTER III.

Lucy's troubles.

The evening after the affair with the sheet went off quietly, as did many days and many evenings. Mrs. Dosett was wise enough to forget the little violence and to forget also the feeling which had been displayed. When Lucy first asked for some household needlework, which she did with a faltering voice and shame-faced remembrance of her fault, her aunt took it all in good part and gave her a task somewhat lighter as a beginning than the handling of a sheet. Lucy sat at it and suffered. She went on sitting and suffering. She told herself that she was a martyr at every stitch she made. As she occupied the seat opposite to her aunt's accustomed chair she would hardly speak at all, but would keep her mind always intent on Ayala and the joys of Ayala's life. That they who had been born together, sisters, with equal fortunes, who had so closely lived together, should be sundered so utterly one from the other; that the one should be so exalted and the other so debased! And why? What justice had there been? Could it be from heaven or even from earth that the law had gone forth for such a division of the things of the world between them ?

" You have got very little to say to a person ?" said Aunt Dosett, one morning. Thisj too, was a reproach. This, too, was scolding. And yet Aunt Dosett had intended to be as pleasant as she knew how.

" I have very little to say," replied Lucy, with repressed anger.

"But why?"

" Because I am stupid," said Lucy. " Stupid people can't talk. You should have had Ayala."

" I hope you do not envy Ayala her fortune, Lucy?" A woman with any tact would not have asked such a question at such a time. She should have felt that a touch of such irony might be natural, and that unless it were expressed loudly, or shown actively, it might be left to be suppressed by affection and time. But she, as she had grown old, had taught herself to bear disappointment, and thought it wise to teach Lucy to do the same.

" Envy I" said Lucy, not passionately, but after a little pause for thought. " I sometimes think it is \ery hard to know what envy is."

" Envy, hatred, and malice," said Mrs. Dosett, hardly knowing what she meant by the use of the well-worn words.

I do know what hatred and malice are," said Lucy. " Do you think I hate Ayala?"

I am sure you do not."

" Or that I bear her malice ?"

" Certainly not."

" If I had the power to take anything from her, would I do it ? I love Ayala with my whole heart. Whatever be my misery I would rather bear it than let Ayala have even a share of it. Whatever good things she may have I would not rob her even of a part of them. If there be joy and sorrow to be divided between us I would wish to have the sorrow so that she might have the joy. That is not hatred and malice." Mrs. Dosett looked at her over her spectacles. This was the girl who had declared that she could not speak because she was too stupid ! " But, when you ask me whether I envy her, I hardly know," continued Lucy. " I think one does covet one's neighbour's house, in spite of the tenth commandment, even though one does not want to steal it»"

Mrs. Dosett repented herself that she had given rise to any conversation at all. Silence, absolute silence, the old silence which she had known for a dozen years before Lucy had come to her, would have been better than this. She was very angry, more angry than she had ever yet been with Lucy; and yet she was afraid to show her anger. Was this the girl's gratitude for all that her uncle was doing for her,—for shelter, food, comfort, for all that she had in the world ? Mrs. Dosett knew, though Lucy did not, of the little increased pinchings which had been made necessary by the advent of another inmate in the house ; so many pounds of the meat in the week, and so much bread, and so much tea and sugar! It had all been calculated. In genteel houses such calculation must often be made. And when by degrees,—degrees very quick,—the garments should become worn which Lucy had brought with her, there must be something taken from the tight-fitting income for that need. Arrangements had already

been made of which Lucy knew nothing, and already the two glasses of port wine a day had been knocked off from poor Mr. Dosett's comforts. His wife had sobbed in despair when he had said that it should be so. He had declared gin and water to be as supporting as port wine, and the thing had been done. Lucy inwardly had been disgusted by the gin and water, knowing nothing of its history. Her father, who had not always been punctual in paying his wine-merchant's bills, would not have touched gin and water, would not have allowed it to contaminate his table ? Everything in Mr., Dosett's house was paid for weekly.

And now Lucy, who had been made welcome to all that the genteel house could afford, who had been taken in as a child, had spoken of her lot as one which was all sorrowful. Bad as it is,—this living in Kingsbury Crescent,—I would rather bear it myself than subject Ayala to such misery I It was thus that she had, in fact, spoken of her new home when she had found it necessary to defend her feelings towards her sister. It was impossible that her aunt should be altogether silent under such treatment. " We have done the best for you that is in our power, Lucy," she said, with a whole load of reproach in her tone.

" Have I complained, aunt ? "

" I thought you did."

" Oh, no I You asked me whether I envied Ayala. What was I to say ? Perhaps 1 should have said nothing, but the idea of envying Ayala was painful to me. Of course she "

" I had better say nothing more, aunt. If I were to pretend to be cheerful I should be false. It is as yet only a few weeks since papa died." Then the work went on in silence between them for the next hour.

And the work went on in solemn silence between them through the winter. It came to pass that the sole excitement of Lucy's life came from Ayala's letters,—the sole excitement except a meeting which took place between the sisters one day. When Lucy was taken to Kingsbury Crescent Ayala was at once carried down to Glenbogie, and from thence there came letters twice a week for six weeks. Ayala's letters, too, were full of sorrow. She, too, had lost her mother, her father, and her sister. Moreover, in her foolish petulance she said things of her Aunt Emmeline, and of the girls, and of Sir Thomas, which ought not to have been written of those who were kind to her. Her cousin Tom, too, she ridiculed,—Tom Tringle, the son-and-heir,— saying that he was a lout who endeavoured to make eyes at her. Oh, how distasteful, how vulgar they were after all that she had known. Perhaps the eldest girl, Augusta, was the worst. She did not think that she could put up wdth the assumed authority of Augusta. Gertrude was better, but a simpleton. Ayala declared herself to be sad at heart. But then the sw^eet scenery of Glenbogie, and the colour of the moors, and the glorious heights of Ben Alchan, made some amends. Even in her sorrow^ she would rave about the beauties of Glenbogie. Lucy, as she read the letters, told herself that

Ayala's grief was a grief to be borne, a grief almost to be enjoyed. To sit and be sad with a stream purling by you, how different from the sadness of that dining-room in the Crescent. To look out upon the glories of a mountain, while a tear would now and again force itself into the eye, how much less bitter than the falling of salt drops over a tattered towel.

Lucy, in her answers, endeavoured to repress the groans of her spirit. In the first place she did acknowledge that it did not become her to speak ill of those who were, in truth, her benefactors; and then she was anxious not to declare to Ayala her feeling of the injustice by which their two lots had been defined to them. Though she had failed to control herself once or twice in speaking to her aunt she did control herself in writing her letters. She would never, never, write a word which should make Ayala unnecessarily unhappy. On that she was determined. She Would say nothing to explain to Ayala the unutterable tedium of that downstairs parlour in which they passed their lives, lest Ayala should feel herself to be wounded by the luxurious comforts around her.

It was thus she wrote. Then there came a time in which they were to meet,—just at the beginning of November. The Tringles were going to Rome. They generally did go somewhere.

Glenbogie, Merle Park, and the house in Queen's Gate, were not enough for the year. Sir Thomas was to take them to Rome, and then return to London for the manipulation of the millions in Lombard Street. He generally did remain nine months out of the

twelve in town, because of the millions, making his visits at Merle Park very short; but Lady Tringle found that change of air was good for the girls. It was her intention now to remain at Rome for two or three months.

The party from Scotland reached Queen's Gate late one Saturday evening, and intended to start early on the Monday. To Ayala, who had made it quite a matter of course that she should see her sister. Lady Tringle had said that in that case a carriage must be sent across. It was awkward, because there were no carriages in London. She had thought that they had all intended to pass through London just as though they were not stopping. Sunday, she had thought, was not to be regarded as being a day at all. Then Ayala flashed up. She had flashed up some times before. Was it supposed that she was not going to see Lucy ? Carriage ! She would walk across Kensington Gardens, and find the house out all by herself She would spend the whole day with Lucy, and come back alone in a cab. She was strong enough, at any rate, to have her way so far, that a carriage, wherever it came from, was sent for Lucy about three in the afternoon, and did take her back to Kingsbury Crescent after dinner.

Then at last the sisters were together in Ayala's bedroom. " And now tell me about everything," said Ayala.

But Lucy was resolved that she would not tell anything. "I am so wretched!" That would have been all; but she would not tell her wretchedness. " We are so quiet in Kingsbury Crescent," she said; " you have so much more to talk of."

VOL. I. D

" Oh, Lucy, I do not like it."

" Not your aunt ?"

" She is not the worst, though she sometimes is hard to bear. I can't tell you what it is, but they all seem to think so much of themselves. In the first place they never will say a word about papa."

*^ Perhaps that is from feeling, Ayey."

" No, it is not. One would know that. But they look down upon papa, who had more in his little finger than they have with all their money."

" Then I should hold my tongue."

" So I do,—about him; but it is very hard. And then Augusta has a way with me, as though she had a right to order me. I certainly will not be ordered by Augusta. You never ordered me,"

" Dear Ayey!"

" Augusta is older than you,—of course, ever so much. They make her out twenty-three at her last birthday, but she is twenty-four. But that is not difference enough for ordering,— certainly between cousins. I do hate Augusta."

" I would not hate her."

How is one to help one's-self ? She has a way of whispering to Gertrude, and to her mother, when I am there, which almost kills me. ' If you'll only give me notice I'll go out of the room at once,' I said the other day, and they were all so angry."

" I would not make them angry if I were you, Ayey.'

"Why not?"

" Not Sir Thomas, or Aunt Emmeline."

" I don't care a bit for Sir Thomas. I am not sure but he is the most good-natured, though he is so podgy. Of course, when Aunt Emmehne tells me anything I do it."

" It is so important that you should be on good terms with them."

" I don't see it all," said Ayala, flashing round.

" Aunt Emmeline can do so much for you. We have nothing of our own,—you and I."

" Am I to sell myself because they have got money! No, indeed ! No one despises money so much as I do. I will never be other to them than if I had the money, and they were the poor relations."

" That will not do, Ayey."

^' I will make it do. They may turn me out if they like. Of course, I know that I should obey my aunt, and so I will. If Sir Thomas told me anything I should do it. But not Augusta." Then, while Lucy was tliinking how she might best put into soft words advice which was so clearly needed, Ayala declared another trouble. " But there is worse still."

"What is that?"

" Tom!"

"What does Tom do?"

" You know Tom, Lucy?"

" I have seen him."

" Of all the horrors he is the horridest."

" Does he order you about?"

" No ; but he "

" What is it, Ayey?"

d2

" Oh! Lucy, he is so dreadful. He "

" You don't mean that he makes love to you?"

 He does. What am I to do, Lucy ?"

"Do they know it?"

" Augusta does, I'm sure; and pretends to think that ife is my fault. I am sure that there will be a terrible quarrel some day. I told him the day before we left Glenbogie that I should tell his mother. I did indeed. Then he grinned. He is such a fool. And when I laughed he took it all as kindness. I couldn't have helped laughing if I had died for it."

" But he has been left behind."

" Yes, for the present. But he is to come over to us some time after Christmas, when Uncle Tringle has gone back."

" A girl need not be bothered by a lover unless she chooses, Ayey."

" But it will be such a bother to have to talk about it. He looks at me, and is such an idiot. Then Augusta frowns. When I see Augusta frowning I am so angry that I feel like boxing her ears. Do you know, Lucy, that I often think that it will not do, and that I shall have to be sent away. I wish it had been you that they had chosen."

Such was the conversation between the girls. Of what was said everything appertained to Ayala. Of the very nature of Lucy's life not a word was spoken. As Ayala was talking Lucy was constantly thinking of all that might be lost by her sister's imprudence. Even though Augusta might be disagreeable, even though Tom might be a bore, it should all be borne,—borne at any rate for a while,— seeing how terrible would be the alternative. The alternative to Lucy seemed to be Kingsbury Crescent and Aunt Dosett. It did not occur to her to think whether in any possible case Ayala would indeed be added to the Crescent family, or what in that case would become of herself, and whether they two might live with Aunt Dosett, and whether in that case life would not be infinitely improved. Ayala had all that money could do for her, and would have such a look-out into the world from a wealthy house as might be sure at last to bring her some such husband as would be desirable. Ayala, in fact, had everything before her, and Lucy had nothing. Wherefore it became Lucy's duty to warn Ayala, so that she should bear with much, and throw away nothing. If Ayala could only know what life might be, what life was at Kingsbury Crescent, then she would be patient, then she w^ould softly make a confidence with her aunt as to Tom's folly, then she would propitiate Augusta. Not care for money ! Ayala had not yet lived in an ugly room and darned sheets all the morning. Ayala had never sat for two hours between the slumbers of Uncle Dosett and the knitting of Aunt Dosett. Ayala had not been brought into contact with gin and water.

"Oh, Ayala!" she said, as they were going down to dinner together, "do struggle; do bear it. Tell Aunt Emmeline. She will like you to tell her. If Augusta wants you to go anywhere, do go. What does it signify? Papa and mamma are gone, and we are alone." All this

she said without a word of allusion to her own sufferings. Ayala made a half promise. She did not think she would go anywhere for Augusta's telling ; but she would do her best to satisfy Aunt Emmeline. Then they went to dinner, and after dinner Lucy was taken home without further words between them.

Ayala wrote long letters on her journey, full of what she saw, and full of her companions. From Paris she wrote, and then from Turin, and then again on their immediate arrival at Kome. Her letters were most imprudent as written from the close vicinity of her aunt and cousin. It was such a comfort that that oaf Tom had been left behind. Uncle Tringle was angry because he did not get what he liked to eat. Aunt Emmeline gave that courier such a terrible life, sending for him every quarter of an hour. Augusta would talk first French and then Italian, of which no one could understand a word. Gertrude was so sick with travelling that she was as pale as a sheet. Nobody seemed to care for anything. She could not get her aunt to look at the Campanile at Florence, or her cousins to know one picture from another. '^ As for pictures, I am quite sure that Mangle's angels would do as well as Eaffael's." Mangle was a brother academician whom their father had taught them to despise. There was contempt, most foolish contempt, for all the Tringles; but, luckily, there had been no quarrelling. Then it seemed that both in Paris and in Florence Ayala had bought pretty things, from which it was to be argued that her uncle had provided her liberally with money. One pretty

thing had been sent from Paris to Lucj, which could not have been bought for less than many franks. It would not be fair that Ayala should take so much without giving something in return.

Lucy knew that she too should give something in return. Though Kingsbury Crescent was not attractive, though Aunt Dosett was not to her a pleasant companion, she had begun to realise the fact that it behoved her to be grateful, if only for the food she ate, and for the bed on which she slept. As she thought of all that Ayala owed she remembered also her own debts. As the winter went on she struggled to pay them. But Aunt Dosett was a lady not much given to vacillation. She had become aware at first that Lucy had been rough to her, and she did not easily open herself to Lucy's endearments. Lucy's life at Kingsbury Crescent had begun badly, and Lucy, though she understood much about it, found it hard to turn a bad beginning to a good result.

CAAPTER lY.
ISADORE HAMEL.

It was suggested to Lucy before she had been long in Kingsbury Crescent that she should take some exercise. For the first week she had hardly been out of the house; but this was attributed to her sorrow. Then she had accompanied her aunt for a few days during the half-hour's marketing which took place every morning, but in this there had been no sympathy. Lucy would not interest herself in the shoulder of mutton which must be of just such a weight as to last conveniently for two days,—twelve pounds,—of which, it was explained to her, more than one-half was intended for the two servants, because there was always a more lavish consumption in the kitchen than in the parlour. Lucy would not appreciate the fact that eggs at a penny a piece, whatever they might be, must be used for puddings, as eggs with even a reputation of freshness cost twopence. Aunt Dosett, beyond this, never left the house on week-days except for a few calls which were made perhaps once a month, on which occasion the Sunday gloves and the Sunday silk dress were used. On Sunday they all went to church. But this was not enough for exercise, and as Lucy was becoming pale she was recommended to take to walking in Kensington Gardens.

It is generally understood that there are raging lions about the metropolis, who would certainly eat up young ladies whole if young ladies were to walk about the streets or even about the parks by themselves. There is, however, beginning to be some vacillation as to the received belief on this subject as regards London. In large continental towns, such as Paris and Vienna, young ladies would be devoured certainly. Such, at least, is the creed. In New York and Washington there are supposed to be no lions, so that young ladies go about free as air. In London there is a rising doubt, under which before long, probably, the lions will succumb altogether. Mrs. Dosett did believe somewhat in lions, but she believed also in exercise. And she was aware that the lions eat up chiefly rich people. Young ladies who must go about without mothers, brothers, uncles, carriages, or attendants of any sort, are not often eaten or even roared at. It is the dainty darlings for whom the roarings have to be feared. Mrs. Dosett, aware that daintiness was no longer within the reach of her and hers, did assent to these walkings in Kensington Gardens. At some hour in the afternoon Lucy would walk from the house by herself, and within a quarter of an hour would find herself on the broad gravel path which leads down to the Round Pond. From thence she would go by the back of the Albert Memorial, and then across by the Serpentine and return to the same gate, never leaving Kensington Gardens. Aunt Dosett had expressed some old-fashioned idea that lions were more likely to roar in Hyde Park than within the comparatively retired purlieus of Kensington.

Now the reader must be taken back for a few moments to the bijou, as the bijou was before either the artist or his wife had died. In those days there had been a frequent concourse of people in the artist's house. Society there had not consisted chiefly of eating and drinking. Men and women would come in and out as though really for a purpose of talking. There would be three or four constantly with Dormer in his studio, helping him but little perhaps in the real furtherance of his work, though discussing art subjects in a manner calculated to keep alive art-feeling among them. A novelist or two of a morning might perhaps aid me in my general pursuit, but would, I think, interfere with the actual tally of pages. Egbert Dormer did not turn out from his hand so much work as some men that I know, but he was overflowing with art up to his ears;—and with tobacco, so that, upon the whole, the bijou was a pleasant rendezvous.

There had come there of late, quite of late, a young sculptor, named Isadore Hamel. Hamel was an Englishman, who, however, had been carried very early to Eome and had been bred there. Of his mother question never was made, but his father had been well known as an English sculptor resident at Rom-c. The elder Hamel had been a man of mark, who had a fine suite of rooms in the city and a villa on one of the lakes, but who never came to England. English connections were, he said, to him abominable, by which he perhaps meant that the restrictions of decent life were not to his taste. But his busts came, and his groups in marble, and now and again some

great work for some public decoration : so that money[was plentiful with him, and he was a man of note. It must be acknowledged of him that he spared nothing in bringing up his son, giving him such education as might best suit his ftiture career as an artist, and that money was always forthcoming for the lad's wants and fantasies.

Then young Hamel also became a sculptor of much promise ; but early in life differed from his father on certain subjects of importance. The father was wedded to Rome and to Italy. Isadore gradually expressed an opinion that the nearer a man was to his market the better for him, that all that art could do for a man in Eome was as nothing to the position which a great artist might make for himself in London,—that, in fact, an Englishman had better be an Englishman. At twenty-six he succeeded in his attempt, and became known as a young sculptor with a workshop at Brompton. He became known to many both by his work and his acquirements; but it may not be surprising that after a year he was still unable to live, as he had been taught to live, without drawing upon his father. Then his father threw his failure in his teeth, not refusing him money indeed, but making the receipt of it unpleasant to him.

At no house had Isadore Hamel been made so welcome as at Dormer's. There was a sympathy between them both on that great question of art, whether to an artist his art should be a matter to him of more importance than all the world besides. So said Dormer,—who simply died because his wife died, who could not have touched his

brush if one of his girls had been suffering, who, with all his genius, was but a faineant workman. His art more than all the world to him! No, not to him. Perhaps here and again to some enthusiast, and him hardly removed from madness! Where is the painter who shall paint a picture after his soul's longing though he shall get not a penny for it,—though he shall starve as he put his last touch to it, when he knows that by drawing some duchess of the day he shall in a fortnight earn a ducal price ? Shall a wife and child be less dear to him than to a lawyer, —or to a shoemaker ; or the ver\'7d^ craving of his hunger less obdurate ? A man's self, and what he has within him and nis belongings, with his outlook for this and other worlds,—let that be the first, and the work, noble or otherwise, be the second. To be honest is greater than to have painted the San Sisto, or to have chiselled the Apollo; to have assisted in making others honest,— infinitely greater. All of which were discussed at great length at the bijou, and the bijouites always sided with the master of the house. To an artist, said Dormer, let his art be everything,—above wife and children, above money, above health, above even character. Then he would put out his hand with his jewelled finger, and stretch forth his velvet-clad arm, and soon after lead his friend away to the little dinner at which no luxury had been spared. But young Hamel agreed with the sermons, and not the less because Lucy Dormer had sat by and listened to them with rapt attention.

Not a word of love had been spoken to her by the

sculptor v/hen her mother died, but there had been glances and little feelings of which each was half conscious. It is so hard for a young man to speak of love, if there be real love,—so impossible that a girl should do so ! Not a word had been spoken, but each had thought that the other must have known. To Lucy a word had been spoken by her mother,—" Do not think too much of him till you know," the mother had said,—not quite prudently. " Oh, no! I will think of him not at all," Lucy had replied. And she had thought of him day and night. " I wonder why Mr.

Hamel is so different with you ?" Ayala had said to her sister. " I am sure he is not diifferent with me," Lucy had replied. Then Ayala had shaken her full locks and smiled.

Things came quickly after that. Mrs. Dormer had sickened and died. There was no time then for thinking of that handsome brow, of that short jet black hair, of those eyes so full of fire and thoughtfulness, of that perfect mouth, and the deep but yet soft voice. Still even in her sorrow this new god of her idolatry was not altogether forgotten. It was told to her that he had been summoned off to Eome by his father, and she wondered whether he was to find his home at Eome for ever. Then her father was ill, and in his illness Hamel came to say one word of farewell before he started.

" You fiad me crushed to the ground," the painter said. Something the young man whispered as to the consolation which time would bring. " Not to me," said Dormer, " It is as though one had lost his eyes. One cannot see

without his eyes." It was true of him. His light had been put out.

Then, on the landing at the top of the stairs, there had been one word between Lucy and the sculptor. " I ought not to have intruded on you perhaps," he said; " but after so much kindness I could hardly go without a word."

" I am sure he will be glad that you have come."

"And you?"

" I am glad too,—so that I may say good-bye." Then she put out her hand, and he held it for a moment as he looked into her eyes. There was not a word more, but it seemed to Lucy as though there had been so many words.

Things went on quickly. Egbert Dormer died, and Lucy was taken away to Kingsbury Crescent. When once Ayala had spoken about Mr. Hamel, Lucy had silenced her. Any allusion to the idea of love wounded her, as though it was too impossible for dreams, too holy for words. How should there be words about a lover when father and mother were both dead ? He had gone to his old and natural home. He had gone, and of course he would not return. To Ayala, when she came up to London early in November, to Ayala, who was going to Rome, where Isadore Hamel now was, Isadore Hamel's name was not mentioned. But through the long mornings of her life, through the long evenings, through the long nights, she still thought of him,—she could not keep herself from thinking. To a girl whose life is full of delights her lover need not be so very much,—need not, at least, be everything. Though he be a lover to be loved at all points, her

friends will be something, her dancing, her horse, her theatre-going, her brothers and sisters, even her father and mother. But Lucy had nothing. The vision of Isadore Hamel had passed across her life, and had left with her the only possession that she had. It need hardly be said that she never alluded to that possession at Kingsbury Crescent. It was not a possession from which any enjoyment could come except that of thinking of it. He had passed away from her, and there was no point of life at which he could come across her again. There was no longer that half-joint studio. If it had been her lot to be as was Ayala, she then would have been taken to Kome. Then again he would have looked into her eyes and taken

her hand in his. Then perhaps . But now, even

though he were to come back to London, he would know nothing of her haunts. Even in that case nothing would bring them together. As the idea was crossing her mind,—as it did cross it so frequently,—she saw him turning from the path on which she was walking, making his way towards the steps of the Memorial.

Though she saw no more than his back she was sure that it was Isadore Hamel. For a moment there was an impulse on her to run after him and to call his name. It was then early in

January, and she was taking her daily walk through Kensington Gardens. She had walked there daily now for the last two months and had never spoken a word or been addressed,—had never seen a face that she had recognised. It had seemed to her that she had not an acquaintance in the world except Uncle Reg and Aunt

Dosett. And now, almost within reach of her hand, was the one being in all the world whom she most longed to see. She did stand, and the word was formed within her lips ; but she could not speak it. Then came the thought that she would run after him, but the thought was expelled quickly. Though she might lose him again and for ever she could not do that. She stood almost gasping till he was out of sight, and then she passed on upon her usual round.

She never omitted her walks after that, and always paused a moment as the path turned away to the Memorial. It was not that she thought that she might meet him there, —there rather than elsewhere,—but there is present to us often an idea that when some object has passed from us that we have desired then it may be seen again. Day after fday, and week after week, she did not see him. During this time there came letters from Ayala, saying that their return to England was postponed till the first week in February,—that she would certainly see Lucy in February,—that she was not going to be hurried through London in half-an-hour because her aunt wished it; and that she would do as she pleased as to visiting her sister. Then there was a word or two about Tom,—" Oh, Tom— that idiot Tom!" And another word or two about Augusta. " Augusta is worse than ever. We have not spoken to each other for the last day or two." This came but a day or two before the intended return of the Tringles.

No actual day had been fixed. But on the day before

that on which Lucy thought it probable that the Tringles might return to town she was again walking in the Gardens. Having put two and two together, as people do, she felt sure that the travellers could not be away more than a day or two longer. Her mind was much intent upon Ayala, feeling that the imprudent girl was subjecting herself to great danger, knowing that it was wrong that she and Augusta should be together in the house without speaking,—thinking of her sister's perils,—when, of a sudden, Hamel was close before her! There was no question of calling to him now,—no question of an attempt to see him face to face. She had been wandering along the path with eyes fixed upon the ground, when her name was sharply called, and they two were close to each other. Hamel had a friend with him, and it seemed to Lucy at once, that she could only bow to him, only mutter something, and then pass on. How can a girl stand and speak to a gentleman in public, especially when that gentleman has a friend with him? She tried to look pleasant, bowed, smiled, muttered something, and was passing on. But he was not minded to lose her thus immediately. " Miss Dormer," he said, " I have seen your sister at Rome. May I not say a word about her ? "

Why should he not say a word about Ayala? In a minute he had left his friend, and was walking back along the path with Lucy. There was not much that he had to say about Ayala. He had seen Ayala and the Tringles, and did manage to let it escape him that Lady Tringle had not been very gracious to himself when once, in public, he

VOL. I. E

had claimed acquaintance with Ayala. But at that he simply smiled. Then he had asked of Lucy where she lived. " With my uncle, Mr. Dosett," said Lucy, " at Kingsbury Crescent." Then, when he asked whether he might call, Lucy, with many blushes, had said that her aunt did not receive many visitors,—that her uncle's house was different from what her father's had been.

" Shall I not see you at all, then ? " he asked.

She did not like to ask him after his own purposes of life, whether he was now a resident in London, or whether he intended to return to Rome. She was covered with bashfulness, and dreaded to seem even to be interested in his affairs. '^ Oh, yes," she said; " perhaps we may meet some day."

" Here ? " he asked.

" Oh, no ; not here ! It was only an accident." As she said this she determined that she must walk no more in Kensington Gardens. It would be dreadful, indeed, were he to imagine that she would consent to make an appointment with him. It immediately occurred to her that the lions were about, and that she must shut herself up.

" I have thought of you every day since I have been back," he said, " and I did not know where to hear of you. Now that we have met am I to lose you again! " Lose her ! What did he mean by losing her ? She, too, had found a friend,—she who had been so friendless! Would it not be dreadful to her, also, to lose him? "Is there no place where I may ask of you?"

" When Ayala is back, and they are in town, perhaps I

shall sometimes be at Lady Tringle's," said Lucy, resolved that she would not tell him of her immediate abode. This was, at any rate, a certain address from where he might commence further inquiries, should he wish to make inquiry ; and as such he accepted it. "I think I had better go now," said Lucy, trembling at the apparent impropriety of her present conversation.

He knew that it was intended that he should leave her, and he went. " I hope I have not offended you in coming so far."

" Oh, no." Then again she gave him her hand, and again there was the same look as he took his leave.

When she got home, which was before the dusk, having resolved that she must, at any rate, tell her aunt that she had met a friend, she found that her uncle had returned from his office. This was a most unusual occurrence. Her uncle, she knew, left Somerset House exactly at half-past four, and always took an hour and a quarter for his walk. She had never seen him in Kingsbury Crescent till a quarter before six. " I have got letters from Rome," he said, in a solemn voice.

"FromAyala?"

" One from Ayala, for you. It is here. And I have had one from my sister, also; and one, in the course of the day, from your uncle in Lombard Street. You had better read them! " There was something terribly tragic in Uncle Dosett's voice as he spoke.

And so must the reader read the letters; but they mus be delayed for a few chapters.

e2

CHAPTER V.

AT GLENBOGIE.

We must go back to Ayala's life during the autumn and winter. She was rapidly whirled away to Glenbogie amidst the affectionate welcomings of her aunt and cousins. All manner of good things were done for her, as to presents and comforts. Young as she was, she had money given to her, which was not without attraction; and though she was, of course, in the depth of her mourning, she was made to understand that even mourning might be made becoming if no expense were spared. No expense among the Tringles ever was spared, and at first Ayala liked the bounty of profusion. But before the end of the first fortnight there grew upon her a feeling that even bank notes become tawdry if you are taught to use them as curl-papers. It may be said that nothing in the world is charming unless it be achieved at some trouble. If it rained " '64 Leoville,"—which I regard as the most divine of nectars,—I feel sure that I should never raise it to my lips. Ayala did not argue the matter out in her mind, but in very early days she began to entertain a dislike to Tringle magnificence. There had been a good deal of luxury at the bijou, but always with a feeling that it ought not to be there,—that more money was being spent

than prudence authorised,—which had certainly added a savour to the luxuries. A lovely bonnet, is it not more lovely because the destined wearer knows that there is some wickedness in achieving it ? All the bonnets, all the claret, all the horses, seemed to come at Queen's Gate and at Glenbogie without any wickedness. There was no more question about them than as to one's ordinary bread and butter at breakfast. Sir Thomas had a way,—a merit shall we call it or a fault ?—of pouring out his wealth upon the family as though it were water running in perpetuity from a mountain tarn. Ayala the romantic, Ayala the poetic, found very soon that she did not like it.

Perhaps the only pleasure left to the very rich is that of thinking of the deprivations of the poor. The bonnets, and the claret, and the horses, have lost their charm; but the Gladstone, and the old hats, and the four-wheeled cabs of their neighbours, still have a little flavour for them. From this source it seemed to Ayala that the Tringles drew much of the recreation of their lives. Sir Thomas had his way of enjoying this amusement, but it was a w^ay that did not specially come beneath Ayala's notice. When she heard that Break-at-last, the Huddersfield manufacturer, had to sell his pictures, and that all Shoddy and Stuffgoods' grand doings for the last two years had only been a flash in the pan, she did not understand enough about it to feel wounded; but when she heard her aunt say that people like the Poodles had better not have a place in Scotland than have to let it, and when Augusta hinted that Lady Sophia Small ware had pawned her

diamonds, then she felt that her nearest and dearest relatives smelt abominably of money.

Of all the family Sir Thomas was most persistently the kindest to her, though he was a man who did not look to be kind. She was pretty, and though he was ugly himself he liked to look at things pretty. He was, too, perhaps, a little tired of his own wife and daughters,— who were indeed what he had made them, but still were not quite to his taste. In a general way he gave instructions that Ayala should be treated exactly as a daughter, and he informed Jiis wife that he intended to add a codicil to his will on her behalf. " Is that necessary?" asked Lady Tringle, who began to feel something like natural jealousy. " I suppose I ought to do something for a girl if I take her by the hand," said Sir Thomas, roughly. " If she gets a husband I will give her something, and that will do as well." Nothing more was said about it, but when Sir Thomas went up to town the codicil was added to his will.

Ayala was foolish rather than ungrateful, not understanding the nature of the family to which she was relegated. Before she had been taken away she had promised Lucy that she would be "obedient" to her aunt. There had hardly been such a word as obedience known at the bijou. If any were obedient, it was the mother and the father to the daughters. Lucy, and Ayala as well, had understood something of this; and therefore Ayala had promised to be obedient to her aunt. " And to Uncle Thomas," Lucy had demanded, with an imploring embrace. " Oh, yes,"

said Ayala, dreading her uncle at that time. She soon learned that no obedience whatsoever was exacted from Sir Thomas. She had to kiss him morning and evening, and then to take whatever presents he made her. An easy uncle he was to deal with, and she almost learned to love him. Nor was Aunt Emmeline very exigeant, though she was fantastic and sometimes disagreeable. But Augusta was the great difficulty. Lucy had not told her to obey Augusta, and Augusta she would not obey. Now Augusta demanded obedience.

" You never ordered me," Ayala had said to Lucy when they met in London as the Tringles were passing through. At the bijou there had been a republic, in which all the inhabitants and all the visitors had been free and equal. Such republicanism had been the very mainspring of life at the bijou. Ayala loved equality, and she specially felt that it should exist among sisters. Do anything for Lucy ? Oh, yes, indeed, anything; abandon anything; but for Lucy as a sister among sisters, not for an elder as from a younger! And if she were not bound to serve Lucy then certainly not Augusta. But Augusta liked to be served. On one occasion she sent Ayala upstairs, and on another she sent Ayala down-stairs. Ayala went, but determined to be equal with her cousin. On the morning following, in the presence of Aunt Emmeline and of Gertrude, in the presence also of two other ladies who were visiting at the house, she asked Augusta if she would mind running upstairs and fetching her scrap-book ! She had been thinking about it all the night and all the morning, plucking up her

courage. But she had been determined. She found a great difficulty in saying the words, but she said them. The thing was so preposterous that all the ladies in the room looked aghast at the proposition. " I really think that Augusta has got something else to do," said Aunt Emmeline. '^ Oh, very well," said Ayala, and then they were all silent. Augusta, who was employed on a silk purse, sat still and did not say a word.

Had a great secret, or rather a great piece of news which pervaded the family, been previously communicated to Ayala, she would not probably have made so insane a suggestion. Augusta was engaged to be married to the Honourable Septimus Traffic, the member for Port Glasgow. A young lady who is already half a bride is not supposed to run up and down stairs as readily as a mere girl. For running up and down stairs at the bijou Ayala had been proverbial. They were a family who ran up and down with the greatest alacrity. " Oh, papa, my basket is out on the seat"—for there had been a seat in the two-foot garden behind the house. Papa would go down in two jumps and come up with three skips, and there was the basket, only because his girl liked him to do something for her. But for him Ayala would run about as though she were a tricksy Ariel. Had he important matrimonial news been conveyed to Ariel, with a true girl's spirit she would have felt that during the present period Augusta was entitled to special exemption from all ordering. Had she herself been engaged she would have run more and quicker than ever,— would have been excited thereto by the pecu-

liar vitality of her new prospects; but to even Augusta she would be subservient, because of her appreciation of bridal importance. She, however, had not been told till that afternoon.

" You should not have asked Augusta to go up stairs," said Aunt Emmeline, in a tone of mitigated reproach.

" Oh ! I didn't know," said Ayala.

" You had meant to say that because she had sent you you were to send her. There is a difference, you know."

" I didn't know," said Ayala, beginning to think that she would fight her battle if told of such differences as she believed to exist.

" 1 had meant to tell you before, but I may as well tell you now, Augusta is engaged to be married to the Honourable Mr. Septimus Traffick. He is second son of Lord Boardotrade, and is in the House."

" Dear me!" said Ayala, acknowledging at once within her heart that the difference alleged was one against which she need not rouse herself to the fight. Aunt Emmeline had, in truth, intended to insist on that difference—and another ; but her courage had failed her.

" Yes, indeed. He is a man very much thought of just now in public life, and Augusta's mind is naturally much occupied. He writes all those letters in The Tim es about supply and demand."

"Does he, aunt?" Ayala did feel that if Augusta's mind was entirely occupied with supply and demand she ought not to be made to go upstairs to fetch a scrap-book.

But she had her doubts about Augusta's mind. Nevertheless, if the forthcoming husband were true, that might be a reason. " If anybody had told me before I wouldn't have asked her," she said.

Then Lady Tringle explained that it had been thought better not to say anything heretofore as to the coming matrimonial hilarities because of the sadness which had fallen upon the Dormer family. Ayala accepted this as an excuse, and nothing further was said as to the iniquity of her request to her cousin. But there was a general feeling among the women that Ayala, in lieu of gratitude, had exhibited an intention of rebelling.

On the next day Mr. Traffick arrived, whose coming had probably made it necessary that the news should be told. Ayala was never so surprised in her life as when she saw him. She had never yet had a lover of her own, had never dreamed of a lover, but she had her own idea as to what a lover ought to be. She had thought that Isadore Hamel would be a very nice lover—for her sister. Hamel was young, handsome, with a great deal to say on such a general subject as art, but too bashful to talk easily to the girl he admired. Ayala had thought that all that was just as it should be. She was altogether resolved that Hamel and her sister should be lovers, and was determined to be devoted to her future brother-in-law. But the Honourable Septimus Traffick! It was a question to her whether her Uncle Tringle would not have been better as a lover.

And yet there was nothing amiss about Mr. Traffick.

He was very much like an ordinary hard-working member of the House of Commons, over perhaps rather than under forty years of age. He was somewhat bald, somewhat grey, somewhat fat, and had lost that look of rosy plumpness which is seldom, I fear, compatible with hard work and late hours. He was not particularly ugly, nor was he absurd in appearance. But he looked to be a disciple of business, not of pleasure, nor of art. " To sit out on the bank of a stream and have him beside one would not be particularly nice," thought Ayala to herself. Mr. Traffick no doubt would have enjoyed it very well if he could have spared the time; but to Ayala it seemed that such a man as that could have cared nothing for love. As soon as she saw him, and realised in her mind the fact that Augusta was to become his wife, she felt at once the absurdity of sending Augusta on a message.

Augusta that evening was somewhat more than ordinarily kind to her cousin. Now that the great secret was told, her cousin no doubt would recognise her importance. *' I suppose you had not heard of him before ?" she said to Ayala.

" I never did."

" That's because you have not attended to the debates."

" I never have. What are debates ? "

" Mr. Traffick is yqyj much thought of in the House of Commons on all subjects affecting commerce."

"Oh!"

"It is the most glorious study which the world affords."

" The House of Commons. I don't think it can be equal to art."

Then Augusta turned up her nose with a double turn, — first as against painters, Mr. Dormer having been no more, and then at Ayala's ignorance in supposing that the House of Commons could have been spoken of as a study. " Mr. Traffick will probably be in the government some day," she said.

" Has not he been yet?" asked Ayala.

" Not yet."

"Then won't he be very old before he gets there?" This w^as a terrible question. Young ladies of five-and-twenty, when they marry gentlemen of four-and-fifty, make up their minds for well-understood and well-recognised old age. They see that they had best declare their purpose, and they do declare it. " Of course, Mr. Walker is old enough to be my father, but I have made up my mind that I like that better than anything else." Then the wall has been jumped, and the thing can go smoothly. But at forty-five there is supposed to be so much of youth left that the difference of age may possibly be tided over and not made to appear abnormal. Augusta Tringle had determined to tide it over in this way. The forty-five had been gradually reduced to " less than forty,"—though all the Peerages were there to give the lie to the assertion. She talked of her lover as Septimus, and was quite prepared to sit with him beside a stream if only half-an-hour for the amusement could be found. When, therefore, Ayala suggested that if her lover wanted to get into office

he had better do so quickly, lest he should be too old, Augusta was not well pleased.

" Lord Boardotrade was much older when he began," said Augusta. " His friends, indeed, tell Septimus that he should not push himself forward too quickly. But I don't think that I ever came across any one who was so ignorant of such things as you are, Ayala."

" Perhaps he is not so old as he looks," said Ayala. After this it may be imagined that there was not close friendship between the cousins. Augusta's mind was filled with a strong conception as to Ayala's ingratitude. The houseless, penniless orphan had been taken in, and had done nothing but make herself disagreeable. Young! No doubt she was young. But had she been as old as Methuselah she could not have been more insolent. It did not, however, matter to her, Augusta. She was going away; but it would be terrible to her mamma and to Gertrude ! Thus it was that Augusta spoke of her cousin to her mother.

And then there came another trouble, which was more troublesome to Ayala even than the other. Tom Tringle, who w^as in the house in Lombard Street, who was the only son, and heir to the title and no doubt to much of the wealth, had chosen to take Ayala's part and to enlist himself as her special friend. Ayala had, at first, accepted him as a cousin, and had consented to fraternise w^itli him. Then, on some unfortunate day, there had been some word or look which she had failed not to understand, and immediately she had become afraid of Tom. Tom w^as not like

Isadore Hamel,—was very far, indeed, from that idea of a perfect lover which Ayala's mind had conceived ; but he was by no means a lout, or an oaf, or an idiot, as Ayala in her letters to her sister had described him. He had been first at Eton and then at Oxford, and having spent a great deal of money recklessly, and done but little towards his education, had been withdrawn and put into the office. His father declared of him now that he would do fairly well in the world. He had a taste for dress, and kept four or five hunters which he got but little credit by riding. He made a fuss about his shooting, but did not shoot much. He was stout and awkward looking,— very like his father, but without that settled air which age gives to heavy men. In appearance he was not the sort of loverv to satisfy the preconceptions of such a girl as Ayala. But he was good-natui'ed and true. At last he became to her terribly true. His love, such as it seemed at first, was absurd to her. " If you make yourself such a fool, Tom, I'll never speak to you again," she had said, once. Even after that she had not understood that it was more than a stupid joke. But the joke, while it was considered as such, was very distasteful to her; and afterwards, when a certain earnestness in it was driven in upon her, it became worse than distasteful.

She repudiated his love with such power as she had, but she could not silence him. She could not at all understand that a young man, who seemed to her to be an oaf, should really be in love,—honestly in love with her. But such was the case. Then she became afraid lest others should

see it,—afraid, though she often told herself that she would appeal to her aunt for protection. " I tell you I don't care a bit about you, and you oughtn't to go on," she said. But he did go on, and though her aunt did not see it Augusta did.

Then Augusta spoke a word to her in scorn. " Ayala," she said, " you should not encourage Tom."

Encourage him! What a word from one girl to another ! What a world of wrong there was in the idea which had created the word! What an absence of the sort of feeling which, according to Ayala's theory of life, there should be on such a matter between two sisters, two cousins, or two friends! Encourage him! When Augusta ought to have been the first to assist her in her trouble! " Oh, Augusta," she said, turning sharply round, " what a spiteful creature you are."

" I suppose you think so, because I do not choose to approve."

" Approve of what! Tom is thoroughly disagreeable. Sometimes he makes my life such a burden to me that I think I shall have to go to my aunt. But you are worse. " Oh!" exclaimed Ayala, shuddering as she thought of the unwomanly treachery of which her cousin was guilty towards her.

Nothing more came of it at Glenbogie. Tom was required in Lombard Street, and the matter was not suspected by Aunt Emmeline,—as far, at least, as Ayala was aware. When he was gone it was to her as though there would be a world of time before she would see him

again. They were to go to Rome, and he would not be at Rome till January. Before that he might have forgotten his folly. But Ayala was quite determined that she would never forget the ill offices of Augusta. She did hate Augusta, as she had told her sister. Then, in this frame of mind, the family was taken to Rome.

CHAPTER VI.

AT ROME.

During her journeying and during her sojourn at Rome Ayala did enjoy much; but even these joys did not come to her without causing some trouble of spirit. At Glenbogie everybody had known that she was a dependent niece, and that as such she was in truth nobody. On that morning when she had ordered Augusta to go upstairs the two visitors had stared with amazement,— who would not have stared at all had they heard Ayala ordered in the same way. But it came about that in Rome Ayala was almost of more importance than the Tringles, It was absolutely true that liady Tringle and Augusta and Gertrude were asked here and there because of Ayala; and the worst of it was that the fact was at last suspected by the Tringles themselves. Sometimes they would not always be asked. One of the Tringle girls would only be named. But Ayala was never forgotten. Once or twice an effort was made by some grand lady, whose taste was perhaps more conspicuous than her goodnature, to get Ayala without burdening herself with any of the Tringles. When this became clear to the mind of Augusta,—of Augusta, engaged as she was to the

VOL. T. P

Honourable Septimus Traffick, Member of Parliament,— Augusta's feelings were—such as may better be understood than described ! " Don't let her go, mamma," she said to Lady Tringle one morning.

*' But the Marchesa has made such a point of it."

"Bother the Marchesa! Who is the Marchesa? I believe it is all Ayala's doing because she expects to meet that Mr. Hamel. It is dreadful to see the way she goes on."

" Mr. Ham el was a very intimate friend of her father's."

"I don't believe a bit of it."

** He certainly used to be at his house. I remember seeing him."

'^ I daresay; but that doesn't justify Ayala in running after him as she does. I believe that all this about the Marchesa is because of Mr. Hamel." This was better than believing that Ayala was to be asked to sing, and that Ayala was to be f^ted and admired and danced with, simply because Ayala was Ayala, and that they, the Tringles, in spite of Glenbogie, Merle Park, and Queen's Gate, were not wanted at all. But when Aunt Em-meline signified to Ayala that on that particular morning she had better not go to the Marchesa's picnic, Ayala simply said that she had promised;—and Ayala went.

At this time no gentleman of the family was with them. Sir Thomas had gone, and Tom Tringle had not come. Then, just at Christmas, the Honourable Septimus Traffick came for a short visit,—a very short visit, no more than

four or five days, because Supply and Demand were requiring all his services in preparation for the coming Session of Parliament. But for five halcyon days he was prepared to devote himself to the glories of Home under the guidance of Augusta. He did not of course sleep at the Palazzo Ruperti, where it delighted Lady Tringle to inform her friends in Eome that she had a suite of apartments " au premiere," but he ate there and drank there and almost lived there; so that it became absolutely necessary to inform the world of Rome that it was Augusta's destiny to become in course of time the Honourable Mrs. Trafiick, otherwise the close intimacy would liardly have been ch'screet,—unless it had been thought, as the ill-natured Marchesa had hinted, that Mr. Trafiick was Lady Tringle's elder brother. Augusta, however, was by no means ashamed of her lover. Perhaps she felt that when it was known that she was about to be the bride of so great a man then doors would be open for her at any rate as wide as for her cousin. At this moment she was very important to herself. She was about to convey no less a sum than ;£ 120,000 to Mr. Traffick, who, in truth, as younger son of Lord Boardo trade, was himself not well endowed. Considering her own position and her future husband's rank and standing, she did not know how a young woman could well be more important. She was very important at any rate to Mr. Traffick. She was sure of that. When, therefore, she learned that Ayala had been asked to a grand ball at the Marchesa's, that Mr. Traffick was also to be among the

F 2

guests, and that none of the Tringles had been invited,— then her anger became hot.

She must have been very stupid when she took it into her head to be jealous of Mr. Traffick's attention to her cousin; stupid, at any rate, vhen she thought that her cousin was laying out feminine lures for Mr. Traffick. Poor Ayala! We shall see much of her in these pages, and it may be well to declare of her at once that her ideas at this moment about men,—or rather about a possible man,— were confined altogether to the abstract. She had floating in her young mind some fancies as to the beauty of love. That there should be a hero must of course be necessary. But in her day-dreams this hero was almost celestial,—or, at least, aethereal. It was a concentration of poetic perfection to which there was not as yet any appanage of apparel, of features, or of wealth. It was a something out of heaven which should think it well to spend his whole time in adoring her and making her more blessed than had ever yet been a woman upon the earth. Then her first approach to a mundane feeling had been her acknowledgment to herself that Isadore Hamel would do as a lover for Lucy. Isadore Hamel was certainly very handsome,— was possessed of infinite good gifts; but even he would by no means have come up to her requirements for her own hero. That hero must have wings tinged with azure, whereas Hamel had a not much more aBtherealised than ordinary coat and waistcoat. She knew that heroes with azure wings were not existent save in the imagination, and, as she desired a real lover for Lucy, Hamel would do. But for herself her

imagination was too valuable then to allow her to put her foot upon earth. Such as she was, must not Augusta have been very stupid to have thought that Ayala should become fond of her Mr. Traffick !

Her cousin Tom had come to her, and had been to her as a Newfoundland dog is when he jumps all over you just when he has come out of a horsepond. She would have liked Tom had he kept his dog-like gambols at a proper distance. But when he would cover her with muddy water he was abominable. But this Augusta had not understood. With Mr. Traffick there would be no doglike gambols; and, as he was not harsh to her, Ayala liked him. She had liked her uncle. Such men were, to her thinking, more like dogs than lovers. She sang when Mr. Traffick asked her, and made a picture for him, and went with him to the Coliseum, and laughed at him about Supply and Demand. She was very pretty, and perhaps Mr. Traffick did like to look at her.

" I really think you were too free with Mr. Traffick last night," Augusta said to her one morning.

"Free I How free?"

" You were—laughing at him."

" Oh, he likes that," said Ayala. " All that time we were up at the top of St. Peter's I was quizzing him about his speeches. He lets me say just what I please."

This was wormwood. In the first place there had been a word or two between the lovers about that going up of St. Peter's, and Augusta had refused to join them. She had wished Septimus to remain down with her,—which

would have been tantamount to preventing any of the p^tiy from going up ; but Septimus had persisted on ascending. Then Augusta had been left for a long hour alone with her mother. Gertrude had no doubt gone up^ but Gertrude had lagged during the ascent. Ayala had skipped up the interminable stairs and Mr. Traffick had trotted after her with admiring breathless industry. This itself, with the thoughts of the good time which Septimus might be having at the topj was very bad. But now to be told that she^ Ayala, should laugh at him; and that he, Septimus, should like it! "I suppose he takes you to be a child," said Augusta\'7d "but if you are a child you ought to conduct yourself."

" I suppose he does perceive the difference," said Ayala.

She had not in the least known what the words might convey,—had probably meant nothing. But to Augusta it was apparent that Ayala had declared that her lover, her Septimus, had preferred her extreme youth to the more mature charms of his own true love,—or had, perhapsj^ preferred Ayala's raillery to Augusta's serioijs demeanour. ^' You are the most impertinent person I ever knew in my life," said Augusta, rising from her chair and walking slowly out of the room. Ayala stared after her, not above half comprehending th« cause of the anger.

Then came the very serious affair of the ball. The Mar-chesa had asked that her dear little friend Ayala Dormer might be allowed to come over to a little dance which her own girls were going to have. Her own girls were so fond

I

of Ayala! There would be no trouble. There was a carriage which would be going somewhere else, and she would be fetched and taken home. Ayala at once declared that she intended to go, and her Aunt Emmeline did not refuse her sanction. Augusta was shocked, declaring that the little dance was to be one of the great balls of the season, and pronouncing the whole to be a falsehood; but the affair was arranged before she could stop it.

But Mr. Traffick's affair in the matter came more within her range. *^ Septimus," she said, " I would rather you would not go to that woman's party." Septimus had been asked only on the day before the party,—as soon, indeed, as his arrival had become known to the Marchesa.

" Why, my own one ?"

" She has not treated mamma well,—nor yet me."

" Ayala is going»" He had no right to call her Ayala, So Augusta thought

" My cousin is behaving badly in the matter, and mamma ought not to allow her to go. Who knows anything about the Marchesa Baldoni ?"

" Both he and she are of the very best families in Rome," said Mr. Traffick, who knew everything about it.

" At any rate they are behaving very badly to us, and I will take it as a favour that you do not go. Asking Ayala, and then asking you, as good as from the same house, is too marked. You ought not to go>"

Perhaps Mr. Traffick had on some former occasion felt some little interference with his freedom of action. Perhaps he liked the acquaintance of the Marchesa. Perhai>s

he liked Ayala Dormer. Be that as it might, he would not yield. " Dear Augusta, it is right that I should go there, if it be only for half-an-hour." This he said in a tone of voice with which Augusta was already acquainted, which she did not love, and which, when she heard it, would make her think of her £120,000. When he had spoken he left her, and she began to think of her £120,000.

They both went, Ayala and Mr. Traffick,—and Mr. Traffick, instead of staying half-an-hour, brought Ayala back at three o'clock in the m.orning. Though Mr. Traffick was nearly as old as Uncle Tringle, yet he could dance. Ayala had been astonished to find how well he could dance, and thought that she might please her cousin Augusta by praising the juvenility of her lover at luncheon the next day. She had not appeared at breakfast, but had been full of the ball at lunch. " Oh, dear, yes, I dare say there were two hundred people there."

" That is what she calls a little dance," said Augusta, with scorn.

" I suppose that is the Itahan way of talking about it," said Ayala.

" Itahan way I I hate Italian ways."

" Mr, Traffick liked it very much. I'm sure he^U tell you so. I had no idea he would care to dance."

Augusta only shook herself and turned up her nose. Lady Tringle thought it necessary to say something in defence of her daughter's choice. " Why should not Mr. Traffick dance like any other gentleman ?"

" Oh, I don't know, I thought-"that a man who makes

AT HOMK ?3

so many speeches in Parliament would think of something else. I was very glad he did, for he danced three times

with me. He can waltz as lightly as " As though

he were young, she was going to say, but then she stopped herself.

" He is the best dancer I ever danced with," said Augusta.

" But you almost never do dance," said Ayala.

" I suppose I may know about it as well as another," said Augusta, angrily.

The next day was the last of Mr Traffick's sojourn in Bome, and on that day he and Augusta so quarrelled that, for a certain number of hours, it was almost supposed in the family that the match would be broken off. On the afternoon of the day after the dance Mr. Traffick was walking with Ayala on the Pincian, while Augusta was absolutely remaining behind with her mother* For a quarter-of-an-hour,-"the whole day, as it seemed to Augusta, there was a full two hundred yards between them. It was not that the engaged girl could not bear the severance, but that she could not endure the attention paid to Ayala. On the next morning " she had it out," as some people say, with her lover. " If I am to be treated in this way you had better tell me so at once," she said.

" I know no better way of treating you," said Mr. Traffick.

" Dancing with that chit all night, turning her head, and then walking with her all the next day! I will not put up with such conduct."

U AYALA'S AmUL

Mr. Traffick valued £120,000 very highly, as do most men, and would have done much to keep it; but he believed that the best waj of making sure of it would be by showing himself to be the master* " My own one,"he said, **you are really making an ass of yourself*"

*' Very well I Then 1 will write to papa, and let him know that it must be all over."

For three hours there was terrible trouble in the apartments in the Palazzo Rupertij during which Mr. Traffick was enjoying himself by walking up and down the Forum, and calculating how many Romans could have congregated themselves in the space which is supposed to have seen so much of the world's doings. During this time Augusta was very frequently in hysterics; but, whether in hysterics or out of them, she would not allow Ayala to come near her* She gave it to be understood that Ayala had interfered fatally, foully, damnably, with all her happiness. She demanded, from fit to fit, that telegrams should be sent over to bring her father to Italy for her protection. She would rave about Septimus, and then swear that, under no consideration whatever, would she ever see him again. At the end of three hours she was told that Septimus was in the drawing-room* Lady Tringle had sent half-a-dozen messengers after him, and at last he was found looking up at the Arch of Titus. " Bid him go," said Augusta. " I never want to behold him again." But within two minutes she was in his arms, and before dinner she was able to take a stroll with him on the Pincian.

He left, like a thriving lover, high in the good graces of his beloved ; but the anger which had fallen on Ayala had not been removed. Then came a rumour that the Marchesa, who was half English, had called Ayala Cinderella, and the name had added fuel to the fire of Augusta's wrath. There was much said about it between Lady Tringle and her daughter, the aunt really feeling that more blame was being attributed to Ayala than she deserved. ^* Perhaps she gives herself airs," said Lady Tringle, " but really it is no more."

" She is a viper," said -Augusta.

Gertrude rather took Ayala's part, telling her mother, in private, that the accusation about Mr. Traffick was absurd. *^ The truth is,'* said Gertrude, " that Ayala thinks herself very clever and very beautiful, and Augusta will not stand it»" Gertrude acknowledged that Ayala Was upsetting and ungrateful* Poor Lady Tringle, in her husband's absence, did not know what to do about her niece*

Altogether, they were uncomfortable after Mr. Traffick went and before Tom Tringle had come. On no consideration whatsoever would Augusta speak to her cousin* She declared that Ayala was a viper, and would give no other reason. In all such quarrelings the matter most distressing is that the evil cannot be hidden. Everybody at Home who knew the Tringles, or who knew Ayala, was aware that Augusta Tringle would not speak to her cousin* When Ayala was asked she would shake her locks, and open her eyes, and declare that she knew nothing about it In truth she knew very little about it. She remembered that passage-at-arms about the going upstairs at Glenbogie, but she could hardly understand that for so small an affront, and one so distant, Augusta would now refuse to speak to her. That Augusta had always been angry with her, and since Mr. Traffick's arrival more angry than ever, she had felt; but that Augusta was jealous in respect to her lover had never yet at all come home to Ayala. That she should have wanted to captivate Mr. Traffick,—she with her high ideas of some transcendental, more than human, hero I

But she had to put up with it, and to think of it. She had sense enough to know that she was no more than a stranger in her aunt's family, and that she must go if she made herself unpleasant to them. She was aware that hitherto she had not succeeded with her residence among them. Perhaps she might have to go. Some things she would bear, and in them she would endeavour to amend her conduct. In other matters she would hold her own, and go, if necessary. Though her young imagination was still full of her unsubstantial hero,—though she still had her castles in the air altogether incapable of terrestrial foundation,-^—still there was a common sense about her which told her that she must give and take. She would endeavour to submit herself to her aunt. She would be kind,-—as she had always been kind,—to Gertrude. She would in all matters obey her uncle. Her misfortune with the "Newfoundland dog had almost dwindled out of her mind. To Augusta she could not submit herself

But then Augusta, as soon as the next session of Parliament should be over, would be married out of the way. And, on her own part, she did think that her aunt was inclined to take her part in the quarrel with Augusta.

Thus matters were going on in Rome when there came up another and a worse cause for trouble.

CHAPTER VII.

TOM TRINGLE IN EARNEST.

Tom Tringle, though he had first appeared to his cousin Ayala as a Newfoundland dog which might perhaps be pleasantly playful, and then, as the same dog, very unpleasant because dripping with muddy water, was nevertheless a young man with so much manly truth about him as to be very much in love. He did not look like it; but then perhaps the young men who do fall most absolutely into love do not look like it. To Ayala her cousin Tom was as unloveable as Mr. Septimus Traffick. She could like them both well enough while they would be kind to her. But as to regarding cousin Tom as a lover,—the idea was so preposterous to her that she could not imagine that any one else should look upon it as real. But with Tom the idea had been real, and was, moreover, permanent. The black locks which would be shaken here and there, the bright glancing eyes which could be so joyous and could be so indignant, the colour of her face which had nothing in it of pink, which was brown rather, but over which the tell-tale blood would rush with a quickness which was marvellous to him, the lithe quick figure which had in it nothing of the weight of earth, the little foot which in itself was a perfect joy, the step with all the

elasticity of a fawn,—these charms together had mastered him. Tom was not romantic or poetic, but the romance and poetry of Ayala had been divine to him. It is not always like to like in love. Titania loved the weaver Bottom with the ass's head. Bluebeard, though a bad husband, is supposed to have been fond of his last wife The Beauty has always been beloved by the Beast. To Ayala the thing was monstrous;—but it was natural. Tom Tringle was determined to have his way, and when he started for Rome was more intent upon his love-making than all the glories of the Capitol and the Vatican.

When he first made his appearance before Ayala's eyes he was bedecked in a manner that was awful to her. Down at Glenbogie he had aflPected a rough attire, as is the custom with young men of ample means when fishing, shooting, or the like, is supposed to be the employment then in hand. The roughness had been a little overdone, but it had added nothing to his own uncouthness. In London he was apt to run a little towards ornamental gilding, but in London his tastes had been tempered by the ill-natured criticism of the world at large. He had hardly dared at Queen's Gate to wear his biggest pins ; but he had taken upon himself to think that at Rome an Englishman might expose himself with all his jewelry. " Oh, Tom, I never saw anything so stunning," his sister Gertrude said to him. He had simply frowned upon her, and had turned himself to Ayala, as though Ayala, being an artist, would be able to appreciate something beautiful in art. Ayala had looked at him and had marvelled, and had ventured to hope that, with his

Glenbogie dress, his Glenbogie manners and Glenbogie propensities would be changed.

At this time the family at Rome was very uncomfortable. Augusta would not speak to her cousin, and had declared to her mother and sister her determination never to speak to Ayala again. For a time Aunt Emmeline had almost taken her niece's part, feeling that she might best ring things back to a condition of peace in this manner. Ayala, she had thought, might thus be decoyed into a state of submission. Ayala, so instigated, had made her attempt. ^' What is the matter, Augusta," she had said, ^' that you are determined to quarrel with me ?'* Then had followed a little offer that bygones should be bygones.

" I have quarrelled with you," said Augusta, '^ because you do not know how to behave yourself.'* Then Ayala had flashed forth, and the little attempt led to a worse condition than ever, and words were spoken which even Aunt Emmeline had felt to be irrevocable, irremediable.

" Only that you are going away I would not consent to live here," said Ayala. Then Aunt Emmeline had asked her where she would go to live should it please her to remove herself, Ayala had thought of this for a moment, and then had burst into tears. " If I could not live I could die. Anything would be better than to be treated as she treats me." So the matters were when Tom came to Rome with all his jewelry.

Lucy Tringle had already told herself that, in choosing Ayala, she had chosen wrong. Lucy, though not so attractive as Ayala, was pretty, quiet, and ladylike. So she

thought now. And as to Ayala's attractions, they were not at all of a nature to be serviceable to such a family as hers. To have her own girls outshone, to be made to feel that the poor orphan was the one person most worthy of note among them, to be subjected to the caprices of a pretty, proud, ill-conditioned minx;—thus it was that Aunt Emmeline was taught to regard her own charity and goodnature towards her niece. There was, she said, no gratitude in Ayala. Had she said that there was no humility she would have been more nearly right. She was entitled, she thought, to expect both gratitude and humility, and she was sorry that she had opened the Paradise of her opulent home to one so little grateful and so little humble as Ayala. She saw now her want of judgment in that she had not taken Lucy.

Tom, who was not a fool, in spite of his trinkets, saw the state of the case, and took Ayala's part at once. " I think you are quite right," he said to her, on the first occasion on which he had contrived to find himself alone with her after his arrival.

Right about what?"

In not giving up to Augusta. She was always like that when she was a child, and now her head is turned about Traffick."

I shouldn't grudge her her lover if she would only let me alone." I don't suppose she hurts you much ?"

She sets my aunt against me, and that makes me unhappy. Of course I am wretched."

" Oh, Ayala, don't be wretched."

How is one to help it ? I never said an ill-natured word to her, and now I am so lonely among them !" In saying this,—in seeking to get one word of sympathy from her cousin, she forgot for a moment his disagreeable pretensions. But, no sooner had she spoken of her loneliness, than she saw that ogle in his eye of which she had spoken with so much ludicrous awe in her letters from Glenbogie to her sister.

" I shall always take your part," said he.

" I don't want any taking of parts."

" But I shall. I am not going to see you put upon. You are more to me, Ayala, than any of them." Then he looked at her, whereupon she got up and ran away.

, But she could not always run away, nor could she always refuse when he asked her to go with him about the show-places of the city. To avoid starting alone with him was within her power ; but she found herself compelled to join herself to Gertrude and her brother in some of those little excursions which were taken for her benefit. At this time there had come to be a direct quarrel between Lady Tringle and the Marchesa, which, however, had arisen altogether on the part of Augusta. Augusta had forced her mother to declare that she was insulted, and then there was no more visiting between them. This had been sad enough for Ayala, who had struck up an intimacy with the Marchesa's daughters. But the Marchesa had explained to her that there was no help for it. " It won't do for you to separate yourself from your aunt," she had

said. " Of course we shall be friends, and at some future time you shall come and see us." So there had been a division, and Ayala would have been quite alone had she declined the proffered companionship of Gertrude.

Within the walls and arches and upraised terraces of the Coliseum they were joined one day by young Hamel, the sculptor, who had not, as yet, gone back to London,— and had not, as yet, met Lucy in the gardens at Kensington ; and with him there had been one Frank Houston, who had made acquaintance with Lady Tringle, and with the Tringles generally, since they had been at Eome. Frank Houston was a young man of family^ with a taste for art, very good-looking, but not specially well off in regard to income. He had heard of the good fortune of Septimus Traffick in having prepared for himself a connection with so wealthy a family as the Tringles, and had thought it possible that a settlement in life might be comfortable for himself. What few soft words he had hitherto been able to say to Gertrude had been taken in good part, and when, therefore, they met among the walls of the Coliseum, she had naturally straggled away to see some special wonder which he had a special aptitude for showing. Hamel remained with Ayala and Tom, talking of the old days at the bijou, till he found himself obliged to leave them. Then Tom had his opportunity.

" Ayala," he said, " all this must be altered."

" What must be altered ?"

" If you only knew, Ayala, how much you are to

" I wish you wouldn't, Tom. I don't want to be anything to anybody in particular."

" What I mean is, that I won't have them sit upon you. They treat you as—as,—well, as though you had only half a right to be one of them."

" No more I have. I have no right at all."

" But that^s not the way I want it to be. If you were my wife "

" Tom, pray don't."

" Why not ? I'm in earnest. Why ain't I to speak as I think ? Oh, Ayala, if you knew how much I think of you."

" But you shouldn't. You haven't got a right."

" I have got a right."

'^ But I don't want it, Tom, and I won't have it." He had carried her away now to the end of the terrace, or ruined tier of seats, on which they were walking, and had got her so hemmed into a corner that she could not get away from him. She was afraid of him, lest he should put out his hand to take hold of her,—lest something even more might be attempted. And yet his manner was manly and sincere, and had it not been for his pins and his chains she could not but have acknowledged his goodness to her, much as she might have disliked his person. " I want to get out," she said. " I won't stay here any more." Mr. Traffick, on the top of St. Peter's, had been a much pleasanter companion.

" Don't You believe me when I tell you that I love you better than anybody?" pleaded Tom.

" No."

" Not believe me ? Oh, Ayala!"

" I don't want to believe anything. I want to get out. If you go on, I'll tell my aunt."

Tell her aunt! There was a want of personal consideration to himself in this way of receiving his addresses which almost angered him. Tom Triugle was not in the least afraid of his mother,—was not even afraid of his father as long as he was fairly regular at the office in Lombard Street. He was quite determined to please himself in marriage, and was disposed to think that his father and mother would like him to be settled. Money was no object. There was, to his thinking, no good reason why he should not marry his cousin. For her the match was so excellent that he hardly expected she would reject him when she could be made to understand that he was really in earnest. " You may tell all the world," he said proudly. " All I want is that you should love me."

" But I don't. There are Gertrude and Mr. Houston, and I want to go to them."

" Say one nice word to me, Ayala."

" I don't know how to say a nice word. Can't you be made to understand that I don't like it?"

" Ayala."

" Why don't you let me go away ?"

" Ayala,—give me—one—kiss." Then Ayala did go away, escaping by some kid-like manoeuvre among the ruins, and running quickly, while he followed her, joined herself to the other pair of lovers, who probably were less

in want of her society than she of theirs. " Ayala, I am quite in earnest," said Tom, as they were walking home, " and I mean to go on with it."

Ayala thought that there was nothing for it but to tell her aunt. That there would be some absurdity in such a proceeding she did feel,—that she would be acting as though her cousin were a naughty boy who was merely teasing her. But the felt also the peculiar danger of her ow^n position. Her aunt must be made to understand that she, Ayala, was innocent in the matter. It would be terrible to her to be suspected even for a moment of a desire to inveigle the heir. That Augusta would bring such an accusation against her she thought probable. Augusta had said as much even at Glenbogie. She must therefore be on the alert, and let it be understood at once that she was not leagued with her cousin Tom. There would be an absurdity 5—but that would be better than suspicion.

She thought about it all that afternoon, and in the evening she came to a resolution. She would write a letter to her cousin and persuade him if possible to desist. If he should again annoy her after that she would appeal to her aunt. Then she wrote and sent her letter^ which was as follows ;—

" Dear Tom,

You don't know how unhappy you made me at the Coliseum to-day. I don't think you ought to turn against me when you know what I have to, bear. It is turning

against me to talk as you did. Of course it means nothing; but you shouldn't do it. It never never could mean anything. I hope you will be good-natured and kind to me, and then I shall be so much obliged to you. If you won't say anything more like that I will forget it altogether. "
Your affectionate cousin,

" Atala."

The letter ought to have convinced him. Those two underscored nevers should have eradicated from his mind the feeling which had been previously produced by the assertion that he had " meant nothing." But he was so assured in his own meanings that he paid no attention whatever to the nevers. The letter was a delight to him because it gave him the opportunity of a rejoinder,—and he wrote his rejoinder on a scented sheet of note-paper and copied it twice ;—

Dearest Ayala,

" Why do you say that it means nothing ? It means everything. No man was ever more in earnest in speaking to a lady than I am with you. Why should J not be in earnest when I am so deeply in love ? From the first moment in which I saw you down at Glenbogie I knew how it was going to be with me.

" As for my mother I don't think she would say a word. Why should she ? But I am not the sort of man to be talked out of my intentions in such a matter as this. I have set my heart upon having you and nothing will ever turn me off.

" Pearest Ajala, let me have one look to say that you will love me, and I shall be the happiest man in England. I think you so beautiful! I do, indeed. The governor has always said that if I would settle down and marry there should be lots of money. What could I do better with it than make my darling look as grand as the best of them.

" Yours, always meaning it,

" Most affectionately,

" T. Tringle."

It almost touched her,—not in the way of love but of gratitude. He was still to her like Bottom with the ass's head, or the Newfoundland dog gambolling out of the water. There was the heavy face, and there were the big chains and the odious rings, and the great hands and the clumsy feet,—making together a creature whom it was impossible even to think of with love. She shuddered as she remembered the proposition which had been made to her in the Coliseum.

And now by writing to him she had brought down upon herself this absolute love-letter. She had thought that by appealing to him as " Dear Tom," and by signing herself his affectionate cousin, she might have prevailed. If he could only be made to understand that it could never mean nothing ! But now, on the other hand, she had begun to understand that it did mean a great deal. He had sent to her a regular offer of marriage! The magnitude of the thing struck her at last. The heir of all the wealth of her mighty uncle wanted to make her his wife !

But it was to her exactly as though the heir had come to her wearing an ass's head on his shoulders. Love him! Marry him !—or even touch him ? Oh, no. They might ill-use her ; they might scold her; they might turn her out of the house ; but no consideration would induce her to think of Tom Tringle as a lover.

And yet he was in earnest, and honest, and good. And some answer,—some further communication must be made to him. She did recognise some nobility in him, though personally he was so distasteful to her. Now* his appeal to her had taken the guise of an absolute offer of marriage he was entitled to a discreet and civil answer. Eomantic, dreamy, poetic, childish as she was, she knew as much as that. " Go away, Tom, you fool, you," would no longer do for the occasion. As she thought of it all that night it was borne in upon her more strongly than ever that her only protection would be in telling her aunt, and in getting her aunt to make Tom understand that there must be no more of it. Early on the following morning she found herself in her aunt's bedroom.

CHAPTER VIIL

THE LOUT.

" Aunt Emmeline, I want you to read this letter/' So it was that Ayala commenced the interview. At this moment Ajala was not on much better terms with her aunt than she was with her cousin Augusta. Ayala was a trouble to her, —Lady Tringle,—who was altogether perplexed with the feeling that she had burdened herself with an inmate in her house who was distasteful to her and of whom she could not rid herself. Ayala had turned out on her hands something altogether different from the girl she had intended to cherish and patronise. Ayala was independent ; superior rather than inferior to her own girls; more thought of by others; apparently without any touch of that subservience which should have been produced in her by her position. Ayala seemed to demand as much as though she were a daughter of the house, and at the same time to carry herself as though she were more gifted than the daughters of the house. She was less obedient even than a daughter. All this Aunt Emmeline could not endure with a placid bosom. She was herself kind of heart. She acknowledged her duty to her dead sister. She wished to protect and foster the orphan. She did not even yet wish to punish Ayala by utter desertion. She

would protect lier in opposition to Augusta^s more declared malignity; but she did wish to be rid of Ayala, if she only knew how.

She took her son's letter and read it, and as a matter of course misunderstood the position. At Glcnbogie something had been whispered to her about Tom and Ayala, but she had not believed much in it. Ayala was a child, and Tom was to her not much more than a boy. But now here was a genuine love-letter,—a letter in which her son had made a distinct proposition to marry the orphan. She did not stop to consider why Ayala had brought the letter to her, but entertained at once an idea that the two young people were going to vex her very soul by a lamentable love affair. How imprudent she had been to let the two young people be together in Home, seeing that the matter had been whispered to her at Glenbogie I " How long has this been going on ?'* she asked, severely.

" He used to tease me at Glenbogie, and now he is doing it again," said Ayala.

" There must certainly be put an end to it. You must go away."

Ayala knew at once that her aunt was angry with her, and was indignant at the injustice. '^ Of course there must be put an end to it, Aunt Emmeline. He has no right to annoy me when I tell him not."

" T suppose you have encouraged him."

This was too cruel to be borne! Encouraged him! Ayala's anger was caused not so much by a feeling that her aunt had misappreciated the cause of her coming as

that it should have been thought possible that she should have " encouraged such a lover. It was the outrage to her taste rather than to her conduct which afflicted her. " He is a lout she said; "a stupid lout I" thus casting her scorn upon the mother as vell as on the son, and, indeed, upon the whole family. " I have not encouraged him. It is untrue."

" Ayala, you are very impertinent."

" And you are very unjust. Because I want to put a stop to it I come to you, and you tell me that I encourage him. You are worse than Augusta."

This was too much for the good nature even of Aunt Emmeline. Whatever may have been the truth as to the love affair, however iimocent Ayala may have been in that matter, or however guilty Tom, such words from a niece to her aunt,—from a dependent to her superior,—were unpardonable. The extreme youthfulness of the girl, a peculiar look of childhood which she still had with her, made the feeling so much the stronger. " You are worse than Augusta I"

And this was said to her who was specially conscious of her endeavours to mitigate Augusta's just anger. She bridled up, and tried to look big and knit her brows. At that moment she could not think what must be the end of it, but she felt that Ayala must be crushed. " How dare you speak to me like that, ' Miss' ?" she said.

" So you are. It is very cruel. Tom will go on saying all this nonsense to me, and when I come to you you say I encourage him ! I never encouraged him. I despise him

too much. I did not think my own aunt could have told me that I encouraored any man. No, I didn't. You drive me to it, so that I have got to be impertinent."

" You had better go to your room," said the aunt. Then Ayala, lifting her head as high as she knew how, walked towards the door. " You had better leave that letter with me." Ayala considered the matter for a moment, and then handed the letter a second time to her aunt. It could be nothing to her who saw the letter. She did not want it. Having thus given it up she stalked off in silent disdain and went to her chamber.

Aunt Emmeline, when she was left alone, felt herself to be enveloped in a cloud of doubt. The desirableness of Tom as a husband first forced itself upon her attention, and the undesirableness of Ayala as a wife for Tom. She was perplexed at her own folly in not having seen that danger of this kind would arise when she first proposed to take Ayala into the house. Aunts and uncles do not like the marriage of cousins, and the parents of rich children do not, as a rule, approve of marriages with those which are poor. Although Ayala had been so violent. Lady Tringle could not rid herself of the idea that her darling boy was going to throw himself away. Then her cheeks became red with anger as she remembered that her Tom had been called a lout,—a stupid lout. There was an ingratitude in the use of such language which was not alleviated even by the remembrance that it tended against that matrimonial danger of which she was so much afraid. Ayala was behaving very badly. She ought not to have

coaxed Tom to be her lover, and she certainly ought not to have called Tom a lout. And then Ayala had told her aunt that she was unjust and worse than Augusta! It was out of the question that such a state of things should be endured. Ayala must be made to go away.

Before the day was over Lady Tringle spoke to her son, and was astonished to find that the "lout" was quite in earnest,— so much in earnest that he declared his purpose of marrying his cousin in opposition to his father and mother, in opposition even to Ayala herself. He was so much in earnest that he would not be roused to wrath even when he was told that Ayala had called him a lout. And then grew upon the mother a feeling that the young man had never been so little loutish before. For there had been, even in her maternal bosom, a feeling that Tom was open to the criticism expressed on him. Tom had been a hobble-de-hoy, one of those overgrown lads who come late to their manhood, and who are regarded by young ladies as louts. Though he had spent his money only too freely when away, his sisters had sometimes said that he could not say " bo to a goose " at home. But now, —now Tom was quite an altered young man. When his own letter was shown to him he simply said that he meant to stick to it. When it was represented to him that his cousin would be quite an unfit wife for him he assured his mother that his own opinion on that matter was very different. When his father's anger was threatened he declared that his father would have no right to be angry with him if he married a lady. At the word "lout" he simply

smiled. " She'll come to think different from that before she's done with me," he said, with a smile. Even the mother could not but perceive that the young man had been much improved by his love.

But what was she to do ? Two or three days went on, during which there was no reconciliation between her and Ayala. Between Augusta and Ayala no word was spoken. Messages were taken to her by Gertrude, the object of which was to induce her to ask her aunt's pardon. But Ayala was of opinion that her aunt ought to ask her pardon, and could not be beaten from it. " Why did she say that I encouraged him ?" she demanded indignantly of Gertrude. " I don't think she did encourage him," said Gertrude to her mother. This might possibly be true, but not the less had she misbehaved. And though she might not yet have encouraged her lover it was only too probable that she might do so when she found that her lover was quite in earnest.

Lady Tringle was much harassed. And then there came an additional trouble. Gertrude informed her mother that she had engaged herself to Mr. Francis Houston, and that Mr. Houston was going to write to her father with the object of proposing himself as a son-in-law. Mr. Houston came also to herself, and told her, in the most natural tone in the world, that he intended to marry her daughter. She had not known what to say. It was Sir Thomas who managed all matters of money. She had an idea that Mr. Houston was very poor. But then so also had been Mr. Traffick, who had been received into the family with

open arms. But then Mr. Traffick had a career, whereas Mr. Houston was lamentably idle. She could only refer Mr. Houston to Sir Thomas, and beg him not to come among them any more till Sir Thomas had decided. Upon this Gertrude also got angry, and shut herself up in her room. The apartments Ruperti were, therefore, upon the whole, an uncomfortable home to them.

Letters upon letters were written to Sir Thomas, and letters upon letters came. The first letter had been about Ayala. He had been much more tender towards Ayala than her aunt had been. He talked of calf-love, and said that Tom was a fool; but he had not at once thought it necessary to give imperative orders for Tom's return. As to Ayala's impudence, he evidently regarded it as nothing. It was not till Aunt Emmeline had spoken out in her third letter that he seemed to recognise the possibility of getting rid of Ayala altogether. And this he did in answer to a suggestion which had been made to him. " If she likes to change with her sister Lucy, and you like it, I shall not object," said Sir Thomas. Then there came an order to Tom that he should return to Lombard Stree at once; but this order had been rendered abortive by the sudden return of the whole family. Sir Thomas, in his first letter as to Gertrude, had declared that the Houston marriage would not do at all. Then, when he was told that Gertrude and Mr. Houston had certainly met each other more than once since an order had been given for their separation, he desired the whole family to come back at once to Merle Park.

The proposition as to Lucy had arisen in this wise. Tom being in the same house with Ayala, of course had her very much at advantage, and would cany on his suit in spite of any abuse which she might lavish upon him. It was quite in vain that she called him lout. " You'll think very different from that some of these days, Ayala," he said, more seriously.

" No, I shan't; I shall think always the same."

" When you know how much I love you, you'll change."

" I don't want you to love me," she said ; " and if you were anything that is good you wouldn't go on after I have told you so often. It is not manly of you. You have brought me to all manner of trouble. It is your fault, but they make me suffer."

After that Ayala again went to her aunt, and on this occasion the family misfortune was discussed in more seemly language. Ayala was still indignant, but she said nothing insolent. Aunt Emmeline was still averse to her niece, but she abstained from crimination. They knew each as enemies, but recognised the wisdom of keeping the peace. *' As for that. Aunt Emmeline," Ayala said, " you may be quite sure that I shall never encourage him. I shall never like him well enough."

" Very well. Then we need say no more about that, my dear. Of course, it must be unpleasant to us all, being in the same house together."

"It is very unpleasant to me, when he will go on bothering me like that. It makes me wish that I were anywhere else."

VOL. I. H

Then Aunt Emmeline began to think about it very seriously. It was very unpleasant- Ayala had made herself disagreeable to all the ladies of the family, and only too agreeable to the young gentleman. Nor did the manifest favour of Sir Thomas do much towards raising Ayala in Lady Tringle's estimation. Sir Thomas had only laughed when Augusta had been requested to go upstairs for the scrap-book. Sir Thomas had been profuse with his presents even when Ayala had been most persistent in her misbehaviour. And then all that affair of the Mar-chesa, and even Mr. Traffick's infatuation I If Ayala wished that she were somewhere else would it not be well to indulge her wish! Aunt Emmeline certainly wished it. " If you think so, perhaps some arrangement can be made said Aunt Emmeline, very slowly.

" What arrangement ?"

" You must not suppose that I wish to turn you out?"

" But what arrangement?"

" You see, Ayala, that unfortunately we have not all of us hit it off nicely; have we ?"

*^ Not at all. Aunt Emmeline. Augusta is always angry with me. And you,—you think that I have encouraged Tom."

" I am saying nothing about that, Ayala."

" But what arrangement is it, Aunt Emmeline ?" The matter was one of fearful import to Ayala. She was prudent enough to understand that well. The arrangement must be one by which she would be banished from all the wealth of the Tringles. Her coming among them had not been a success. She had already made them tired of her by her petulance and independence. Young as she was she could see that, and comprehend the material injury she had done herself by her folly. She had been very wrong in telling Augusta to go upstairs. She had been wrong in the triumph of her exclusive visits to the Marchesa. She had been wrong in walking away with Mr. Traffick on the Pincian. She could see that. She had not been wrong in regard to Tom,—except in calling him a lout; but whether wrong or right she had been most unfortunate. But the thing had been done, and she must go.

At this moment the wealth of the Tringles seemed to be more to her than it had ever been before,—and her own poverty and destitution seemed to be more absolute. When the word '^ arrangement" was whispered to her there came upon her a clear idea of all that which she was to lose. She was to be banished from Merle Park, from Queen's Gate, and from Glenbogie. For her there were to be no more carriages, and horses, and pretty trinkets;—none of that abandon of the luxury of money among which the Tringles lived. But she had done it for herself, and she would not say a word in opposition to the fate which was before her. " What arrangement, aunt ?" she said again, in a voice which was intended to welcome any arrangement that might be made.

Then her aunt spoke very softly. " Of course, dear Ayala, we do not wish to do less than we at first intended.

But as you are not happy here " Then she paused,
almost ashamed of herself.

H 2

" I am not happy here," said Ayala, boldly.

" How would it be if you were to change,—with Lucy?"

The idea which had been present to Lady Tringle for some weeks past had never struck Ayala. The moment she heard it she felt that she was more than ever bound to assent. If the home from which she was to be banished was good, then would that good fall upon Lucy. Lucy would have the carriages and the horses and the trinkets, Lucy, who certainly was not happy at: Kingsbury Crescent, I should be very glad, indeed," said Ayala.

Her voice was so brave and decided that, in itself, it gave fresh offence to her aunt. Was there to be no regret after so much generosity ? But she misunderstood the girl altogether. As the words were coming from her lips, —" I should be very glad, indeed,Ayala's heart was sinking with tenderness as she remembered how much after all had been done for her. But as they wished her to go there should be not a word, not a sign of unwillingness on her part.

" Then perhaps it can be arranged," said Lady Tringle.

" I don't know what Uncle Dosett may say. Perhaps they are very fond of Lucy now."

" They wouldn't wish to stand in her way, I should think."

" At any rate, won't. If you, and my uncles, and Aunt Margaret, will consent, I will go whenever you choose. Of course I must do just as I'm told."

Aunt Emmeline made a faint demur to this; but still the matter was held to be arranged. Letters were written

to Sir Thomas, and letters came, and at last even Sir Thomas had assented. He suggested, in the first place, that all the facts which would follow the exchange should be explained to Ayala; but he was obliged after a while to acknowledge that this would be inexpedient. The girl was willing; and knew no doubt that she was to give up the great wealth of her present home. But she had proved herself to be an unfit participator, and it was better that she should go.

Then the departure of them all from Rome was hurried on by the indiscretion of Gertrude. Gertrude declared that she had a right to her lover. As to his having no income, what matter for that. Everyone knew that Septimus Traffick had no income. Papa had income enough for them all. Mr. Houston was a gentleman. Till this moment no one had known of how strong a will of her own Gertrude was possessed. When Gertrude declared that she would not consent to be separated from Mr. Houston then they were all hurried home.

CHAPTER IX.

THE EXCHANGE.

Such was the state of things when Mr. Dosett brought the three letters home with him to Kingsbury Crescent,]iaving been so much disturbed by the contents of the two which were addressed to himself as to have found himself compelled to leave his office two hours before the proper time. The three letters were handed together by her uncle to Lucy, and she, seeing the importance of the occasion, read the two open ones before she broke the envelope of her own. That from Sir Thomas came first, and was as follows ;—

Lombard Street, January, 187—. " My dear Dosett,
I have had a correspondence with the ladies at Rome
which has been painful in its nature, but which I had better
perhaps communicate to you at once. Ayala has not got
on as well with Lady Tringle and the girls as might have
been wished, and they all think it will be better that she
and Lucy should change places. I chiefly write to give my
assent. Your sister will no doubt write to you. I may as
well mention to you, should you consent to take charge of
Ayala, that I have made some provision for her in my will,and that I shall not change it. I have to add on my own account that I have no complaint of my own to make against Ayala.

Yours sincerely,
T. Tringle."

Lucy, when she had read this, proceeded at once to the letter from her aunt. The matter to her was one of terrible importance, but the importance was quite as great to Ayala. She had been allowed to go up alone into her own room. The letters were of such a nature that she could hardly have read them calmly in the presence of her Aunt Dosett. It was thus that her Aunt Emmeline had written;—

Palazzo Ruperti, Rome, Thursday. My DEAR Reginald,
I am sure you will be sorry to hear that we are in great trouble here. This has become bo bad that we are obliged to apply to you to help us. Now you must understand that I do not mean to say a word against dear Ayala; —only she does not suit. It will occur sometimes that people who are most attached to each other do not suit. So it has been with dear Ayala. She is not happy with us. She has not perhaps accommodated herself to her cousins quite as carefully as she might have done. She is fully as sensible of this as I am, and is, herself, persuaded that there had better be a change.

Now, my dear Reginald, I am quite aware that when poor Egbert died it was I who chose Ayala, and that you took Lucy partly in compliance with my wishes. Now I write to suggest that there should be a change. I am sure you will give me credit for a desire to do the best I can for both the poor dear girls. T did think that this might be best done by letting Ayala come to us. I now think that Lucy would do better with her cousins, and that Ayala would be more attractive without the young people around her.

^^ When I see you 1 will tell you everything. There has been no great fault. She has spoken a word or two to me to which had been better unsaid, but I am well convinced that it has come from hot temper and not from a bad heart. Perhaps I had better tell you the truth. Tom has admired her. She has behaved very well; but she could not bear to be spoken to, and so there have been unpleasantnesses. And the girls certainly have not got on well together. Sir Thomas quite agrees with me that if ysu will consent there had better be a change.

" I will not write to dear Lucy herself because you and Margaret can explain it all so much better,—if you will consent to our plan. Ayala also will write to her sister. But pray tell her from me that I will love her very dearly if she will come to me. And indeed I have loved Ayala almost as though she were my own, only we have not been quite able to hit it off together.

" Of course neither has Sir Thomas or have I any idea of escaping from a responsibility. I should be quite unhappy if I did not have one of poor dear Egbert's girls with me. Only I do think that Lucy would be the best for us; and Ayala thinks so too. I should be quite unhappy if I were doing this in opposition to Ayala.

" We shall be in England almost as soon as this letter, and I should be so glad if this could be decided at once. If a thing like this is to be done it is so much better for all parties that it should be done quickly. Pray give my best love to Margaret, and tell her that Ayala shall bring everything with her that she wants.

Your most affectionate sister,
Emmeline Tringle."

The letter, though it was much longer than her uncle's, going into details, such as that of Tom's unfortunate passion for his cousin, had less effect upon Lucy, as it did not speak with so much authority as that from Sir Thomas. What Sir Thomas said would surely be done; whereas Aunt Emmeline was only a woman, and her letter, unsupported, might not have carried conviction. But, if Sir Thomas wished it, surely it must be done. Then, at last, came Ayala's letter;—

" Rome, Thursday.

" Dearest, dearest Lucy,

" Oh, I have such things to write to you ! Aunt Emmeline has told it all to Uncle Reginald. You are to come and be the princess, and I am to go and be the milkmaid at home. I am quite content that it should be so because I know that it will be the best. You ought to be a princess and I ought to be a milkmaid.

" It has been coming almost ever since the first day that I came among them,- since I told Augusta to go upstairs

for the scrap-book. I felt from the very moment in which the words were uttered that I had gone and done for myself. But I am not a bit sorry, as you will come in my place. Augusta will very soon be gone now, and Aunt Emmeline is not bad at all if you will only not contradict her. I always contradicted her, and I know that I have been a fool. But I am not a bit sorry, as you are to come instead of me.

'^ But it is not only about Augusta and Aunt Emmeline. There has been that oaf Tom. Poor Tom ! I do believe that he is the most good-natured fellow alive. And if he had not so many chains I should not dislike him so very much. But he will go on saying horrible things to me. And then he wrote me a letter ! Oh dear ! 1 took the letter to Aunt Emmeline, and that made the quarrel. She said that I had—encouraged him ! Oh, Lucy, if you will think of that! I was so angry that I said ever so much to her,—till she sent me out of the room. She had no business to say that I encouraged him. It was shameful ! But she has never forgiven me, because I scolded her. So they have decided among them that I am to be sent away, and that you are to come in my place.

My own darling Lucy, it will be ever so much better. I know that you are not happy in Kingsbury Crescent, and that I shall bear it very much better. I can sit still and mend sheets.*'

Poor Ayala, how little she knew herself! And you will make a beautiful grand lady, quiescent and dignified as a grand lady ought to be. At any rate it would be impossible that I should remain here.

Tom is bad enougli, but to be told that I encourage him is more than I can bear.

I shall see you very soon, but I cannot help writing and telling it to you all. Give my love to Aunt Dosett. If she will consent to receive me I will endeavour to be good to her. In the meantime good-bye.

Your most affectionate sister,

"Ayala.

When Lucy had completed the reading of the letters she sat for a considerable time wrapped in thought. There was, in truth, very much that required thinking. It was proposed that the whole tenour of her life should be changed, and changed in a direction which would certainly suit her *aste. She had acknowledged to herself that she had hated the comparative poverty of her Uncle Dosett's life, hating herself in that she was compelled to make such acknowledgment. But there had been more than the poverty which had been distasteful to her,—a something which she had been able to tell herself that she might be justified in hating without shame. There had been to her an absence of intellectual charm in the habits and manners of Kingsbury Crescent which she had regarded as unfortunate and depressing. There had been no thought of art delights. No one read poetry. No one heard music. No one looked at pictures. A sheet to be darned was the one thing of greatest importance. The due development of a leg of mutton, the stretching of a pound of butter, the best way of repressing the washerwoman's bills,—these had been the

matters of interest. And they had not been made the less irritating to her by her aunt's extreme goodness in the matter. The leg of mutton was to be developed in the absence of her uncle,—if possible without his knowledge. He was to have his run of clean linen. Lucy did no grudge him anything, but was sickened by that partnership in economy which was established between her and her aunt. Undoubtedly from time to time she had thought of the luxuries which had been thrown in Ayala's way. There had been a regret,—not that Ayala should have them but that she should have missed them. Money she declared that she despised ;— but the easy luxury of the bijou was sweet to her memory.

Now it was suggested to her suddenly that she was to exchange the poverty for the luxury, and to return to a mode of life in which her mind might be devoted to things of beauty. The very scenery of Glenbogie,—what a charm it would have for her ! Judging from her uncle's manner, as well as she could during that moment in which he handed to her the letter, she imagined that he intended to make no great objection. Her aunt disliked her. She was sure that her aunt disliked her in spite of the partnership. Only that there was one other view of the case— how happy might the transfer be. Her uncle was always gentle to her, but there could hardly as yet have grown up any strong affection for her. To him she was grateful, but she could not tell herself that to part from him would be a pang. There was, however, another view of the case.

Ayala ! How would it be with Ayala I Would Ayala like the partnership and the economies ? Would Ayala be cheerful as she sat opposite to her aunt for four hours at a time I Ayala had said that she could sit still and mend sheets, but was it not manifest enough that Ayala knew nothing of the life of which she was speaking. And would she, Lucy, be able to enjoy the glories of Glenbogie while she thought that Ayala was eating out her heart in the sad companionship of Kingsbury Crescent ? For above an hour she sat and thought; but of one aspect which the affair bore she did not think. She did not reflect that she and Ayala were in the hands of Fate, and that they must both do as their elders should require of them.

At last there came a knock at the door, and her aunt entered. She would sooner that it should have been her uncle: but there was no choice but that the matter should be now discussed with the woman whom she did not love, —this matter that was so dreadful to herself in all its bearings, and so dreadful to one for whom she would willingl\'7d^ sacrifice herself if it were possible I She did not know what she could say to create sympathy with Aunt Dosett. ^' Lucy," said Aunt Dosett, " this is a very serious proposal."

" Very serious," said Lucy, sternly.

" I have not read the letters, but your uncle has told me about it." Then Lucy handed her the two letters, keeping that from Ayala to herself, and she sat perfectly still while her aunt read them both slowly. " Your Aunt Emmeline is certainly in earnest," said Mrs. Dosett.

" Aunt Emmeline is very good-natured, and perhaps she will change her mind if we tell her that we wish it."

" But Sir Thomas has agreed to it."

" I am sure my uncle will give way if Aunt Emmeline will ask him. He says he has no complaint to make against Ayala. I think it is Augusta, and Augusta will be married, and will go away very soon."

Then there came a change, a visible change, over the countenance of Aunt Dosett, and a softening of the voice, —so that she looked and spoke as Lucy had not seen or heard her before. There are people apparently so hard, so ungenial, so unsympathetic, that they who only half know them expect no trait of tenderness, think that features so little alluring cannot be compatible with softness. Lucy had acknowledged her Aunt Dosett to be good, but believed her to be incapable of being touched. But a word or two had now conquered her. The girl did not want to leave her,—did not seize the first opportunity of running from her poverty to the splendour of the Tringles I " But, Lucy," she said, and came and placed herself nearer to Lucy on the bed.

" Ayala ," said Lucy, sobbing.

" I will be kind to her,—perhaps kinder than I have been to you."

" You have been kind, and I have been ungrateful. I know it. But I will do better now. Aunt Dosett. I will stay, if you will have me."

" They are rich and powerful, and you will have to do as they direct."

" No ! Who are they that 1 should be made to come and go at their bidding? Tliey cannot make me leave you."

" But they can rid themselves of Ayala, You see what your uncle says about money for Ayala."

" I hate money."

" Money is a thing v»rhich none of us can afford to hate. Do you think it will not be much to your Uncle Reginald to know that you are both provided for ? Already he is wretched because there will be nothing to come to you. If you go to your Aunt Emmeline, Sir Thomas will do for you as he has done for Ayala. Dear Lucy, it is not that 1 want to send you away." Then for the first time Lucy put her arm round her aunt's neck. " But it had better be as is proposed, if your aunt still wishes it, when she comes home. I and your Uncle Reginald would not do right were we to allow you to throw away the prospects that are offered you. It is natural that Lady Tringle should be anxious about her son."

"' She need not, in the least," said Lucy, indignantly.

^^ But you see what they say."

'^ It is his fault, not hers. Why should she be punished ?"

" Because he is Fortune's favourite, and she is not. It is no good kicking against the pricks, my dear. He is his father's son and heir, and everything must give way to him."

" But Ayala does not want him. Ayala despises him. It is too hard that she is to lose everything because a

young man like that will go on making himself disagreeable. They have no right to do it after having accustomed Ayala to such a home. Don't you feel that, Aunt Dosett ?"

" I do feel it."

" However it might have been arranged at first, it ought to remain now. Even though Ayala and I are only girls, we ought not to be changed about as though we were horses. If she had done anything wrong,—but Uncle Tom says that she has done nothing wrong."

" I suppose she has spoken to her aunt disrespectfully."

^^ Because her aunt told her that she had encouraged this man. What would you have a girl say when she is falsely accused like that? Would you say it to me merely because some horrid man would come and speak to me ?" Then there came a slight pang of conscience as she remembered Isadore Hamel in Kensington Gardens. If the men were not thought to be horrid, then perhaps the speaking might be a sin worthy of most severe accusation.

There was nothing more said about it that night, nor till the following afternoon, when Mr. Dosett returned home at the usual hour from his office. Then Lucy was closeted with him for a quarter-of-an-hour in the drawing-room. He had been into the City and seen Sir Thomas. Sir Thomas had been of opinion that it would be much better that Lady Tringle's wishes should be obeyed. It was quite true that he himself had no complaint to make against Ayala, but he did think that Ayala had been pert; and, though it might be true that Ayala had not encou-

raged Tom, there was no knowing what might grow out of such a propensity on Tom's part. And then it could not be pleasant to Lady Tringle or to himself that their son should be banished out of their house. When something was hinted as to the injustice of this, Sir Thomas endeavoured to put all that right by declaring that, if Lady Tringle's wishes could be attended to in this matter, provision would be made for the two girls. He certainly would not strike Ayala's name out of his will, and as certainly would not take Lucy under his wing as his own child without making some provision for her. Looking at the matter in this light hq did not think that Mr. Dosett would be justified in robbing Lucy of the advantages which were offered to her. With this view Mr. Dosett found himself compelled to agree, and with these arguments he declared to Lucy that it was her duty to submit herself to the proposed exchange.

Early in February all the Tringle family were in Queen's Grate, and Lucy on her first visit to the house found that everyone, including Ayala, looked upon the thing as settled. Ayala, who under these circumstances was living on affectionate terms with all the Tringles, except Tom, was quite radiant. " I suppose I had better go to-morrow, aunt?" she said, as though it were a matter of most trivial consequence.

" In a day or two, Ayala, it will be better."

" It shall be Monday, then. You must come over here in a cab, Lucy."

" The carriage shall be sent, my dear."

VOL. I. I

" But then it must go back with me, Aunt Emmeline.'^

" It shall, my clear."

And the horses must be put up, because Lucy and I must change all our things in the drawers." Lucy at the time was sitting in the drawing-room, and Augusta, with most affectionate confidence, was singing to her all the praises of Mr. Traffick. Li this way it was settled, and the change, so greatly affecting the fortunes of our twcy sisters, was arranged.

CHAPTER X.

AYALA AND HER AUNT MARGARET.

Till the last moment for going Ayala seemed to be childish, triumphant, and indifferent. But, till tha t last moment, she was never alone with Lucy. It was the presence of her aunt and cousins which sustained her in her hardihood. Tom was never there,—or so rarely as not to affect her greatly. In London he had his own lodgings, and was not encouraged to appear frequently till Ayala should have gone. But Aunt Emmeline and Gertrude were perseveringly gracious, and even Augusta had somewhat relaxed from her wrath. With them Ayala was always good-humoured, but always brave. She affected to rejoice at the change which was to be made. She spoke of Lucy's coming and of her own going as an unmixed blessing. This she did so effectually as to make Aunt Emmeline declare to Sir Thomas, with tears in her eyes, that the girl was heartless. But when, at the moment of parting, the two girls were together, then Ayala broke down.

They were in the room, together, which one had occupied and the other was to occupy, and their boxes were still upon the floor. Though less than six months had passed since Ayala had come among the rich things and I 2

Lucy had been among the poor, Ayala's belongings had become much more important than her sister's. Though the Tringles had been unpleasant they had been generous. Lucy was sitting upon the bed, while Ayala was now moving about the room restlessly, now clinging to her sister, and now sobbing almost in despair. " Of course I know," she said. " What is the use of telling stories about it any longer ?"

" It is not too late yet, Ayala. If we both go to Uncle Tom he will let us change it."

" Why should it be changed? If I could change it by lifting up my little finger I could not do it. Why should it not be you as well as me ? They have tried me, and,— as Aunt Emmeline says,—I have not suited."

" Aunt Dosett is not ill-natured, my darling."

" No, I dare say not. It is I that am bad. It is bad to like pretty things and money, and to hate poor things. Or, rather, I do not believe it is bad at all, because it is so natural. I believe it is all a lie as to its being wicked to love riches. I love them, whether it is wicked or not."

^'Oh, Ayala!"

" Do not you? Don't let us be hypocritical, Lucy, now at the last moment. Did you like the way in which they lived in Kingsbury Crescent ?"

Lucy paused before she answered. " I like it better than I did," she said. " At any rate, I would willingly go back to Kingsbury Crescent."

" Yes,—for my sake."

" Indeed I would, my pet."

" And for your sake I would rather die than stay. But what is the good of talking about it, Lucy." You and I have no voice in it, though it is all about ourselves. As you say, we are like two tame birds, who have to be moved from one cage into another just as the owner pleases. We belong either to Uncle Tom or Uncle Dosett, just as they like to settle it. Oh, Lucy, I do so wish that I were dead."

Ayala, that is wicked.*'

How can I help it, if I am wicked ? What am I to do when I get there ? What am I to say to them ? How am I to live ? Lucy, we shall never see each other."

" I will come across to you constantly."

I meant to do so, but I didn't. They are two worlds, miles asunder. Lucy, will they let Isadore Hamel come here?" Lucy blushed and hesitated. "I am sure he will come."

Lucy remembered that she had given her friend her address at Queen's Gate, and felt that she would seem to have done it as though she had known that she was about to be transferred to the other uncle's house. ^* It will make no difference if he does," she said.

" Oh, I have such a dream,—such a castle-in-the-air ! If I could think it might ever be so, then I should not want to die."

^* What do you dream ? " But Lucy, though she asked the question, knew the dream.

^^ If you had a little house of your own, oh, ever so tiny ; and if you and he ? "

" There is no he."

There might be. And, if you and he would let me have any corner for myself, then I should be happy. Then I would not want to die. You would, wouldn't you ? "

" How can I talk about it, Ayala ? There isn't such a thing. But yet,—but yet; oh, Ayala, do you not know that to have you with me would be better than anything?"

" No;—not better than anything;—second best. He would be best. I do so hope that he may be he.' Come in." There was a knock at the door, and Aunt Emmeline, herself, entered the room.

 Now, my dears, the horses are standing there, and the men are coming up for the luggage. Ayala, I hope we shall see you very often. And remember that, as regards anything that is unpleasant, bygones shall be bygones." Then there was a crowd of farewell kisses, and in a few minutes Ayala was alone in the carriage on her road up to Kingsbury Crescent.

The thing had been done so quickly that hitherto there had hardly been time for tears. To Ayala herself the most remarkable matter in the whole affair had been Tom's persistence. He had, at last, been allowed to bring them home from Eome, there having been no other gentleman whose services were available for the occasion. He had been watched on the journey very closely, and had had no slant in his favour, as the young lady to whom he was devoted was quite as anxious to keep out of his way as had been the others of the party to separate them. But he had made occasion, more than once, sufficient to express his intention. I don't mean to give you up, you know,"

he had said to her. When I say a thing I mean it. I am not going to be put off by my mother. And as for the governor he would not say a word against it if he thought we were both in earnest."

" But I ain't in earnest," said Ayala; " or rather, I am very much in earnest."

" So am I. That's all I've got to say just at present." From this there grew up within her mind a certain respect for the " lout," which, however, made him more disagreeable to her than he might have been had he been less persistent.

It was late in the afternoon, not much before dinner, when Ayala reached the house in Kingsbury Crescent. Hitherto she had known almost nothing of her Aunt Do-sett, and had never been intimate even with her uncle. They, of course, had heard much of her, and had been led to suppose that she was much less tractable than the simple Lucy. This feeling had been so strong that Mr. Dosett himself would hardly have been led to sanction the change had it not been for that promise from Sir Thomas that he would not withdraw the provision he had made for Ayala, and would do as much for Lucy if Lucy should become an inmate of his family. Mrs. Dosett had certainly been glad to welcome any change, when a change was proposed to her. There had grown up something of affection at the last moment, but up to that time she had certainly disliked her niece. Lucy had appeared to her to be at first idle and then sullen. The girl had seemed to affect a higher nature than her own, and had been wilfully indifferent to the little

things which had given to her life whatever interest it possessed. Lucy's silence had been a reproach to her, though she herself had been able to do so little to abolish the silence. Perhaps Ayala might be better.

But they were both afraid of Ayala,—as they had not been afraid of Lucy before her arrival. They made more of preparation for her in their own minds, and, as to their owm conduct, Mr. Dosett was there himself to receive her, and was conscious in doing so that there had been something of failure in their intercourse with Lucy. Lucy had been allowed to come in without preparation, with an expectation that she would fall easily into her place, and there had been failure. There had been no regular consultation as to this new coming, but both Mr. and Mrs. Dosett were conscious of an intended effort.

Lady Tringle and Mr. Dosett had always been Aunt Emmeline and Uncle Reginald, by reason of the neaniess of their relationship. Circumstances of closer intercourse had caused Sir Thomas to be Uncle Tom. But Mrs. Dosett had never become more than Aunt Dosett to either of the girls. This in itself had been matter almost of soreness to her, and she had intended to ask Lucy to adopt the more endearing form of her Christian name ; but there had been so little endearment between them that the moment for doing so had never come. She was thinking of all this up in her own room, preparatory to the reception of this other girl, while Mr. Dosett was bidding her welcome to Kingsbury Crescent in the drawing-room below.

Ayala had been dissolved in tears during the drive round

by Kensington to Bayswater, and was hardly able to repress her sobs as she entered the house. " My dear," said the uncle, ^' we will do all that we can to make you happy here."

"I am sure you will; but—but—it is so sad coming away from Lucy."

" Lucy I am sure will be happy with her cousins." If Lucy's happiness were made to depend on her cousins, thought Ayala, it would not be well assured. '^ And my sister Emmeline is always good-natured."

" Aunt Emmeline is very good, only "

" Only what?"

" I don't know. But it is such a sudden change, Uncle Reginald."

Yes, it is a very great change, my dear. They are very rich and we are poor enough. I should hardly have consented to this, for your sake, but that there are reasons which will make it better for you both."

" As to that," said Ayala, stoutly, " I had to come away. I didn't suit."

" You shall suit us, my dear."

'* I hope so. I will try. I know more now than I did then. I thought I was to be Augusta's equal."

" We shall all be equal here."

*^ People ought to be equal, I think,—except old people and young people. I will do whatever you and my aunt tell me. There are no young people here, so there won't be any trouble of that kind."

" There will be no other young person, certainly. You shall go upstairs now and see your aunt."

Then there was the interview upstairs, which consisted chiefly in promises and kisses, and Ayala was left alone to unpack her boxes and prepare for dinner. Before she began her operations she sat still for a few moments, and with an effort collected her energies and made her resolution. She had said to Lucy in her passion that she would that she were dead. That that should have been wicked was not matter of much concern to her. But she acknowledged to herself that it had been weak and foolish. There was her life before her, and she would still endeavour to be happy though there had been so much to distress her. She had flung away wealth. She was determined to fling it away still when it should present itself to her in the shape of her cousin Tom. But she had her dreams,—her daydreams,—those castles in the air which it had been the delight of her life to construct, and in the building of which her hours had never run heavy with her. Isadore Hamel would, of course, come again, and would, of course, marry Lucy, and then there would be a home for her after her own heart. With Isadore as her brother, and her own own Lucy close to her, she would not feel the want of riches and of luxury. If there were only some intellectual charm in her life, some touch of art, some devotion to things beautiful, then she could do without gold and silver and costly raiment. Of course, Isadore would come; and then—then—in the far distance, something else would come, something of which in her castle-building she had

not yet developed the form, of which she did not yet know the bearing, or the manner of its beauty, or the music of its voice ; but as to which she was very sure that its form would be beautiful and its voice full of music. It can hardly be said that this something was the centre of her dreams, or the foundation of her castles. It was the extreme point of perfection at which she would arrive at last, when her thoughts had become sublimated by the intensity of her thinking. It was the tower of the castle from which she could look down upon the inferior world below,—the last point of the dream in arranging which she would all but escape from earth to heaven,—when in the moment of her escape the cruel waking back into the world would come upon her. But this she knew,— that this something, whatever might be its form or whatever its voice, would be exactly the opposite of Tom Tringle.

She had fallen away from her resolution to her dreams for a time, when suddenly she jumped up and began her work with immense energy. Open went one box after another, and in five minutes the room was strewed with her possessions. The modest set of drawers which was to supply all her wants was filled w^ith immediate haste. Things were deposited in whatever nooks might be found, and every corner was utilized. Her character for tidiness had never stood high. At the bijou Lucy, or her mother, or the favourite maid, had always been at hand to make good her deficiencies with a reproach which had never gone beyond a smile or a kiss. At Glenbogie and even on the

journey there had been attendant lady's maids. But here she was all alone.

Everything was still in confusion w^hen she was called to dinner. As she went down she recalled to herself her second resolution. She would be good;—whereby she intimated to herself that she would endeavour to do what might be pleasing to her Aunt Dosett. She had little doubt as to her uncle. But she was aware that there had been differences between her aunt and Lucy. If Lucy had found it difficult to be good how great would be the struggle required from her!

She sat herself down at table a little nearer to her aunt than her uncle, because it was specially her aunt whom she wished to win, and after a few minutes she put out her little soft hand and touched that of Mrs. Dosett. ^* My dear," said that lady, " I hope you will be happy."

" I am determined to be happy," said Ayala, if you will let me love you."

Mrs. Dosett was not beautiful, nor was she romantic. In appearance she was the very reverse of Ayala. The cares of the world, the looking after shillings and their results, had given her that look of commonplace insignificance which is so frequent and so unattractive among middle-aged women upon whom the world leans heavily. But there was a tender corner in her heart which was still green, and from which a little rill of sweet water could be made to flow when it was touched aright. On this occasion a tear came to her eye as she pressed her niece's hand; but she said nothing. She was sure, however, that she

would love Ayala much better than she had been able to love Lucy.

" What would you like me to do ?" asked Ayala, when her aunt accompanied her that night to her bed-room.

" To do, my dear ? What do you generally do ?"

" Nothing. I read a little and draw a little, but I do nothing useful. I mean it to be different now."

" You shall do as you please, Ayala."

" Oh, but I mean it. And you must tell me. Of course things have to be different."

" We are not rich like your uncle and aunt Tringle."

" Perhaps it is better not to be rich, so that one may have something to do. But I want you to tell me as though you really cared for me."

" I will care for you," said Aunt Dosett, sobbing.

" Then first begin by telling me what to do. I will try and do it. Of course I have thought about it, coming away from all manner of rich things; and I have determined that it shall not make me unhappy. I will rise above it. I will begin to-morrow and do anything if you will tell me." Then Aunt Dosett took her in her arms and kissed her, and declared that on the morrow they would begin their work together in perfect confidence and love with each other.

" I think she will do better than Lucy," said Mrs. Dosett to her husband that night.

" Lucy was a dear girl too," said Uncle Eeginald.

" Oh, yes;—quite so. I don't mean to say a word against Lucy; but I think that I can do better with Ayala.

She will be more diligent." Uncle Reginald said nothing to this, but he could not but think that of the two Lucy would be the one most likely to devote herself to hard work.

On the next morning Ayala went out with her aunt on the round to the shopkeepers, and listened with profound attention to the domestic instructions which were given to her on the occasion. When she came home she knew much of which she had known nothing before. What was the price of mutton, and how much mutton she was expected as one of the family to eat per week; what were the necessities of the house in bread and butter, how far a pint of milk might be stretched,—with a proper understanding that her Uncle Reginald as head of the family was to be subjected to no limits. And before their return from that walk,—on the first morning of Ayala's sojourn, —Ayala had undertaken always to call Mrs. Dosett Aunt Margaret for the future*

CHAPTER XI.

TOM TRINGLE COMES TO THE CRESCENT.

During the next three months, up to the end of the winter and through the early spring, things went on without any change either in Queen's Gate or Kingsbury Crescent. The sisters saw each other occasionally, but not as frequently as either of them had intended. Lucy was not encouraged in the use of cabs, nor was the carriage lent to her often for the purpose of going to the Crescent. The reader may remember that she had been in the habit of walking alone in Kensington Gardens, and a walk across Kensington Gardens would carry her the greater part of the distance to Kingsbury Crescent. But Lucy, in her new circumstances, was not advised,—perhaps, I may say, was not allowed,—to walk alone. Lady Tringle, being a lady of rank and wealth, was afraid, or pretended to be afraid, of the lions. Poor Ayala was really afraid of the lions. Thus it came to pass that the intercourse was not frequent. In her daily life Lucy was quiet and obedient. She did not run counter to Augusta, whose approaching nuptials gave her that predominance in the house which is always accorded to young ladies in her recognised position. Gertrude was at this time a subject of trouble at Queen's Gate. Sir Thomas had not been got to approve of Mr.

Frank Houston, and Gertrude had positively refused to give him up. Sir Thomas was, indeed, considerably troubled by his children. There had been a period of disagreeable obstinacy even with Augusta before Mr. Traffick had been taken into the bosom of the family. Now Gertrude had her own ideas, and so also had Tom. Tom had become quite a trouble. Sir Thomas and Lady Tringle, together, had determined that Tom must be weaned; by which they meant that he must be cured of his love. But Tom had altogether refused to be weaned. Mr. Dosett had been requested to deny him admittance to the house in Kingsbury Crescent, and as this request had been fully endorsed by Ayala herself orders had been given to the effect to the parlour-maid. Tom had called more than once, and had been unable to obtain access to his beloved. But yet he resolutely refused to be weaned. He told his father to his face that he intended to marry Ayala, and abused his mother roundly when she attempted to interfere. The whole family was astounded by his perseverance, so that there had already sprung up an idea in the minds of some among the Tringles that he would be successful at last. Augusta was very firm, declaring that Ayala was a viper. But Sir Thomas, himself, began to inquire, within his own bosom, whether Tom should not be allowed to settle down in the manner desired by himself. In no consultation held at Queen's Gate on the subject was there the slightest expression of an opinion that Tom might be denied the opportunity of settling down as he wished through any unwillingness on the part of Ayala.

When things were in this position, Tom sought an interview one morning with his father in Lombard Street. They rarely saw each other at the office, each having his <iwn pecuHar branch of business. Sir Thomas manipulated his millions in a little back room of his own, while Tom, dealing probably with limited thousands, made himself useful in an outer room. They never went to, or left, the office together, but Sir Thomas always took care to know that his son was or was not on the premises. " I want to say a word or two, Sir, about—about the little affair of mine," said Tom.

" What affair ?" said Sir Thomas, looking up from his millions.

I think I should like to—marry."

" The best thing you can do, my boy ; only it depends upon who the young lady may be."

My mind is made up about that, Sir; I mean to marry my cousin. I don't see why a young man isn't to choose for himself" Then Sir Thomas preached his sermon, but preached it in the manner which men are wont to use when they know that they are preaching in vain. There is a tone of refusal, which, though the words used may be manifestly enough w^ords of denial, is in itself indicative of assent. Sir Thomas ended the conference bv taking: a week to think over the matter, and when the week was over gave way. He was still inclined to think that marriages with cousins had better be avoided; but he gave way, and at last promised that if Tom and Ayala were of one mind an income should be forthcoming.

VOL. I. K

For the carrying out of this purpose it was necessary that the door of Uncle Dosett's house should be unlocked, ■and with the object of turning the key Sir Thomas himself called at the Admiralty. " I find my boy is quite in earnest about this," he said to the Admiralty clerk.

"Oh; indeed."

" I can't say I quite like it myself." Mr. Dosett could only shake his head. " Cousins had better be cousins, and nothing more."

" And then you would probably expect him to get money ?"

" Not at all," said Sir Thomas, proudly. ^' I have got money enough for them both. It isn't an affair of money. To make a long story short, I have given my consent; and, therefore, if you do not mind, I shall be glad if you will allow Tom to call at the Crescent. Of course, you may have your own views; but I don't suppose you can hope to do better for the girl. Cousins do marry, you know, very often." Mr. Dosett could only say that he could not expect to do anything for the girl nearly so good, and that, as far as he was concerned, his nephew Tom should he made quite welcome at Kingsbury Crescent. It was not, he added, in his power to answer for Ayala. As to this, Sir Thomas did not seem to have any doubts. The good things of the world, which it was in his power to offer, were so good, that it was hardly probable that a young lady in Ayala's position should refuse them.

My dear," said Aunt Margaret, the next morning,
speaking in her most suasive tone, "your Cousin Tom is to be allowed to call here."

" Tom Tringle ?"

" Yes, my dear. Sir Thomas has consented."

" Then he had better not," said Ayala, bristling up in hot anger. " Uncle Tom has got nothing to do with it, either in refusing or consenting. I won't see him."

" I think you must see him if he calls."

" But I don't want. Oh, Aunt Margaret, pray make him not come. I don't like him a bit. We are doing so very well. Are we not. Aunt Margaret?"

" Certainly, my dear, we are doing very well;—at least, I hope so. But you are old enough now to understand that this is a very serious matter."

" Of course it is serious," said Ayala, who certainly was not guilty of the fault of making light of her future life. Those dreams of hers, in which were contained all her hopes and all her aspirations, were very serious to her. This was so much the case that she had by no means thought of her Cousin Tom in a light spirit, as though he were a matter of no moment to her. He was to her just what the Beast must have been to the Beauty, when the Beast first began to be in love. But her safety had consisted in the fact that no one had approved of the Beast being in love with her. Now she could understand that all the horrors of oppression might fall upon her. Of course it was serious; but not the less was she resolved that nothing should induce her to marry the Beast.

" I think you ought to see him when he comes, and to
k2
remember how different it will be when he comes with the approval of his father. It is, of course, saying that they are ready to welcome you as their daughter."

" I don't want to be anybody's daughter."

" But, Ayala, there are so many things to be thought of. Here is a young man who is able to give you not only every comfort but great opulence."

" I don't want to be opulent."

" And he will be a baronet."

^' I don't care about baronets. Aunt Margaret."

" And you will have a house of your own in which you may be of service to your sister."

" I had rather she should have a house."

" But Tom is not in love with Lucy."

He is such a lout! Aunt Margaret, I won't have anything to say to him. I would a great deal sooner die. Uncle Tom has no right to send him here. They have got rid of me, and I am very glad of it; but it isn't fair that he should come after me now that I'm gone away. Couldn't Uncle Keginald tell him to stay away ?"

A great deal more was said, but nothing that was said had the slightest effect on Ayala. When she was told of her dependent position, and of the splendour of the prospects offered, she declared that she would rather go into the poor-house than marry her cousin. When she was told that Tom was good-natured, honest, and true, she declared that good-nature, honesty, and truth had nothing to do with it. When she was asked what it was that she looked forward to in the world she could merely sob and

say that there was nothing. She could not tell even her sister Lucy of those dreams and castles. How, then, could she explain them to her Aunt Margaret? How could she make her aunt understand that there could be no place in her heart for Tom Tringle seeing that it was to be kept in reserve for some angel of light who would surely make his appearance in due season,—but who must still be there, present to her as her angel of light, even should he never show himself in the flesh. How vain it was to talk of Tom Tringle to her, when she had so visible before her eyes that angel of light with whom she was compelled to compare him !

But, though she could not be brought to say that she would listen patiently to his story, she was nevertheless made to understand that she m.ust see him when he came to her. Aunt Margaret was very full on that subject. A young man who was approved of by the young lady's friends, and who had means at command, was, in Mrs. Dosett's opinion, entitled to a hearing. How otherwise were properly authorised marriages to be made up and arranged? When this was going on there was in some slight degree a diminished sympathy between Ayala and her aunt. Ayala still continued her household duties,— over which, in the privacy of her own room, she groaned sadly; but she continued them in silence. Her aunt, upon whom she had counted, was, she thought, turning against her. Mrs. Dosett, on the other hand, declared to herself that the girl was romantic and silly. Husbands with every immediate comfort, and a prospect of almost unlimited wealth,

are not to be found under every hedge. What right could a girl so dependent as Ayala have to refuse an eligible match ? She therefore in this way became an advocate on behalf of Tom,—as did also Uncle Reginald, more mildly. Uncle Reginald merely remarked that Tom was attending to his business, which was a great thing in a young man. It was not much, but it showed Ayala that in this matter her uncle was her enemy. In this, her terrible crisis, she had not a friend, unless it might be Lucy.

Then a day was fixed on which Tom was to come, which made the matter more terrible by anticipation. " What can be the good ?" Ayala said to her aunt when the hour named for the interview was told her, '^ as I can tell him everything just as well without his coming at all." But all that had been settled. Aunt Margaret had repeated over and over again that such an excellent young man as Tom, with such admirable intentions, was entitled to a hearing from any young lady. In reply to this Ayala simply made a grimace, which was intended to signify the utter contempt in which she held her cousin Tom with all his wealth.

Tom Tringle, in spite of his rings and a certain dash of vulgarity, which was, perhaps, not altogether his own fault, was not a bad fellow. Having taken it into his heart that he was very much in love he was very much in love. He pictured to himself a happiness of a wholesome cleanly kind. To have the girl as his own, to caress her and foster her, and expend himself in making her happy ; to exalt her, so as to have it acknowledged that she was,

at any rate, as important as Augusta ; to learn something from her, so that he, too, might become romantic, and in some degree poetical;—all this had come home to him in a not ignoble manner. But it had not come home to him that Ayala might probably refuse him. Hitherto Ayala had been very persistent in her refusals ; but then hitherto there had existed the opposition of all the family. Now he had overcome that, and he felt therefore that he was entitled to ask and to receive.

On the day fixed, and at the hour fixed, he came in the plenitude of all his rings. Poor Tom ! It was a pity that he should have had no one to advise him as to his apparel. Ayala hated his jewelry. She was not quite distinct in her mind as to the raiment which would be worn by the angel of light when he should come, but she was sure that he would not be chiefly conspicuous for heavy gilding; and Tom, moreover, had a waistcoat which would of itself have been suicidal. Such as he was, however, he was shown up into the drawing-room, where he found Ayala alone. It was certainly a misfortune to him that no preliminary conversation was possible. Ayala had been instructed to be there with the express object of listening to an ofier of marriage. The work had to be done,—and should be done ; but it would not admit of other ordinary courtesies. She was very angry with him, and she looked her anger. Why should she be subjected to this terrible annoyance ? He had sense enough to perceive that there was no place for preliminary courtesy, and therefore rushed away at once to the matter in hand. ^' Ayala!" he ex-

claimed, coming and standing before her as she sat upon the sofa.

" Tom !" she said, looking boldly up into his face.

" Ayala, I love you better than anything else in the world."

But what's the good of it ?"

Of course it was different when I told you so before. I meant to stick to it, and I was determined that the governor should give way. But you couldn't know that. Mother and the girls were all against us."

" They weren't against me," said Ayala.

" They were against our being married, and so they squeezed you out as it were. That is why you have been sent to this place. But they understand me now, and know what I am about. They have all given their consent, and the governor has promised to be liberal. When he says a thing he'll do it. There will be lots of money."

" I don't care a bit about money," said Ayala, fiercely.

" Eo more do 1,—except only that it is comfortable. It wouldn't do to marry without money,—would it?"

^' It would do very well if anybody cared for anybody." The angel of light generally appeared " in form^ pauperis," though there was always about him a tinge of bright azure which was hardly compatible with the draggle-tailed hue of everyday poverty.

" But an income is a good thing, and the governor will come down like a brick."

" The governor has nothing to do with it. I told you before that it is all nonsense. If you will only go away

and say nothing about it I shall always think you very good-natured."

" But I won't go away said Tom speaking out boldly, " I mean to stick to it. Ayala, I don't believe you understand that I am thoroughly in earnest."

" Why shouldn't I be in earnest, too ? "

" But I love you, Ayala. I have set my heart upon it You don't know how well I love you. I have quite made up my mind about it."

" And I have made up my mind."

" But Ayala " Now the tenor of his face changed,

and something of the look of a despairing lover took the place of that offensive triumph which had at first sat upon his brow. ^* I don't suppose you care for any other fellow yet."

There was the angel of light. But even though she might be most anxious to explain to him that his suit was altogether impracticable she could say nothing to him about the angel. Though she was sure that the angel would come, she was not certain that she would ever give herself altogether even to the angel. The celestial castle which was ever being built in her imagination was as yet very much complicated. But had it been ever so clear it would have been quite impossible to explain anything of this to her cousin Tom. " That has nothing to do with it," she said.

" If you knew how I love you ! " This came from him with a sob, and as he sobbed he went down before her on his knees.

" Don't be a fool, Tom,—pray don't. If you won't get up I shall go away. I must go away. I have heard all that there is to hear. I told them that there is no use in your coming."

" Ayala!" with this there were veritable sobs.

" Then why don't you give it up and let us be good friends."

" I can't give it up. 1 won't give it up. When a fellow means it as I do he never gives it up. Nothing on earth shall make me give it up. Ayala, you've got to do it, and so I tell you."

" Nobody can make me," said Ayala, nodding her head, but somewhat tamed by the unexpected passion of the young man.

" Then you won't say one kind word to me ? "

" I can't say anything kinder."

" Very well. Then I shall go away and come again constantly till you do. I mean to have you. When you come to know how very much I love you I do think you will give way at last." With that he picked himself up from the ground and hurried out of the house without saying another word.

CHAPTER XII.

" WOULD YOU ? "

The scene described in the last chapter took place in March. For three days afterwards there was quiescence in Kingsbury Crescent. Then there came a letter from Tom to Ayala, very pressing, frill of love and resolution, offering to wait any time,—even a month,—if she wished il, but still persisting in his declared intention of marrying her sooner or later;—not by any means a bad letter had there not been about it a little touch of bombast which made it odious to Ayala's sensitive appreciation. To this Ayala wrote a reply in the following words:

" When I tell you that I won't, you oughtn't to go on. It isn't manly. " Ayala."

" Pray do not write again for I shall never answer another."

Of this she said nothing to Mrs. Dosett, though the arrival of Tom's letter must have been known to that lady. And she posted her own epistle without a word as to what she was doing.

She wrote again and again to Lucy imploring her sister to come to her, urging that as circumstances now were she could not show herself at the house in Queen's Gate. To

these Lucy always replied; but she did not reply by coming, and hardly made it intelligible why she did not come. Aunt Emmeline hoped, she said, that Ayala would very soon be able to be at Queen's Gate. Then there was a difficulty about the carriage. No one would walk across with her except Tom; and walking by herself was forbidden. Aunt Emmeline did not like cabs. Then there came a third or fourth letter, in which Lucy was more explanatory, but yet not sufficiently so. During the Easter recess, which would take place in the middle of April, Augusta and Mr. Traffick would be married. The happy couple were to be blessed with a divided honeymoon. The interval between Easter and Whitsuntide would require Mr. Traffick's presence in the House, and the bride with her bridegroom were to return to Queen's Gate. Then they would depart again for the second holidays, and when they were so gone Aunt Emmeline hoped that Ayala would come to them for a visit. " They quite understand," said Lucy, '^ that it will not do to have you and Augusta together."

This was not at all what Ayala wanted. " It won't at all do to have me and him together," said Ayala to herself, alluding of course to Tom Tringle. But why did not Lucy come over to her ? Lucy, who knew so well that her sister did not want to see any one of the Tringles, who must have been sure that any visit to Queen's Gate must have been impossible, ought to have come to her. To whom else could she say a word in her trouble ? it was thus that Ayala argued with herself, declaring to herself

that she must soon die in her misery,—unless indeed that angel of light might come to her assistance very quickly.

But Lucy had troubles of her own in reference to the family at Queen's Gate, which did, in fact, make it almost impossible to visit her sister for some weeks. Sir Thomas had given an unwilling but a frank consent to his son's marriage,—and then expected simply to be told that it would take place at such and such a time, when money would be required. Lady Tringle had given her consent, —but not quite frankly. She still would fain have forbidden the banns, had any power of forbidding remained in her hands. Augusta was still hot against the marriage, and still resolute to prevent it. That proposed journey upstairs after the scrap-book at Glenbogie, that real journey up to the top of St. Peter's, still rankled in her heart. That Tom should make Ayala a future baronet's wife; that Tom should endow Ayala with the greatest share of the Tringle wealth; that Ayala should become powerful in Queen's Gate, and dominant probably at Merle Park and Glenbogie,—was wormwood to her. She was conscious that Ayala was pretty and witty, though she could affect to despise the wit and the prettiness. By instigating her mother, and by inducing Mr. Traffick to interfere when Mr. Traffick should be a member of the family, she thought that she might prevail. With her mother she did in part prevail. Her future husband was at present too much engaged with Supply and Demand to be able to irive his thoughts to Tom's affairs. But there would soon be a time when he naturally would be compelled to

divide his thoughts. Then there was Gertrude. Gertrude's own affairs had not as yet been smiled upon, and the want of smiles she attributed very much to Augusta. Why should Augusta have her way and not she, Gertrude, nor her brother Tom ? She therefore leagued herself with Tom, and declared herself quite prepared to receive Ayala into the house. In this way the family was very much divided.

When Lucy first made her petition for the carriage, expressing her desire to see Ayala, both her uncle and her aunt were in the room. Objection was made,—some frivolous objection,—by Lady Tringle, who did not in truth care to maintain much connection between Queen's Gate and the Crescent. Then Sir Thomas, in his burly authoritative way, had said that Ayala had better come to them. That same evening he had settled or intended to settle it with his wife. Let Ayala come as soon as the Trafficks,—as they then would be,—should have gone. To this Lady Tringle had assented, knowing more than her husband as to Ayala's feelings, and thinking that in this way a breach might be made between them. Ayala had been a great trouble to her, and she was beginning to be almost sick of the Dormer connection altogether. It was thus that Lucy was hindered from seeing her sister for six weeks after that first formal declaration of his love made by Tom to Ayala. Tom had still persevered and had forced his way more than once into Ayala's presence, but Ayala's answers had been always the same. " It's a great shame, and you have no right to treat me in this way."

Then came the Traffick marriage with great eclat. There

were no less than four Traffick bridesmaids, all of them no doubt noble, but none of them very young, and Gertrude and Lucy were bridesmaids,—and two of Augusta's friends. Ayala, of course, was not of the party. Tom was gorgeous in his apparel, not in the least depressed by his numerous repulses, quite confident of ultimate success, and proud of his position as a lover with so beautiful a girl. He talked of his affairs to all his friends, and seemed to think that even on this wedding-day his part was as conspicuous as that of his sister, because of his aifair with his beautiful cousin. " Augusta doesn't hit it off with her," he said to one of his friends, who asked why Ayala was not at the wedding,—" Augusta is the biggest fool out, you know. She's proud of her-husband because he's the son of a lord. I wouldn't change Ayala for the daughter of any duchess in Europe:"—thus showing that he regarded Ayala as being almost his own already. Lord Boardotrade was there, making a semi-jocose speech, quite in the approved way for a cognate paterfamilias. Perhaps there was something of a thorn in this to Sir Thomas, as it had become apparent at last that Mr. Traffick himself did not purpose to add anything from his own resources to the income on which he intended to live with his wife. Lord Boardotrade had been obliged to do so much for his eldest son that there appeared to be nothing left for the member for Port Glasgow. Sir Thomas was prepared with his £120,000, and did not perhaps mind this very much. But a man, when he pays his money, likes to have some return for it, and he did 7iot quite like the tone with which the old nobleman,

not possessed of very old standing in the peerage, seemed to imply that he, like a noble old Providence, had enveloped the whole Tringle family in the mantle of his noble blood. He combined the jocose and the paternal in the manner appropriate to such occasions; but there did run through Sir Thomas's mind as he heard him an idea that £120,000 was a sufficient sum to pay, and that it might be necessary to make Mr. Traffick understand that out of the income thenceforth coming he must provide a house for himself and his wife. It had been already arranged that he was to return to Queen's Gate with his wife for the period between Easter and Whitsuntide. It had lately,—quite lately,—been hinted to Sir Thomas that the married pair would run up again after the second holidays. Mr. Septimus Traffick had once spoken of Glenbogie as almost all his own, and Augusta had, in her father's hearing, said a word intended to be very affectionate about " dear Merle Park." Sir Thomas was a father all over, with all a father's feelings; but even a father does not like to be done. Mr. Traffick, no doubt, was a member of Parliament and son of a peer ;—but there might be a question whether even Mr. Traffick had not been purchased at quite his full value.

Nevertheless the marriage was pronounced to have been a success. Immediately after it,—early, indeed, on the following morning,—Sir Thomas inquired when Ayala was coming to Queen's Gate. ^^ Is it necessary that she should come quite at present ?" asked Lady Tringle.

" I thought it was all settled," said Sir Thomas, angrily.

Tliis had been said in the privacy of his own dressing-room, but downstairs at the breakfast-table, in the presence of Gertrude and Lucy, he returned to the subject. Tom, who did not live in the house, was not there. " I suppose we might as well have Ayala now,'^ he said, addressing himself chiefly to Lucy. ^^ Do you go and manage it with her." There v/as not a word more said. Sir Thomas did not always have his own way in his family. What man was ever happy enough to do that ? But he was seldom directly contradicted. Lady Tringlc when the order was given pursed up her lips, and he, had be been observant, might have known that she did not intend to have Ayala if she could help it. But he was not observant,—except as to millions.

When Sir Thomas was gone. Lady Tringle discussed the matter with Lucy. " Of course, my dear," she said, '* if we could make dear Ayala happy "

" I don't think she will come. Aunt Emmeline."

" Not come !" This was not said at all in a voice of anger, but simply as eliciting some further expression of opinion.

She's afraid of—Tom." Lucy had never hitherto expressed a positive opinion on that matter at Queen's Gate. When Augusta had spoken of Ayala as having run after Tom, Lucy had been indignant, and had declared that the running had been all on the other side. Li a side way she had hinted that Ayala, at any rate at present, was far from favourable to Tom's suit. But she had never yet spoken out her mind at Queen's Gate as Ayala had spoken it to her.

VOL. I. L

Afraid of him ?" said Aunt Emmeline.

" I mean that she is not a bit in iove with him, and when a girl is like that I suppose she is—is afraid of a man, if everybody else wants her to marry him."

"Why should everybody want her to marry Tom?" asked Lady Tringle, indignantly. "I am sure I don't want her."

" I suppose it is Uncle Tom, and Aunt Dosett, and Uncle Reginald," said poor Lucy, finding that she had made a mistake.

" I don't see why anybody should want her to marry Tom. Tom is carried away by her baby face, and makes a fool of himself. As to everybody wanting her, I hope she does not flatter herself that there is anything of the kind."

" I only meant that I think she would rather not be brought here, where she would have to see him daily."

After this the loan of the carriage was at last made, and Lucy was allowed to visit her sister at the Crescent. " Has he been there ?" was almost the first question that Ayala asked.

" What he do you mean?"

" Isadore Hamel."

" No ; I have not seen him since I met him in the Park. But I do not want to talk about Mr. Hamel, Ayala. Mr, Hamel is nothing."

" Oh, Lucy."

" He is nothing. Had he been anything, he has gone, and there would be an end to it. But he is nothing."

" If a man is true he may go, but he will come back." Ayala had her ideas about the angel of light very clearly impressed upon her mind in regard to the conduct of the man, though they were terribly vague as to his personal appearance, his condition of life, his appropriateness for marriage, and many other details of his circumstances. It had also often occurred to her that this angel of light, when he should come, might not be in love with herself,— and that she might have to die simply because she had seen him and loved him in vain. But he would be a man sure to come back if there were fitting reasons that he should do so. Isadore Hamel was not quite an angel of light, but he was nearly angelic,—at any rate very good, and surely would come back.

Never mind about Mr. Hamel, Ayala. It is not nice to talk about a man who has never spoken a word."

" Never spoken a word ! Oh, Lucy! "

Mr. Hamel has never spoken a word, and I will not talk about him. There! All my heart is open to you, Ayala. You know that. But I will not talk about Mr. Hamel. Aunt Emmeline wants you to come to Queen's Gate."

" I will not."

" Or rather it is Sir Thomas who wants you to come. I do like Uncle Tom. I do, indeed."

" So do I."

" You ought to come when he asks you."

"Why ought I? That lout would be there,—of

12

'^ I don't know about his being a lout, Ayala." " He comes here, and I have to be perfectly brutal to him. You can't guess the sort of things I say to him, and he doesn't mind it a bit. He thinks that he has to go on long enough, and that I must give way at last. If I were to go to Queen's Gate it would be just as much as to say that I had given way." "Why not?" " Lucy !"

" Why not ? He is not bad. He is honest, and true, and kind-hearted. I know you can't be happy here." " No."

Aunt Dosett, with all her affairs, must be trouble to you. I could not bear them patiently. How can you?"

" Because they are better than Tom Tringle. I read somewhere about there being seven houses of the Devil, each one being lower and worse than the other. Tom would be the lowest,— the lowest,—the lowest." "Ayala, my darling."

" Do not tell me that I ought to marry Tom," said Ayala, almost standing off in anger from the preferred kiss. " Do you think that I could love him ?"

" I think you could if you tried, because he is loveable. It is so much to be good, and then he loves you truly. After all, it is something to have everything nice around you. You have not been made to be poor and uncomfortable. I fear that it must be bad with you here." " It is bad."

" I wish I could have stayed, Ayala. I am more tranquil than you, and could have borne it better."

" It is bad. It is one of the houses,—but not the lowest. I can eat my heart out here, peaceably, and die with a great needle in my hand and a towel in my lap. But if I were to marry him I should kill myself the first hour after I had gone away with him. Things ! What would things be with such a monster as that leaning over one ? Would you marry him?" In answer to this, Lucy made no immediate reply. ^'Why don't you say? You want me to marry him. Would you ?"

" No."

"Then why should I?"

" I could not try to love him."

" Try! How can a girl try to love any man ? It should come because she can't help it, let her try ever so. Trying to love Tom Tringle ! Why can't you try ?"

" He doesn't want me."

" But if he did ? I don't suppose it would make the least difference to him which it was. Would you try if he asked ?"

" No."

" Then why should I ? Am I so much a poorer crea-tnre than you ?"

" "toil are a finer creature. You know that I think so."

" I don't want to be finer. I want to be the same."

" You are free to do as you please. I am not—quite."

" That means Isadore Hamel."

" I try to tell you all the truth, Ayala ; but pray do not talk about him even to me. As for you, you are free; and if you could "

" I can't. I don't know that I am free, as you call it." Then Lucy started, as though about to ask the question which would naturally follow. '^ You needn't look like that, Lucy, There isn't any one to be named."

" A man not to be named ?"

" There isn't a man at all. There isn't anybody. But I may have my own ideas if I please. If I had an Isadore Hamel of my own I could compare Tom or Mr. Traffick, or any other lout to him, and could say how infinitely higher in the order of things was my Isadore than any of them. Though I haven't an Isadore can't I have an image ? And can't I make my image brighter, even higher, than Isadore ? You won't believe that, of course, and I don't want you to believe it yourself. But you should believe it for me. My image can make Tom Tringle just as horrible to me as Isadore Hamel can make him to you." Thus it was that Ayala endeavoured to explain to her sister something of the castle which she had built in the air, and of the angel of light who inhabited the castle.

Then it was decided between them that Lucy should explain to Aunt Emmeline that Ayala could not make a prolonged stay at Queen's Gate. "But how shall I say it ?" asked Lucy.

" Tell her the truth, openly. ' Tom wants to marry Ayala, and Ayala won't have him. Therefore, of course, she can't come, because it would look as though she were

going to change her mind,—which she isn't.' Aunt Emmeline will understand that, and will not be a bit sorry. She doesn't want to have me for a daughter-in-law. She had quite enough of me at B-ome."

All this time the carriage was waiting, and Lucy was obliged to return before half of all that was necessary had been said. What was to be Ayala's life for the future ? How were the sisters to see each other ? What was to be done when, at the end of the coming summer, Lucy should be taken first to Glenbogie and then to Merle Park ? There is a support in any excitement, though it be in the excitement of sorrow only. At the present moment Ayala was kept alive by the necessity of her battle with Tom Tringle, but how would it be with her when Tom should have given up the fight ? Lucy knew, by sad experience, how great might be the tedium of life in Kingsbury Crescent, and knew, also, how unfitted Ayala was to endure it. There seemed to be no prospect of escape in future. " She knows nothing of what I am suffering," said Ayala, " wheii she gives me the things to do, and tells me of more things, and more, and more ! How can there be so many things to be done in such a house as this?" But as Lucy was endeavouring to explain how different were the arrangements in Kingsbmy Crescent firom those which had prevailed at the bijou, the offended coachman sent up word to say that he didn't think Sir Thomas would like it if the horses were kept out in the rain any longer. Then Lucy hurried down, not having spoken of half the things which were down in her mind on the list for discussion.

CHAPTER XIII.

HOW THE TRINGLES FELL INTO TROUBLE.

After the Easter holidays the Trafficks came back to Queen's Gate, making a combination of honeymoon and business which did very well for a time. It was understood that it was to be so. During honeymoon times the fashionable married couple is always lodged and generally boarded for nothing. That opening wide of generous hands, which exhibits itself in the joyous enthusiasm of a coming marriage, taking the shape of a houseful of presents, of a gorgeous and ponderous trousseau, of a splendid marriage feast, and not unfrequently of subsidiary presents from the opulent papa,—presents which are subsidiary to the grand substratum of settled dowry,—generously extends itself to luxurious provision for a month or two. That Mr. and Mrs. Traffick should come back to Queen's Gate for the six weeks intervening between Easter and Whitsuntide had been arranged, and arranged also that the use of Merle Park, for the Whitsun holidays, should be allowed to them. This last boon Augusta, with her sweetest kiss, had obtained from her father only two days before the wedding. But when it was suggested, just before the departure to Merle Park, that Mr. Traffick's unnecessary boots might be left at Queen's Gate, because he would come

back there, then Sir Thomas, who had thought over the matter, said a word.

It was in this way. " Mamma," said Augusta, " I suppose I can leave a lot of things in the big wardrobe. Jemima says I cannot take them to Merle Park without ever so many extra trunks."

Certainly, my dear. When anybody occupies the room, they won't want all the wardrobe. I don't know that any one will come this summer."

This was only the thin end of the wedge, and, as Augusta felt, was not introduced successfully. The words spoken seemed to have admitted that a return to Queen's Gate had not been intended. The conversation went no further at the moment, but was recommenced the same evening. " Mamma, I suppose Septimus can leave his things here ?"

" Of course, my dear; he can leave anything,—to be taken care of."

It will be so convenient if we can come back,—just for a few days."

Now, there certainly had been a lack of confidence between the married daughter and her mother as to a new residence. A word had been spoken, and Augusta had said that she supposed they would go to Lord Boardotrade when they left Queen's Gate, just to finish the season. Now, it was known that his lordship, with his four unmarried daughters, lived in a small house in a small street in Mayfair. The locality is no doubt fashionable, but the house was inconvenient. Mr. Traffick, himself, had occupied lodgings near the House of Commons, but these had been

given up. iT think you must ask your papa," said Lady Tringle.

" Couldn't you ask him ?" said the Honourable Mrs. Traffick. Lady Tringle was driven at last to consent, and then put the question to Sir Thomas,—beginning with the suggestion as to the unnecessary boots.

" I suppose Septimus can leave his things here ? "

" Where do they mean to live when they come back to town ? " asked Sir Thomas, sharply.

" I suppose it would be convenient if they could come here for a little time," said Lady Tringle.

*' And stay till the end of the season,—and then go down to Glenbogie, and then to Merle Park! Where do they mean to live ? "

" I think there was a promise about Glenbogie," said Lady Tringle.

" I never made a promise. I heard Traffick say that he would like to have some shooting,—though, as far as I know, he can't hit a haystack. They may come \o Glenbogie for two or three weeks, if they like, but they shan't stay here during the entire summer."

" You won't turn your own daughter out, Tom."

^^ I'll turn Traffick out, and I suppose he'll take his wife with him," said Sir Thomas, thus closing the conversation in wrath.

The Trafficks went and came back, and were admitted into the bed-room with the big wardrobe, and to the dressing-room where the boots were kept. On the very first day of his arrival Mr. Traffick was in the House at four,

and remained there till four the next morning,—certain Irish Members having been very eloquent. He was not down when Sir Thomas left the next morning at nine, and was again at the House when Sir Thomas came home to dinner. " How long is it to be ?" said Sir Thomas, that night, to his wife. There was a certain tone in his voice which made Lady Tringle feel herself to be ill all over. It must be said, in justice to Sir Thomas, that he did not often use this voice in his domestic circle, though it was well known in Lombard Street. But he used it now, and his wife felt herself to be unv/ell. " I am not going to put up with it, and he needn't think it."

" Don't destroy poor Augusta's happiness so soon."

" That be d d," said the father, energetically.

" Who's going to destroy her happiness. Her happiness ought to consist in living in her husband's house. What have I given her all that money for?" Then Lady Tringle did not dare to say another word.

It was not till the third day that Sir Thomas and his son-in-law met each other. By that time Sir Thomas had got it into his head that his son-in-law was avoiding him. But on the Saturday there was no House. It was then just the middle of June,—Saturday, June 15,—and Sir Thomas had considered, at the most, that there would be yet nearly two months before Parliament would cease to sit and the time for Grlenbogie would come. He had fed his anger warm, and was determined that he would not be done. "Well, Traffick, how are you ?",he said, encountering his son-in-law in the hall, and leading him into the

dining-room. " T haven't seen you since you've been back."

" I've been in the House morning, noon, and night, pretty near."

" I dare say. I hope you found yourself comfortable at Merle Park."

"A charming house,—quite charming. I don't know whether I shouldn't build the stables a little further from "

Very likely. Nothing is so easy as knocking other people's houses about. I hope you'll soon have one to knock about of your own."

"All in good time," said Mr. Traffick, smiling.

Sir Thomas was one of those men who during the course of a successful life have contrived to repress their original roughnesses, and who make a not ineffectual attempt to live after the fashion of those with whom their wealth and successes have thrown them. But among such will occasionally be found one whose roughness does not altogether desert him, and who can on an occasion use it with a purpose. Such a one will occasionally surprise his latter-da^' associates by the sudden ferocity of his brow, by the hardness of his voice, and by an apparently unaccustomed use of violent words. The man feels that he must fight, and, not having learned the practice of finer weapons, fights in this way. Unskilled with foils or rapier he falls back upon the bludgeon with which his hand has not lost all its old familiarity. Such a one was Sir Thomas Tringle, and a time for such exercise had seemed to him to have come

now. There are other men who by the possession of imperturbable serenity seem to be armed equally against rapier and bludgeon, whom there is no wounding with any weapon. Such a one was Mr. Traffick. When he was told of knocking about a house of his own, he quite took the meaning of Sir Thomas's words, and was immediately prepared for the sort of conversation which would follow. " I wish I might;—a Merle Park of my own for instance. If I had gone into the city instead of to Westminster it might have come in my way."

" It seems to me that a good deal has come in your way without very much trouble on your part."

" A seat in the House is a nice thing,—but I work harder I take it than you do, Sir Thomas."

" I never have had a shilling but what I earned. When you leave this where are you and Augusta going to live ?"

This was a home question, which would have disconcerted most gentlemen in Mr.

Traffick's position, were it not that gentlemen easily disconcerted would hardly find themselves there.

"Where shall we go when we leave this? You were so kind as to say something about Glenbogie when Parliament is up."

"No, I didn't."

"I thought I understood it."

'^ You said something and I didn't refuse."

'^ Put it any way you like, Sir Thomas."

"But what do you mean to do before Parliament is up? The long and the short of it is, we didn't expect you to

come back after the holidays. I like to be plain. This might go on for ever if I didn't speak out."

"And a very comfortable way of going on it would be." Sir Thomas raised his eyebrows in unaffected surprise, and then again assumed his frown. "Of course I'm thinking of Augusta chiefly."

"Augusta made up her mind no doubt to leave her father's house when she married."

"She shows her affection for her parents by wishing to remain in it. The fact, I suppose, is, you want the rooms."

^^ But even if we didn't? You're not going to live here for ever, I suppose."

"That, Sir, is too good to be thought of, I fear. The truth is we had an idea of staying at my father's. He spoke of going down to the country and lending us the house. My sisters have made him change his mind and so here we are. Of course we can go into lodgings."

"Or to an hotel."

"Too dear! You see you've made me pay such a sum for insuring my life. I'll tell you what I'll do. If you'll let us make it out here till the 10th of July we'll go into an hotel then." Sir Thomas, surprised at his own compliance, did at last give way. "And then we can have a month at Glenbogie from the 12th."

Three weeks," said Sir Thomas, shouting at the top of his voice.

"Very well; three weeks. If you could have made it the month it would have been convenient; but I hate to

be disagreeable." Thus the matter was settled, and Mr. Traffick was altogether well pleased with the arrangement.

"What are we to do?" said Augusta, with a very long face. "What are we to do when we are made to go away?"

"I hope I shall be able to make some of the girls go down by that time, and then we must squeeze in at my father's."

This and other matters made Sir Thomas in those days irritable and disagreeable to the family. "Tom," he said to his wife, "is the biggest fool that ever lived."

"What is the matter with him now?" asked Lady Tringle, who did not like to have her only son abused.

"He's away half his time, and when he does come he'd better be away. If he wants to marry that girl why doesn't he marry her and have done with it?"

Now this was a matter upon which Lady Tringle had ideas of her own which were becoming every day stronger. "I'm sure I should be very sorry to see it," she said.

"Why should you be sorry? Isn't it the best thing a young man can do? If he's set his heart that way all the world won't talk him off. I thought all that was settled."

*^ You can't make the girl marry him."

" Is that it ?" asked Sir Thomas, with a whistle. " You used to say she was setting her cap at him."

" She is one of those girls you don't know what she would be at. She's full of romance and nonsense, and isn't half as fond of telling the truth as she ought to be. She made my life a burden to me while she was with us, and I don't think she would be any better for Tom."

" But he's still determined."

" What's the use of that ?" said Lady Tringle.

" Then he shall have her. I made him a promise and I'm not going to give it up. I told him that if he was in earnest he should have her."

" You can't make a girl marry a young man."

" You have her here, and then we'll take her to Glen-bogie. Now when I say it I mean it. You go and fetch her, and if you don't I will. I'm not going to have her turned out into the cold in that way."

" She won't come, Tom." Then he turned round and frowned at her.

The immediate result of this was that Lady Tringle herself did drive across to Kingsbury Crescent accompanied by Gertrude and Lucy, and did make her request in form. " My dear, your uncle particularly wants you to come to us for the next month." Mrs. Dosett was sitting by. " I hope Ayala may be allowed to come to us for a month."

" Ayala must answer for herself," said Mrs. Dosett, firmly. There had never been any warm friendship between Mrs. Dosett and her husband's elder sister.

" I can't," said Ayala, shaking her head.

" Why not, my dear?" said Lady Tringle.

"• I can't," said Ayala.

Lady Tringle was not in the least offended or annoyed at the refusal. She did not at all desire that Ayala should come to Glenbogie. Ayala at Glenbogie would make her life miserable to her. It would, of course, lead to Tom's marriage, and then there would be internecine fighting between Ayala and Augusta. But it was necessary that she should take back to her husband some reply;—and this reply, if in the form of refusal, must come from Ayala herself. " Your uncle has sent me," said Lady Tringle, " and I must give him some reason. As for expense, you know,"—then she turned to Mrs. Dosett with a smile,— *^ that of course would be our affair."

" If you ask me," said Mrs. Dosett, " I think that as Ayala has come to us she had better remain with us. Of course things are very different, and she would be only discontented." At this Lady Tringle smiled her sweetest smile,—as though acknowledging that things certainly were different,—and then turned to Ayala for a further reply.

" Aimt Emmeline, I can't," said Ayala.

" But why, my dear ? Can't isn't a courteous answer to a request that is meant to be kind."

^' Speak out, Ayala," said Mrs. Dosett. " There is nobody here but your aunts."

" Because of Tom."

"Tom wouldn't eat you," said Lady Tringle, again smiling.

" It's worse than eating me," said Ayala. " He will go on when I tell him not. If I were down there he'd be doing it always. And then you'd tell me that I—encouraged him!"

Lady Tringle felt this to be unkind and undeserved. Those passages in Rome had been very disagreeable to every one concerned. The girl certainly, as she thought,

VOL. I. M

had been arrogant and impertinent. She had been accepted from charity and had then domineered in the family. She had given herself airs and had gone out into company almost without authority, into company which had rejected her,—Lady Tringle. It had become absolutely necessary to get rid of an inmate so troublesome, so unbearable. The girl had been sent away,—almost ignominiously* Now she, Lady Tringle, the oiFended aunt, the aunt who had so much cause for ojfFence, had been good enough, gracious enough, to pardon all this, and was again offering the fruition of a portion of her good things to the sinner* No doubt she was not anxious that the offer should be accepted, but not the less was it made graciously,—as she felt herself In answer to this she had thrown back upon her the only hard word she had ever spoken to the girl I " You wouldn't be told anything of the kind, but you needn't come if you don't like it."

'* Then I don't," said Ayala, nodding her head.

" But I did think that after all that has passed, and when I am trying to be kind to you, you would have made yourself more pleasant to me. I can only tell your uncle that you say you won't."

" Give my love to my uncle, and tell him that I am much obliged to him and that I know how good he is; but I can't—because of Tom."

" Tom is too good for you," exclaimed Aunt Emmeline, who could not bear to have her son depreciated even by the girl whom she did not wish to marry him.

" I didn't say he wasn't," said Ayala, bursting into

tears. " The Archbishop of Canterbury would be too good for me, but I don't want to marry him." Then she got up and ran out of the room in order that she might weep over her troubles in the privacy of her own chamber. She was thoroughly convinced that she was being ill-used. No one had a right to tell her that any man was too good for her unless she herself should make pretensions to the man. It was an insult to her even to connect her name with that of any man unless she had done something to connect it. In her own estimation her cousin Tom was infinitely beneath her,—worlds beneath her,—a denizen of an altogether inferior race, such as the Beast was to the Beauty! Not that Ayala had ever boasted to herself of her own face or form. It was not in that respect that she likened herself to the Beauty when she thought of Tom as the Beast. Her assumed superiority existed in certain intellectual or rather artistic and sesthetic gifts,—certain celestial gifts. But as she had boasted of them to no one, as she had never said that she and her cousin were poles asunder in their tastes, poles asunder in their feelings, poles asunder in their intelligence, was it not very, very cruel that she should be told, first that she encouraged him, and then that she was not good enough for him ? Cinderella did not ask to have the Prince for her husband. When she had her own image of which no one could rob her, and was content with that, why should they treat her in this cruel way ?

" I am afraid you are having a great deal of trouble with her," said Lady Tringle to Mrs. Dosett.

M 2

" No, indeed. Of course she is romantic, which is very objectionable."

" Quite detestable I " said Lady Tringle.

" But she has been brought up like that, so that it is not her fault. Now she endeavours to do her best."

She is so upsetting."

" She is angry because her cousin persecutes her."

" Persecutes her, indeed I Tom is in a position to ask any girl to be his wife. He can give her a home of her own, and a good income. She ought to be proud of the offer instead of speaking like that. But nobody wants her to have him."

" He wants it, I suppose."

Just taken by her baby face ;—that's all. It won't last, and she needn't think so. However, I've done my best to be kind, Mrs. Dosett, and there's an end of it. If you please I'll ring the bell for the carriage. Good-bye." After that she swam out of the room and had herself carried back to Queen's Gate-

CHAPTER XIV.

FRANK HOUSTON.

Three or four days afterwards Sir Thomas asked whether Ayala was to come to Glenbogie. " She positively refused," said his wife, " and was so rude and impertinent that I could not possibly have her now." Then Sir Thomas frowned and turned himself away, and said not a word further on that occasion.

There were many candidates for Glenbogie on this occasion. Among others there was Mr. Frank Houston, whose candidature was not pressed by himself,—as could not well have been done,—but was enforced by Gertrude on his behalf. It was now July. Gertrude and Mr. Houston had seen something of each other in Rome, as may be remembered, and since then had seen a good deal of each other in town. Gertrude was perfectly well aware that Mr. Houston was impecunious; but Augusta had been allowed to have an impecunious lover, and Tom to throw himself at the feet of an impecunious love. Gertrude felt herself to be entitled to her £120,000; did not for a moment doubt but that she would get it. Why shouldn't she give it to any young man she liked as long as he belonged to decent people ? Mr. Houston wasn't a Member of Parliament,—but then he was young and good-looking. Mr.

Houston wasn't son to a lord, but he was brother to a county squire, and came of a family much older than that of those stupid Boardotrade and TrafHck people. And then Frank Houston was very presentable, was not at all bald, and was just the man for a girl to like as a husband. It was dinned into her ears that Houston had no income at all,—^just a few hundreds a year on which he never could keep himself out of debt. But he was a generous man, who would be more than contented with the income coming from £120,000. He would not spunge upon the house at Queen's Gate. He would not make use of Merle Park and Glenbogie. He would have a house of his own for his old boots. Four-per-cent. would give them nearly £5,000 a year. Gertrude knew all about it already. They could have a nice house near Queen's Gate ;—say somewhere about Onslow Gardens. There would be quite enough for a carriage for three months upon a mountain in Switzerland, and three more among the art treasures of Italy. It was astonishing how completely Gertrude had it all at her finger's ends when she discussed the matter with her mother. Mr. Houston was a man of no expensive tastes. He didn't want to hunt. He did shoot, no doubt, and perhaps a little shooting at Glenbogie might be nice before they went to Switzerland. In that ease two months on the top of the mountain would suffice. But if he was not asked he would never condescend to demand an entry at Glenbogie as a part of his wife's dower. Lady Tringle was thus talked over, though she did think that at least one of her daughter's husbands ought to have an in-

come of his own. There was another point which Gertrude put forward very frankly, and which no doubt had weight with her mother. " Mamma, I mean to have him," she said, when Lady Tringle expressed a doubt.

But papa?"

" I mean to have him. Papa can scold, of course, if he pleases."

But where would the income come from if papa did not give it? "

Of course he'll give it. IVe a right to it as much as Augusta." There was something in Gertrude's face as she said this which made her mother think that she would have her way.

But Sir Thomas had hitherto declined. When Frank Houston, after the manner of would-be sons-in-law, had applied to Sir Thomas, Sir Thomas, who already knew all about it, asked after his income, his prospects, and his occupation. Fifty years ago young men used to encounter the misery of such questions, and to live afterwards often in the enjoyment of the stern questioner's money and daughters. But there used in those days to be a bad quarter of an hour while the questions were being asked, and not un-frequently a bad six months afterwards, while the stern questioner was gradually undergoing a softening process under the hands of the females of the family. But the young man of to-day has no bad quarter of an hour. " You are a mercantile old brick, with money and a daughter. I am a jeunesse doree,—gilded by blood and fashion, though so utterly impecunious! Let us know

your terms. How much is it to be, and then I can say whether we can afford to live upon it." The old brick surrenders himself more readily and speedily to the latter than to the former manner;—but ho hardly surrenders himself quite at once. Frank Houston, when inquired into, declared at once, without blushing, that he had no income at all to speak of in reference to matrimonial life. As to family prospects he had none. His elder brother had four blooming boys, and was likely to have more. As for occupation, he was very fond of painting, very fond of art all round, could shoot a little, and was never in want of anything to do as long as he had a book. But for the earning of money he had no turn whatever. He was quite sure of himself that he could never earn a shilling. But then on the other hand he was not extravagant,—which was almost as good as earning. It was almost incredible ; but with his means, limited as they were to a few hundreds, he did not owe above a thousand pounds;—a fact which he thought would weigh much with Sir Thomas in regard to his daughter's future happiness.

Sir Thomas gave him a flat refusal. I think that I may boast that your daughter's happiness is in my charge," said Frank Houston.

" Then she must be unhappy," said Sir Thomas. Houston shrugged his shoulders. " A fool like that has no right to be happy."

" There isn't another man in the world by whom I would allow her to be spoken of like that," said Houston.

" Bother I"

" I regard her as all that is perfect in woman, and you must forgive me if I say that I shall not abandon my suit. I may be allowed, at any rate, to call at the house ?"

" Certainly not."

" That is a kind of thing that is never done nowadays ; —never," said Houston, shaking his head.

" I suppose my own house is my own."

" Yours and Lady Tringle's, and your daughters', no doubt. At any rate, Sir Thomas, you will think of this again. I am sure you will think of it again. If you find that your daughter's happiness depends upon it "

'^ I shall find nothing of the kind. Good morning."

"Good morning. Sir Thomas." Then Mr. Houston, bowing graciously, left the little back room in Lombard Street, and jumping into a cab, had himself taken straight away to Queen's Gate.

Papa is always like that," said Gertrude. On that day Mrs. Trafiick, with all the boots, had taken herself away to the small house in Mayfair, and Gertrude, with her mother, had the house to herself. At the present moment Lady Tringle was elsewhere, so that the young lady was alone with her lover.

" But he comes round, I suppose." " If he doesn't have too much to eat,—which disagrees with him,—he does. He's always better down at Glen-bogie because he's out of doors a good deal, and then he can digest things."

Then take him down to Glen bogie and let him digest it at once."

" Of course we can't go till the 12th. Perhaps we shall start on the 10th, because the 11th is Sunday. What will you do, Frank ?" There had been a whisper of Frank's going to the Tyrol in August, there to join the Mudbury Docimers, who were his far-away cousins. Imogene Docimer was a young lady of marvellous beauty,—not possessed indeed of £120,000,—of whom Gertrude had heard, and was already anxious that her Frank should not go to the Tyrol this year. She was already aware that her Frank had-—just an artist's eye for feminine beauty in its various shapes, and thought that in the present condition of things he would be better at Glenbogie than in the Tyrol.

^' 1 am thinking of wandering away somewhere ;—perhaps to the Tyrol. The Mudbury Docimers are there. He's a pal of mine, besides being a cousin. Mrs. Docimer is a very nice woman."

" And her sister ?"

" A lovely creature. Such a turn of the neck ! I've promised to make a study of her back head."

" Come down to Glenbogie," said Gertrude, sternly.

" How can I do that when your governor won't let me enter his house-door even in London ? "

" But you're here."

"Well,—yes;—I am here. But he told me not. I don't see how I'm to drive in at the gate at Glenbogie with all my traps, and ask to be shown my room. I have cheek enough for a good deal, my pet."

" I believe you have, Sir;—cheek enough for anything.

But mamma must manage it,—mamma and me, between us. Only keep yourself disengaged. You won't go to the Tyrol,—eh ?" Then Frank Houston promised that he would not go to the Tjrrol as long as there was a chance open that he might be invited to Glenbogie.

" I won't hear of it," said Sir Thomas to his wife. On that occasion his digestion had perhaps failed him a little. ^' He only wants to get my money."

" But Gertrude has set her heart on it, and nothing will turn her away."

" Why can't she set her heart on some one who has got a decent income. That man hasn't a shilling."

" Nor yet has Mr. Traffick."

"Mr. Traffick has, at any rate, got an occupation. Were it to do again, Mr. Traffick would never see a shilling of my money. By , those fellows, who haven't

got a pound belonging to them, think that they're to live on the fat of the land out of the sweat of the brow of such men as me."

" What is your money for, Tom, but for the children?"

" I know what it's for. I'd sooner build a hospital than give it to an idle fellow like that Houston. When I asked him what he did, he said he was fond of ' picters !' " Sir Thomas would fall back from his usual modes of expression when he was a little excited.

Of course he hasn't been brought up to work. But he is a gentleman, and I do think he would make our girl happy."

My money would make him happy,—till he had spent it."

" Tie it up."

" You don't know what you're talking about. How are you to prevent a man from spending his wife's income ?"

" At any rate, if you have him down at Glenbogie you can see what sort of a man he is. You don't know him now."

" As much as I wish to."

" That isn't fair to the poor girl. You needn't give your consent to a marriage because he comes to Glenbogie. You have only to say that you won't give the money and then it must be off. They can't take the money from you." His digestion could not have been very bad, for ho allowed himself to be persuaded that Houston should be asked to Glenbogie for ten days. This was the letter of invitation ;—

" My dear Mr. Houston,

"We shall start for Glenbogie on the 10th of next month. Sir Thomas wighes you to join us on the 20th if you can, and stay till the end of the month. We shall be a little crowded at first, and therefore cannot name an earlier day.

" I am particularly to warn you that this means nothing more than a simple invitation. I know what passed between you and Sir Thomas, and he hasn't at all changed his mind. I think it right to tell you this. If you like to

speak to him again when you are at Glenbogie of course you can. *^ Very sincerely yours,

" Emmeline Tringle."

At the same time, or within a post of it, he got another letter, which was as follows;—

" Dearest F,

" Papa, you see, hasn't cut up so very rough, after all. You are to be allowed to come and help to slaughter grouse, which will be better than going to that stupid Tyrol. If you want to draw somebody's back head you can do it there. Isn't it a joke papa's giving way like that all in a moment ? He gets so fierce sometimes that we think he's going to eat everybody. Then he has to come down, and he gets eaten worse than anybody else.

" Of course, as you're asked to Glenbogie, you can come here as often as you like. I shall ride on Thursday and Friday. I shall expect you exactly at six, just imder the Memorial. You can't come home to dinner, you know, because he might flare up ; but you can turn in at lunch every day you please except Saturday and Sunday. I intend to be so jolly down at Glenbogie. You mustn't be shooting always. " Ever your own,

" G.'

Frank Houston as he read this threw himself back on the sofa and gave way to a soft sigh. He knew he was doing his duty,—just as another man does who goes forth

from his pleasant home to earn his bread and win his fortune in some dry, comfortless climate, far from the delights to which he has been always accustomed. He must do his duty. He could not live always adding a hundred or two of debt to the burden already round his neck. He must do his duty. As he thought of this he praised himself mightily. How beautiful was his far-away cousin, Imogene Docimer, as she would twist' her head round so as to show the turn of her neck I How delightful it would be to talk love to Imogene ! As to marrying Imogene, who hadn't quite so many hundreds as himself, that he knew to be impossible. As for marriage, he wasn't quite sure that he wanted to marry any one. Marriage, to his thinking, was " a sort of grind," at the best. A man would have to get up and go to bed with some regularity. His wife might want him to come down in a frock coat to breakfast. His wife would certainly object to his drawing the back heads of other young women. Then he thought of the provocation he had received to draw Gertrude's back head. Gertrude hadn't got any turn of a neck to speak of. Gertrude was a stout, healthy girl; and, having £120,000, was entitled to such a husband as himself. If he waited longer he might be driven to worse before he found the money which was so essentially necessary. He was grateful to Gertrude for not being worse, and was determined to treat her well. But as for love, romance, poetry, art,—all that must for the future be out of the question. Of course, there would now be no difficulty with- Sir Thomas, and therefore he must at once

make up his mind. He decided that morning, with many-soft regrets, that he would go to Glenbogie, and let those dreams of wanderings in the mountains of the Tyrol pass away from him. " Dear, dearest Imogene !" He could have loved Imogene dearly had fates been more propitious. Then he got up and shook himself, made his resolution like a man, ate a large allowance of curried salmon for his breakfast,—and then wrote the following letter. *^ Duty first!" he said to himself as he sat down to the table like a hero.

Letter No. 1.

" Dear Lady Tringle,

" So many thanks! Nothing could suit my book so well as a few days at Glenbogie just at the end of August. I will be there, like a book, on the 20th. Of course I understand all that you say. Fathers can't be expected to yield all at once, especially when suitors haven't got very much of their own. I shouldn't have dared to ask hadn't I known myself to be a most moderate man. Of course I shall ask again. If you will help me, no doubt I shall succeed. I really do think that I am the man to make Gertrude happy.

" Yours, dear Lady Tringle, ever so much,

" F. Houston."

Letter No. 2. " My own One,

" Your governor is a brick. Of course, Glenbogie will be better than the Tyrol, as you are to be there. Not but

what the Tyrol is a very jolly place, and we'll go and see it together some day. Ask Tom to let me know whether one can wear heavy boots in the Glenbogie mountains. They are much the best for the heather ; but I have shot generally in Yorkshire, and there they are too hot. What number does he shoot with generally ? I fancy the birds are wilder with you than with us.

" As for riding, I don't dare to sit upon a horse this weather. Nobody but a woman can stand it. Indeed, now I think of it, I sold my horse last week to pay the fellow I buy paints from. I've got the saddle and bridle, and if I stick them up upon a rail, under the trees, it would be better than any horse while the thermometer is near 80. All the ladies could come round and talk to one so nicely.

" I hate lunch, because it makes me red in the face, and nobody will give me my breakfast before eleven at the earliest. But I'll come in about three as often as you like to have me. I think I perhaps shall run over to the Tyrol after Glenbogie. A man must go somewhere when he has been turned out in that fashion. There are so many babies at Buncombe Hall!"—Buncombe Hall is the family seat of the Houstons,—" and I don't like to see my own fate typified before the time.

Can I do anything for you except riding or eating lunch,—which are simply feminine exercises? Always your own, Frank."

Letter No. 3. Dear Cousin Im,

"Sow pleasant it is that a little strain of thin blood should make the use of that pretty name allowable ! What a stupid world it is when the people who like each other best cannot get together because of proprieties, and marriages, and such balderdash as we call love. T do not in the least want to be in love with you,—but I do want to sit near you, and listen to you, and look at you, and to know that the whole air around is impregnated by the mysterious odour of your presence. When one is thoroughly satisfied with a woman there comes a scent as of sweet flowers, which does not reach the senses of those whose feelings are not so awakened.

" And now for my news ! I suppose that G. T. will in a tremendously short period become Mistress F. H. ^ A long day, my Lord.' But, if you are to be hung, better be hung at once. Pere Tringle has not consented, —has done just the reverse,—has turned me out of his house, morally. That is, out of his London house. . He asked of my ^ house and my home,' as they did of Allan-a-Dale.

" Queen's Gate and Glenbogie stand fair on the hill.

" * My home,' quoth bold Houston, ' shows gallanter still.

" 'Tis the garret up three pair

" Then he told me roughly to get me gone ; but ^ I had laughed on the lass with my bonny black eye.' So the next day I got an invite to Glenbogie, and att the appropriate time in August,

VOL I. N

" She'll go to the mountains to hear a love tale, *' And the youth

it will be told by is to be your poor unfortunate coz, Frank Houston. Who's going to whimper ? Haven't I known all along what was to come ? It has not been my lot in life to see a flower and pick it because I love it. But a good head of cabbage when you're hungry is wholesome food.—Your loving cousin, but not loving as he oughtn't to love, " Frank Houston."

" I shall still make a dash for the Tyrol when this episode at Glenbogie is over."

CHAPTER XV.

AYALA WITH HER FRIENDS.

Some few days after Lady Tringle had been at Kingsbury Crescent, two visitors, who knew little or nothing of each other, came to see Ayala. One was a lady and the other a gentleman, and the lady came first. The gentleman, however, arrived before the lady had gone. Mrs. Dosett was present while the lady remained; but when the gentleman came she was invited to leave him alone with her niece,—as shall be told.

The lady was the Marchesa Baldoni. Can the reader go so fai' back as to remember the Marchesa Baldoni ? It was she who rather instigated Ayala to be naughty to the Tringles in Rome, and would have Ayala at her parties when she did not want the Tringles. The Marchesa was herself an Englishwoman, though she had lived at Rome all her life, and had married an Italian nobleman. She was now in London for a few weeks, and still bore in mind her friendship for Ayala, and a certain promise she had once made her. In Rome Lady Tringle, actuated by Augusta, who at the moment was very angry with everybody including her own lover, had quarrelled with the Marchesa. The Marchesa had then told Ayala that she, Ayala, must stay with her aunt,—must, in fact, cease for

n2

the time to come to the Marchesa's apartments, because ot the quarrel;, but that a time would come in which they might again be friends. Soon afterwards the Marchesa had heard that the Tringle family had discarded poor Ayala,—that her own quarrel had, in fact, extended itself to Ayala, and that Ayala had been shunted off to a poor relation, far away from all the wealth and luxuries which she had been allowed to enjoy for so short a time. Therefore, soon after her arrival in London, the Marchesa had made herself acquainted with the address of the Dosetts, and now was in Kingsbury Crescent in fulfilment of her promise made at Eome.

" So now you have got our friend Ayala," said the Marchesa with a smile to Mrs. Dosett.

" Yes ; we have her now. There has been a change. Her sister, Lucy, has gone to my husband's sister, Lady Tringle."

The Marchesa made a pleasant little bow at each word. She seemed to Mrs. Dosett to be very gorgeously dressed. She was thoroughly well dressed, and looked like a Marchesa;—'or perhaps, even, like a Marchioness. She was a tall, handsome woman, with a smile perhaps a little too continuously sweet, but with a look conscious of her own position behind it. She had seen in a moment of what nature was Ayala, how charming, how attractive, how pretty, how clever,—how completely the very opposite of the Tringles ! Ayala learned Italian so readily that she could talk it almost at once. She could sing, and play^ and draw. The Marchesa had been quite willing that her

own daughter Nina should find a friend in Ayala. Then had come the quarrel. Now she was quite willing to renew the friendship, though Ayala's position was so sadly altered. Mrs. Dosett was almost frightened as the grand lady sat holding Ayala's hand, and patting it. " We used to know her so well in Rome ;—did we not, Ayala ?"

You were very kind to me."

Nina couldn't come, because her father would make her go with him to the pictures. But now, my dear, you must come to us just for a little time. We have a furnished house in Brook Street, near the park, till the end of the season, and we have one small spare room which will just do for you. I hope you will let her come to us, for we really are old friends," said the Marchesa, turning to Mrs. Dosett.

Mrs. Dosett looked black. There are people who always look black when such applications are made to them,— who look black at any allusions to pleasures. And then there came across her mind serious thoughts as to flowers and ribbons,—and then more serious thoughts as to boots, dresses, and hats. Ayala, no doubt, had come there less than six months since with good store of everything ; but Mrs. Dosett knew that such a house as would be that of this lady would require a girl to show herself with the newest sheen on everything. And Ayala knew it too. The Marchesa turned from the blackness of Mrs. Dosett's face with her sweetest smile to Ayala. " Can't we manage it ?" said the Marchesa.

" I don't think we can," said Ayala, with a deep sigh.

"And why not?"

Ayala looked furtively round to her aunt. " I suppose I may tell, Aunt Margaret?" she said.

" You may tell everything, my dear," said Mrs. Dosett.

" Because we are poor," said Ayala.

" What does that matter ?" said the Marchesa, brightening up. " We want you because you are rich in good gifts and pretty ways."

" But I can't get new frocks now as I used to do in Rome. Aunt Emmeline was cruel to me, and said things which I could not bear. But they let me have everything. Uncle Reginald gives me all that he has, and I am much happier here. But we cannot go out and buy things,—can we. Aunt Margaret ?" " No, my dear; we cannot,"

" It does not signify," said the Marchesa. " We are quite quiet, and what you have got will do very well. Frocks! The frocks you had in Rome are good enough for London. I W/on't have a word of all that. Nina has set her heart upon it, and so has my husband, and so have I. Mrs.

Dosett, when we are at home we are the most homely people in the world. We think nothing of dressing. Not to come and see your old friends because ot your frocks I We shall send for you the day after tomorrow. Don't you know, Mrs. Dosett, it will do her good to be with her young friend for a few days." Mrs. Dosett had not succeeded in her remonstrances when Sir Thomas Tringle was shown into the room, and then the Marchesa took her leave. For Sir Thomas Tringle was

the other visitor who came on that morning to see Ayala.

If you wouldn't mind, Mrs. Dosett," said Sir Thomas before he sat down, " I should like to see Ayala alone Mrs. Dosett had not a word to say against such a request, and at once took her leave.

" My dear," he began, coming and sitting opposite to Ayala, with his knees almost touching her, " I have got something very particular to say to you." Ayala was at once much frightened. Her uncle had never before spoken to her in this way,—had never in truth said a word to her seriously. He had always been kind to her, making her presents, and allowing himself to be kissed graciously morning and evening. He had never scolded her, and, better than all, had never said a word to her, one way or the other, about Tom. She had always liked her uncle, because he had never caused her trouble when all the others in his house had been troublesome to her. But now she was afraid of him. He did not frown, but he looked very seriously at her, as he might look, perhaps, when he was counting out all his millions in Lombard Street. " I hope you think that I have always wished to be kind to you, Ayala."

'^ I am sure you have. Uncle Tom."

" When you had come to us I always wished you to stay. I don't like changes of this sort. I suppose you didn't hit it off with Augusta. But she's gone now,"

" Aunt Emmeline said something." That accusation, as to *' encouragement," so rankled in her heart, that when

she looked back at her grievances among the Tringles that always loomed the largest.

" I don't want to hear anything about it," said Sir Thomas. " Let bygones be bygones. Your aunt, I am sure, never meant unkindly by you. Now, I want you to listen to me."

I will. Uncle Tom."

' Listen to me to the end, like a good girl."

" I will."

" Your Cousin Tom ." Ayala gave a visible

shudder, and uttered an audible groan, but as yet she did not say a word. Sir Thomas, having seen the shudder, and heard the groan, did frown as he began again. " Your Cousin Tom is most tjuly attached to you."

" Why won't he leave me alone, then ?"

" Ayala, you promised to listen to me without speak-mg."

" I will, Uncle Tom. Only "

" Listen to me, and then I will hear anything you have to say."

I will," said Ayala, screwing up her lips, so that no words should come out of them, let the provocation be what it might.

Sir Thomas began again. " Your Cousin Tom is most truly attached to you. For some time I and his mother disapproved of this. We thought you were both too young, and there were other reasons which I need not now mention. But when I came to see how thoroughly he was in earnest, how he put his heart into it, how the very fact that he loved you had made a man of him ; then how the fact that you would not return his love unmanned him,— when I saw all that, I gave my permission." Here he paused, almost as though expecting a word; but Ayala gave an additional turn to the screw on her lips, and remained quite silent. Yes ; we gave our permission,—I and your aunt. Of course, our son's happiness is all in all to us; and I do believe that you are so good that you would make him a good wife."

But "

" Listen till I have done, Ayala." Then there was another squeeze. *' I suppose you are what they call romantic. Romance, my dear, won't buy bread and butter. Tom is a very good young man, and he loves you most dearly. If you will consent to be his I will make a rich man of him. He will then be a respectable man of business, and will become a partner in the house. You and he can choose a place to live in almost where you please. You can have your own establishment and your carriage, and will be able to do a deal of good. You will make him happy, and you will be my dear child. I have come here to tell you that I will make you welcome into the family, and to promise that I will do everything I can to make you happy. Now you may say what you like ; but, Ayala, think a little before you speak."

Ayala thought a little;—not as to what she should say, but as to the words in which she might say it. She was conscious that a great compliment was paid to her. And

there was a certain pride in her heart as she thought that this invitation into the family had come to her after that ignominious accusation of encouragement had been made. Augusta had snubbed her about Tom, and her aunt; but now she was asked to come among them, and be one of them, with full observances. She was aware of all this, and aware, also, that such treatment required from her a gracious return. But not on that account could she give herself to the Beastv Not on that account could she be untrue to her image. Not on that account could she rob her bosom of that idea of love which was seated there. Not on that account could she look upon the marriage proposed to her with aught but a shuddering abhorrence. She sat silent for a minute or two, while her heavy eyes were fixed upon his. Then, falling on her knees before him, she put up her little hands to pray to him. *' Uncle Tom, I can't," she said. And then the tears came running down her cheeks.

" Why can't you, Ayala ? Why cannot you be sensible, as other girls are ?" said Sir Thomas, lifting her up, and putting her on his knee,

" I can't," she said. " I don't know how to tell you."

" Do you love some other man ?"

" No ; no; no!" To Uncle Tom, at any rate, she need say nothing of the image.

"Then why is it?"

" Because I can't. I don't know what I say, but I can't. I know how very, very, very good you are."

" I would love you as my daughter."

" But I can't, Uncle Tom. Pray tell him, and make him get somebody else. He would be quite happy if he could get somebody else."

" It is you that he loves."

" But what's the use of it, when I can't ? Dear, dear Uncle Tom, do have it all settled for me. Nothing on earth could ever make me do it. I should die if I were to try."

" That's nonsense."

" I do so want not to make you angry. Uncle Tom. And I do so wish he would be happy with someone else. Nobody ought to be made to marry unless they like it;— ought they ?"

" There is no talk of making," said Sir Thomas, frowning.

"At any rate I can't," said Ayala, releasing herself from her uncle's embrace.

It was in vain that even after this he continued his request, begging her to come down <o

Glenbogie, so that she might make herself used to Tom and his ways. If she could only once more, he thought, be introduced to the luxuries of a rich house, then she would give way. But she would not go to Glenbogie ; she would not go to Merle Park; she would not consent to see Tom anywhere. Her uncle told her that she was romantic and foolish, endeavouring to explain to her over and over again that the good things of the world were too good to be thrown away for a dream. At last there was a touch of dignity in the final repetition of her refusal. " I am sorry to make you angry, but I can't. Uncle Tom." Then he frowned with all his

power of frowning, and, taking his hat, left the room and the house almost without a word.

At the time fixed the Marchesa's carriage came, and Ayala with her boxes was taken away to Brook Street. Uncle Reginald had offered to do something for her in the way of buying a frock, but this she refused, declaring that she would not allow herself to become an expense merely becau&e her friends in Rome had been kind to her. So she had packed up the best of what she had and started, with her heart in her mouth, fearing the grandeur of the Marchesa's house. On her arrival she was received by Nina, who at once threw herself into all her old intimacy. *^ Oh, Ayala," she said, '^ this is so nice to have you again. I have been looking forward to this ever since we left Rome."

" Yes," said Ayala, '^ it is nice."

But why did you tell mamma you would not come ? What nonsense to talk to her about frocks ? Why not come and tell me ? You used to have everything at Rome, much more than I had."

Then Ayala began to explain the great difference between Uncle Tom and Uncle Reginald,—how Uncle Tom had so many thousands that nobody could count them, how Uncle Reginald was so shorn in his hundreds that there was hardly enough to supply the necessaries of life. " You. see," she said, " when papa died Lucy and I were divided. I got the rich uncle, and Lucy got the poor one ; but I made myself disagreeable, and didn't suit, and so we have been changed."

But why did you make yourself disagreeable ?" said Nina, opening her eyes. " I remember when we were at Rome your cousin Augusta was always quarrelling with you. I never quite knew what it was all about'*

" It wasn't only that," said Ayala, whispering.

" Did you do anything very bad ?"

Then it occurred to Ayala that she might tell the whole story to her friend, and she told it. She explained the nature of that great persecution as to Tom. " And that was the real reason why we were changed," said Ayala, as she completed her story.

"I remember seeing the young man," said Nina.

" He is such a lout!"

' But was he very much in love ?' asked Nina.

" Well, I don't know. I suppose he was after his way. I don't think louts like that can be very much in love to signify. Young men when they look like that would do with one girl as well as another."

" I don't see that at all," said Nina.

" I am sure he would if he'd only try. At any rate what's the good of his going on ? They can't make a girl marry unless she chooses."

" Won't he be rich ?"

" Awfully rich," said Ayala.

" Then I should think about it again," said the young lady from Rome.

" Never," said Ayala, with an impressive whisper. " I will never think about it again. If he were made of diamonds I would not think about it again."

" And is that why you were changed ?" said Nina.

" Well, yes. No; it is very hard to explain. Aunt Emmeline told me that—that I encouraged him. I thought T should have rushed out of the house when she said that. Then I had to be changed. I don't know whether they could forgive me, but I could not forgive her."

" And how is it now ?"

" It is different now," said Ayala, softly. " Only that it can't make any real difference."

"How different?"

" They'd let me come if I would, I suppose; but I shall never, never go to them any more."

" I suppose you won't tell me everything ?" said Nina, after a pause.

"What everything?"

" You won't be angry if I ask ?"

" No, I will not be angry."

" I suppose there is someone else you really care for ?"

" There is no one," said Ayala, escaping a little from her friend's embrace.

" Then why should you be so determined against that poor young man ?"

" Because he is a lout and a beast," said Ayala, jumping up. " I wonder you should ask me;—as if that had anything to do with it Would you fall in love with a lout because you had no one else ? I would rather live for ever all alone, even in Kingsbury Crescent, than have to think of becoming the wife of my cousin Tom." At this Nina shrugged her shoulders, showing that her education in Italy had been less romantic than that accorded to Ayala in London.

CHAPTER XVI.

JONATHAN STUBBS.

But, though Nina differed somewhat from Ayala as to their ideas as to life in general, they were close friends, and everything was done both by the Marchesa and by her daughter to make Ayala happy. There was not very much of going into grand society, and that difficulty about the dresses solved itself, as do other difficulties. There came a few presents, with entreaties from Ayala that presents of that kind might not be made. But the presents were, of course, aocepted, and our girl was as prettily arrayed, if not as richly, as the best around her. At first there was an evening at the opera, and then a theatre,— diversions which are easy. Ayala, after her six dull months in Kingsbury Crescent, found herself well pleased to be taken to easy amusements. The carriage in the park was delightful to her, and delightful a visit which was made to her by Lucy. For the Tringle carriage could be spared for a visit in Brook Street, even though there was still a remembrance in the bosom of Aunt Emmeline of the evil things which had been done by the Marchesa in Rome. Then there came a dance,—which was not so easy. The Marchesa and Nina were going to a dance at Lady Putney's, and arrangements were made that Ayala shouM be taken.

Ayala begged that there might be no arrangements, declared that she would be quite happy to see Nina go forth in her finery. But the Marchesa was a woman who always had her way, and Ayala was taken to Lady Putney's dance without a suspicion on the part of any who saw her that her ball-room apparatus was not all that it ought to be.

Ayala when she entered the room was certainly a little bashful. When in Kome, even in the old days at the bijou, when she did not consider herself to be quite out, she had not been at all bashful. She had been able to enjoy herself entirely, being yqyj fond of dancing, conscious that she could dance well, and always having plenty to say for herself. But now there had settled upon her something of the tedium, something of the silence, of Kingsbury Crescent, and she almost felt that she would not know how to behave herself if she were asked to stand up and dance before all Lady Putney's world. In her first attempt she certainly was not successful. An elderly gentleman was brought up to her,—a gentleman whom she afterwards declared to be a hundred, and who was, in truth, over forty, and with him she manoeuvred gently through a quadrille. He asked her two or three questions to which she was able to answer only in monosyllables. Then he ceased his questions, and the manoeuvres were carried on in perfect silence. Poor Ayala did not attribute any blame to the man. It was all because she had been six months in Kingsbury Crescent. Of course this aged gentleman, if he wanted to dance, would have a partner chosen for him out of Kingsbury Crescent. Conversation was

not to be expected from a gentleman who was made to stand up with Kingsbury Crescent. Any powers of talking that had ever belonged to herself had of course evaporated amidst the gloom of Kingsbury Crescent. After this she was returned speedily to the wings of the Marchesa, and during the next dance sat in undisturbed peace. Then suddenly, when the Marchesa had for a moment left her, and when Nina had just been taken away to join a set, she saw the man of silence coming to her from a distance, with an evident intention of asking her to stand up again. It was in his eye, in his toe, as he came bowing forward. He had evidently learned to suppose that they two outcasts might lessen their miseries by joining them together. She was to dance w^ith him because no one else would ask her ! She had plucked up her spirit and resolved that, desolate as she might be, she would not descend so far as that, when, in a moment, another gentleman sprang in, as it were, between her and her enemy, and addressed her with free and easy speech as though he had known her all her life. " You are Ayala Dormer, I am sure," said he. She looked up into his face and nodded her head at him in her own peculiar way. She was quite sure that she had never set her eyes on him before. He was so ugly that she could not have forgotten him. So at least she told herself. He was very, very ugly, but his voice was very pleasant. " I knew you were, and I am Jonathan Stubbs. So now we are introduced, and you are to come and dance with me."

She had heard the name of Jonathan Stubbs. She was sure of that, although she could not at the moment join

VOL. I. 0

any facts with the name. " But I don't know you," she said, hesitating. Though he was so ugly he could not but be better than that ancient dancer whom she saw standing at a dis tance, looking like a dog that has been deprived of his bone.

"Yes, you do," said Jonathan Stubbs, ^^ and if you'll come and dance I'll tell you about it. The Marchesa told me to take you."

"Did she?" said Ayala, getting up, and putting her little hand upon his arm.

" I'll go and fetch her if you like; only she's a long way off, and we shall lose our place. She's my aunt."

" Oh," said Ayala, quite satisfied,—remembering now that she had heard her friend Nina boast of a Colonel cousin, who w^as supposed to be the youngest Colonel in the British army, who had done some wonderful thing,— taken a new province in India, or marched across Africa, or defended the Turks,—or perhaps conquered them. She knew that he was very brave,—but why was he so very ugly ? His hair was ruby red, and very short; and he had a thick red beard: not silky, but bristly, with each bristle almost a dagger,—and his mouth was enormous. His eyes were very bright, and there was a smile about him, partly of fun, partly of good humour. But his mouth! And then that bristling beard! Ayala was half inclined to like him, because he was so completely master of himself, so unlike the unhappy ancient gentleman who was still hovering at a distance. But why was he so ugly ? And why was he called Jonathan Stubbs ?

" There now," he said, " we can't get in at any of the sets. That's your fault."

" No, it isn't," said Ayala.

" Yes, it is. You wouldn't stand up till you had heard all about me."

I don't know anything about you now."

" Then come and walk about and I'll tell you. Then we shall be ready for a waltz. Do you waltz well ? "

"Do you?"

" I'll back myself against any Englishman, Frenchman, German, or Italian, for a large sum of money. I can't come quite up to the Poles. The fact is, the honester the man is the worse he always dances. Yes ; I see what you mean. I must be a rogue. Perhaps I am;—perhaps I'm only an exception. I knew your father."

"Papa!"

" Yes, I did. He was down at Stalham with the Alburys once. That was five years ago, and he told me he had a daughter named Ayala, I didn't quite believe him."

"Why not?"

" It is such an out-of-the-way name."

" It's as good as Jonathan, at any rate." And Ayala again nodded her head.

" There's a prejudice about Jonathan, as there is about Jacob and Jonah. I never could quite tell why. I was going to marry a girl once with a hundred thousand pounds, and she wouldn't have me at last because she couldn't bring her lips to say Jonathan. Do you think she was right?"

" Did she love you ? " said Ayala, looking up into his face.

" Awfully! But she couldn't bear the name ; so within three months she gave herself and all her money to Mr. Montgomery Talbot de Montpellier. He got drunk, and threw her out of the window before a month was over. That's what comes of going in for sweet names."

" I don't believe a word of it," said Ayala.

" Very well. Didn't Septimus Traffick marry your cousin?"

" Of course he did, about a month ago."

" He is another friend of mine. Why didn't you goto your cousin's marriage ? "

" There were reasons," said Ayala.

" I know all about it," said the Colonel. " You quarreled with Augusta down in Scotland, and you don't like poor Traffick becaiuse he has got a bald head."

I believe you're a conjuror," said Ayala.

" And then your cousin was jealous because you went to the top of St. Peter's, and because you would walk with Mr. Traffick on the Pincian. I was in Rome, and saw all about it."

" I won't have anything more to do with you," said Ayala.

" And then you quarreled with one set of uncles and aunts, and now you live with another."

^' Your aunt told you that."

" And I know your cousin, Tom Tringle."

" You know Tom ? " asked Ayala.

Yes; he was ever so good to me in Kome about a horse; I like Tom Tringle in spite of his chains. Don't you thi nk, upon the whole, if that young lady had put up with Jonathan she would have done better than marry Mont-peEier ? But now they're going to waltz, come along."

Thereupon Ayala got up and danced with him for the next ten minutes. Again and again before the evening was over she danced with him; and although, in the course of the night, many other partners had offered themselves, and many had been accepted, she felt that Colonel Jonathan Stubbs had certainly been the partner of the evening. Why should he be so hideously ugly? said Ayala to herself, as she wished him good night before she left the room with the Marchesa and Nina.

" What do you think of my nephew?" said the Marchesa, when they were in the carriage together.

" Do tell us what you think of Jonathan ?" asked Nina.

'^ I thought he was very good-natured."

*^' And very handsome ?"

" Nina, don't be foolish. Jonathan is one of the most rising officers in the British service, and luckily he can be that without being beautiful to look at"

" I declare," said Nina, " sometimes, when he is talking, I think him perfectly lovely. The fire comes out of his eyes, and he rubs his old red hairs about till they sparkle. Then he shines all over like a carbuncle, and every word he says makes me die of laughter."

" I laughed too," said Ayala.

" But you didn't think him beautiful," said Nina.

" No, I did notj" said Ayala. I liked liim very much, but I thought him very ugly. Was it true about the young lady who married Mr. Montgomery de Montpellier and was thrown out of window a week afterwards ?"

" There is one other thing I must tell you about Jonathan," said Nina. " You must not believe a word that he says."

 That I deny," said the Marchesa ; " but here we are. And now, girls, get out of the carriage and go up to bed at once."

Ayala, before she went to sleep, and again when she woke in the morning, thought a great deal about her new friend. As to shining like a carbuncle,—perhaps he did, but that was not her idea of manly beauty. And hair ought not to sparkle. She was sure that Colonel Stubbs was very, very ugly. She was almost disposed to think that he was the ugliest man she had ever seen. He certainly was a great deal worse than her cousin Tom, who, after all, was not particularly ugly. But, nevertheless, she would very much rather dance with Colonel Stubbs. She was sure of that, even without reference to Tom's objectionable love-making. Upon the whole she liked dancing with Colonel Stubbs, ugly as he w^as. Indeed, she liked him very much. She had spent a very pleasant evening because he had been there. " It all depends upon whether any one has anything to say." That was the determination to which she came when she endeavoured to explain to herself how it had come to pass that she had liked dancing with anybody so very hideous. The Angel

of Light would of course have plenty to say for himself, and would be something altogether different in appearance. He would be handsome,—or rather, intensely interesting, and his talk would be of other things. He would not say of himself that he danced as well as though he were a rogue, or declare that a lady had been thrown out of a window the week after she was married. Nothing could be more unlike an Angel of Light than Colonel Stubbs,— unless, perhaps, it were Tom Tringle. Colonel Stubbs, however, was completely unangelic,—so much so that the marvel was that he should yet be so pleasant. She had no horror of Colonel Stubbs at all. She would go anywhere with Colonel Stubbs, and feel herself to be quite safe . She hoped she might meet him again very often. He was, as it were, the Genius of Comedy, without a touch of which life would be very dull. But the Angel of Light must have something tragic in his composition,—must verge, at any rate, on tragedy. Ayala did not know that beautiful description of a " Sallow, sublime, sort of Werther-faced man," but I fear that in creating her Angel of Light she drew a picture in her imagination of a man of that kind.

Days went on, till the last day of Ayala's visit had come, and it was necessary that she should go back to Kingsbury Crescent. It was now August, and everybody was leaving town. The Marchesa and Nina were going to their relations, the Alburys, at Stalham, and could not, of. course, take Ayala with them. The Dosetts would remain in town for another month, with a distant hope of being able to run down to Pegwell Bay for a fortnight in September. But even that had not yet been promised. Colonel Stubbs had been more than once at the house in Brook Street, and Ayala had come to know him almost as she might some great tame dog. It was now the afternoon of the last day, and she was sorry because she would not be able to see him again. She was to be taken to the theatre tliat night,—and then to Kingsbury Crescent and the realms of Lethe early on the following morning.

It was very hot, and they were sitting with the shutters nearly closed, having resolved not to go out, in order that they might be ready for the theatre—when the door was opened and Tom Tringle w^as announced. Tom Tringle had come to call on his cousin.

Lady Baldoni," he said, I hope you won't think me intrusive, but I thought I'd come and see my cousin once whilst she is staying here." The Marchesa bowed, and assured him that he was very welcome. " It's tremendously hot," said Tom.

Very hot, indeed," said the Marchesa.

" I don't think it's ever so hot as this in Eome," said Nina, fanning herself.

" I find it quite impossible to walk a yard," said Tom, " and therefore I've hired a Hansom cab all to myself. The man goes home and changes his horse regularly when I go to dinner; then he comes for me at ten, and sticks to me till I go to bed. I call that a very good plan." Nina asked him why he didn't drive the cab himself. " That would be a grind," said he, " because it would be so hot

all day, and there might be rain at night. Have you read what my brother-in-law, Traffick, said in the House last night, my Lady?"

" I'm afraid I passed it over," said the Marchesa. " Indeed, I am not very good at the debates."

"They are dull," said Tom, "but when it's one's brother-in-law, one does like to look at it. I thought he made that very clear about the malt tax." the Marchesa smiled and bowed.

" What is—malt tax ?" asked Nina.

"' Well, it means beer," said Tom. " The question is whether the poor man pays it who drinks the beer, or the farmer who grows the malt. It is very interesting when you come to think of it."

" But I fear I never have come to think of it," said the Marchesa.

During all this time Ayala never said a word, but sat looking at her cousin, and remembering how much better Colonel Jonathan Stubbs would have talked if he had been there. Then, after a pause, Tom got up, and took his leave, having to content himself with simply squeezing his cousin's hand as he left the room.

" He is a lout," said Ayala, as soon as she knew that the door was closed behind him.

" I don't see anything loutish at all," said the Marchesa.

" He's just like most other young men," said Nina.

" He's not at all like Colonel Stubbs," said Ayala.

Then the Marchesa preached a little sermon. " Colonel Stubbs, my dear," she said, " hapens to have been thrown a good deal about the world, and has thus been able to pick up that easy mode of talking which young ladies like, perhaps because it means nothing. Your cousin is a man of business, and will probably have amassed a large fortune when my poor nephew will be a do-nothing old general on half-pay. His chatter will not then have availed him quite so much as your cousin's habits of business."

" Mamma," said Nina, Jonathan will have money of his own."

" Never mind, my dear. I do not like to hear a young man called a lout because he's more like a man of business than a man of pleasure." Ayaia felt herself to be snubbed, but was not a whit the less sure that Tom was a lout, and the Colonel an agreeable partner to dance with. But at the same time she remembered that neither the one nor the other was to be spoken of in the same breath, or thought of in the same spirit, as the Angel of Light.

When they were dressed, and just going to dinner, the ugly man with the red head was announced, and declared his purpose of going with them to the theatre. " I've been to the office," said he, " and got a stall next to yours, and have managed it all. It now only remains that you should give me some dinner and a seat in the carriage." Of course he was told that there was no dinner sufficient for a man to eat; but he put up with a feminine repast, and spent the whole of the evening sitting next to his aunt, on a back tier, while the two girls were placed in front. In this way, leaning forward, with his

Ugly head between them, he acted as a running chorus to the play during the whole performance. Ayala thoroughly enjoyed herself, and thought that in all her experience no play she'd seen had ever been so delightful. On their return home the two girls were both told to go to bed in the Marchesa's good-natured authoritative tone; but, nevertheless, Ayala did manage to say a word before she finally adjusted herself on her pillow. ^^ It is all very well, Nina, for your mamma to say that a young man of business is the best; but I do know a lout when I see him; and I am quite sure that my cousin Tom is a lout, and that Colonel Jonathan is not."

" I believe you are falling in love with Colonel Jonathan," said Nina.

" I should as soon think of falling in love with a wild bear ;—but he's not a lout, and therefore I like him."

CHAPTER XVII.

LUCY IS VERY FIRM.

It was just before the Tringles had returned from Rome, during the winter, that Lucj Dormer had met Mr. Hamel in Kensington Gardens for the second time, had walked there with him perhaps for half-an-hour, and had then returned home with a conviction that she had done a wicked thing. But she had other convictions also, which were perhaps stronger. " Now that we have met, am I to lose you again ?" he had said. What could he mean by losing, except that she was the one thing which he desired to find ? But she had not seen him since, or heard a word of his whereabouts, although, as she so well remembered, she had given him an address at her Aunt Emmeline's,— not knowing then that it would be her fate to become a resident in her Aunt Emmeline's house. She had told him that Ayala would live there, and that perhaps she might sometimes be found visiting Ayala. Now, she was herself filling Ayala's place, and might so easily have been found. But she knew nothing of the man who had once asked whether he was " to lose her again."

Her own feelings about Isadore Hamel were clear enough to herself now. Ayala in her hot humour had asked her whether she could give her hand and her heart to

such a one as their cousin Tom, and she had found herself constrained to say that she could not do so, because she was not free,—not quite free,—to do as she pleased with her hand and her heart. She had striven hard not to acknowledge anything, even to Ayala,—even to herself. But the words had been forced from her, and now she was conscious, terribly conscious, that the words were true. There could be no one else now, whether Tom or another, —whether such as Tom or such as any other. It was just that little word that had won her. " Am I to lose you again?" A girl loves most often because she is loved,—not from choice on her part. She is won by the flattery of the man's desire. " Am I to lose you again ?" He had seemed to throw all his soul into his voice and into his eyes as he had asked the question. A sudden thrill had filled her, and, for his sake,—for his sake,—she had hoped that she might not be lost to him. Now she began to fear that he was lost to her.

Something has been told of the relations between Isadore Hamel and his father. They were both sculptors, the father having become a successful artist. The father was liberal, but he was essentially autocratic. If he supplied to his son the means of living,—and he was willing to supply the means of very comfortable life,—he expected that his son should live to some extent in accordance with his fancies. The father wished his son to live in Rome, and to live after the manner of Romans. Isadore would prefer to live in London, and after the manner of Londoners. For a time he had been allowed to do so, and

had achieved a moderate success. But a young artist may-achieve a moderate success with a pecuniary result that shall be almost less than moderate. After a while the sculptor in Rome had told his son that if he intended to remain in London he ought to do so on the independent proceeds of his own profession. Isadore, if he would return to Eome, would be made welcome to join his affairs to those of his father. In other words, he was to be turned adrift if he remained in London, and petted with every luxury if he would consent to follow his art in Italy. But in Rome the father lived after a fashion which was distasteful to the son. Old Mr. Hamel had repudiated all conventions. Conventions are apt to go very quickly, one after another, when the first has been thrown aside. The man who ceases to dress for dinner soon finds it to be a trouble to wash his hands. A house is a bore. Calling is a bore. Church is a great bore. A family is a bore. A wife is an unendurable bore. All laws are bores, except. those by which inferiors can be constrained to do their work. Mr. Hamel had got rid of a great many bores, and had a strong opinion that bores prevailed more mightily in London than in Rome. Isadore was not a bore to him. He was always willing to have Isadore near to him. But if Isadore chose to enter the conventional mode of life he must do it at his own expense. It may be said at once that Isadore's present view of life was very much influenced by Lucy Dormer, and by a feeling that she certainly was conventional. A small house, very prettily furnished, somewhat near the Fulham Road, or perhaps verging a

little towards South Kensington, with two maids, and perhaps an additional one as nurse in the process of some months, with a pleasant English breakfast and a pleasant English teapot in the evening, afforded certainly a very conventional aspect of life. But, at the present moment, it was his aspect, and therefore he could not go upon all fours with his father. In this state of things there had, during the last twelvemonth, been more than one journey made to Eome and back. Ayala had seen him at Rome, and Lady Tringle, remembering that the man had been intimate with her brother, was afraid of him. They had made inquiry about him, and had fdlly resolved that he should not be allowed into the house if he came after Ayala. He had no mother,—to speak of; and he had little brothers and sisters, who also had no mother,—to speak of. Mr. Ilamel, the father, entertained friends on Sunday, with the express object of playing cards. That a Papist should do so was to be borne;—but Mr. Hamel

was not a Papist, and, therefore, would certainly be .

All this and much more had been learned at Kome, and therefore Lucy, though she herself never mentioned Mr. Hamel's name in Queen's Gate, heard evil things said of the man who was so dear to her.

It was the custom of her life to be driven out every day with her aunt and Gertrude. Not to be taken two or three times round the park would be to Lady Tringle to rob her of the best appreciated of all those gifts of fortune which had come to her by reason of the banker's wealth. It was a stern law;—and as stern a law that Lucy should accompany her. Gertrude, as being an absolute daughter of the house, and as having an almost acknowledged lover of her own, was allowed some choice. But for Lucy there was no alternative. Why should she not go and be driven ? Two days before they left town she was being driven, while her aunt was sitting almost in a slumber beside her, when suddenly a young man, leaning over the railings, took off his hat so close to Lucy that she could almost have put out her hand to him. He was standing there all alone, and seemed simply to be watching the carriages as they passed. She felt that she blushed as she bowed to him, and saw also that the colour had risen to his face. Then she turned gently round to her aunt, whom she hoped to find still sleeping; but Aunt Em-meline could slumber with one eye open. " Who was that young man, my dear ?" said Aunt Emmeline.

" It was Mr. Hamel."

Mr. Isadore Hamel!" said Aunt Emmeline, horrified. " Is that the young man at Kome who has got the horrible father ?"

" I do not know his father," said Lucy ; " but he does live at Kome."

Of course, it's the Mr. Hamel I mean. He scraped some acquaintance with Ayala, but I would not have it for a moment. He is not at all the sort of person any young girl ought to know. His father is a horrible man. I hope he is no friend of yours, Lucy !"

He is a friend of mine." Lucy said this in a tone of voice which was very seldom heard from her, but which.

when heard, was evidence that beneath the softness of her general manner there lay a will of her own.

" Then, my dear, I hope that such friendship may be discontinued as long as you remain with us."

" He was a friend of papa's," said Lucy.

" That's all very well. I suppose artists must know artists, even though they are disreputable." ' " Mr. Hamel is not disreputable."

Aunt Emmeline, as she heard this, could almost fancy that she was renewing one of her difficulties with Ayala. '^ My dear," she said,—and she intended to be very impressive as she spoke,—" in a matter such as this I must beg you to be guided by me. You must acknowledge that I know the world better than you do. Mr. Hamel is not a fit person to be acquainted with a young lady who occupies the place of my daughter. I am sure that will be sufficient." Then she leant back in the carriage, and seemed again to slumber; but she still had one eye open, so that if Mr. Hamel should appear again at any corner and venture to raise his hand she might be aware of the impropriety. But on that day Mr. Hamel did not appear again.

Lucy did not speak another word during the drive, and on reaching the house went at once to her bed-room. While she had been out with her aunt close to her, and while it had been possible that the man she loved should appear again, she had been unable to collect her thoughts or to make up her mind what she would do or say. One thing simply was certain to her, that if Mr. Hamel should

YOL. I. p

present himself again to her she would not desert him. All that her aunt had said to her as to improprieties and the like had no effect at all upon her. The man had been welcomed at her father's house, had been allowed there to be intimate with her, and was now, as she was well aware, much dearer to her than any other human being. Not for all the Aunt Emmelines in the world would she regard him otherwise than as her dearest friend.

When she was alone she discussed the matter with herself. It was repugnant to her that there should be any-secret on the subject between herself and her aunt after what had been said,—much more that there should be any deceit. " Mr. Ham el is not fit to be acquainted with a lady who occupies the position of my daughter." It was thus that her aunt had spoken. To this, the proper answer seemed to be,—seemed "at least to Lucy,—" In that case, my dear aunt, I cannot for a moment longer occupy the position of your daughter, as I certainly am acquainted and shall remain acquainted with Mr. Hamel." But to such speech as this on her own part there were two impediments. In the first place it would imply that Mr. Hamel was her lover,—for implying which Mr. Hamel had given her no authority; and then what should she immediately do when she had thus obstinately declared herself to be unfit for that daughter's position which she was supposed now to occupy ? With all her firmness of determination she could not bring herself to tell her aunt that Mr. Hamel was her lover. Not because it was not as yet true. She would have been quite willing that her

aunt should know the exact truth, if the exact truth could be explained. But how could she convey to such a one as Aunt Emmeline the meaning of those words,—" Am I to lose you again?" How could she make her aunt understand that she held herself to be absolutely bound, as by a marriage vow, by such words as those,—words in which there was no promise, even had they come from some fitting suitor, but which would be regarded by Aunt Emmeline as being simply impertinent coming as they did from such a one as Isadore Hamel. It was quite out of the question to tell all that to Aunt Emmeline, but yet it was necessary that something should be told. She had been ordered to drop her acquaintance with Isadore, and it was essential that she should declare that she would do nothing of the kind. She would not recognise such obedience as a duty on her part. ' The friendship had been created by her father, to whom her earlier obedience had been due. It might be that, refusing to render such obedience, her aunt and her uncle might tell her that there could be no longer shelter for her in that house. They could not cherish and foster a disobedient child. If it must be so, it must. Though there should be no home left to her in all the wide world she would not accept an order which shoukl separate her from the man she loved. She must simply tell her aunt that she could not drop Mr. HameFs acquaintance,—because Mr. Hamel was a friend.

Early on the next morning she did so. " Are you aware," said Aunt Emmeline, with a severe face, " that

p2

lie is—illegitimate." Lucy blushed, but made no answer. " Is he—is he—engaged to you?"

" No," said Lucy, sharply.

" Has he asked you to marry him ?" *

" No," said Lucy.

*^ Then what is it ?" asked Lady Tringle, in a tone which was intended to signify that as nothing of that kind had taken place such a friendship could be a matter of no consequence.

" He was papa's friend."

" My dear, what can that matter ? Your poor papa has gone, and you are in my charge and your uncle's. Surely you cannot object to choose your friends as we should wish, Mr. Hamel is a gentleman of whom we do not approve. You cannot have seen very much of him, and it would be very easy for you, should he bow to you again in the park, to let him see that you do not like it."

" But I do like it," said Lucy, with energy.

" Lucy!"

" I do like to see Mr. Hamel, and I feel almost sure that he will come and call here now that he has seen me. Last winter he asked me my address, and I gave him this house.'^

^^ When you were living with your Aunt Dosett?"

" Yes, I did. Aunt Emmeline. I thought Aunt Margaret would not like him to come to Kingsbury Crescent, and, as Ayala was to be here, I told him he might call at Queen's Gate."

Then Lady Tringle was really angry. It was not only that her house should have been selected for so improper a use but that Lucy should hare shown a fear and a respect for Mrs. Dosett which had not been accorded to herself. It was shocking to her pride that that should have appeared to be easy of achievement at Queen's Gate which was too wicked to be attempted at Kingsbury Crescent. And then the thing which had been done seemed in itself to her to be so horrible ! This girl, when living under the care of her aunt, had made an appointment with an improper young man at the house of another aunt! Any appointment made by a young lady with a young man must, as she thought, be wrong. She began to be aghast at the very-nature of the girl who could do such a thing, and on reflecting that that girl was at present under her charge as an adopted daughter. " Luoy," she said, very impressively, " there must be an end of this."

" There cannot be an end of it," said Lucy.

" Do you mean to say that he is to come here to this house whether I and your uncle like it or not ? "

" He will come," said Lucy; "I am sure he will come. Now he has seen me he will come at once."

" Why should he do that if he is not your lover? "

*' Because," said Lucy,—and then she paused ; "because . It is very hard to tell you, Aunt Emeline."

'^ Why should he come so quickly ? " demanded Aunt Emmeline again.

" Because . Though he has said nothing to me such as that you mean," stammered out Lucy, determined to tell the whole truth, " I believe that he will."

"And you?"

" If he did I should accept him."

" Has he any means ? "

" I do not know."

" Have you any?"

" Certainly not."

"And you would consent to be his wife after what I've told you?"

" Yes," said Lucy, " I should."

" Then it must not be in this house. That is all. 1 will not have him here on any pretence whatsoever."

" 1 thought not. Aunt Emmeline, and therefore I have told you."

" Do you mean that you will make an appointment with him elsewhere ? " ^

" Certainly not. I have not in fact ever made an appointment with him. I do not know his address. Till yesterday I thought that he was in Rome. I i^ver had a line from him in my life, and of course have never written to him." Upon hearing all this Lady Tringle sat in silence, not quite knowing how to carry on the conversation. The condition of L ucy's mind was so strange to her, that she felt herself to be incompetent to dictate. She could only resolve that under no circumstances should the objectionable man be allowed into her house. " Now, Aunt Emmeline," said Lucy, " I have told you everything. Of course you have a right to order, but I also have some right. You told me I was to drop Mr. Hamel, but I cannot drop him. If he comes in my way I certainly shall not drop

liim. If he comes here I shall see him if I can. If you and Uncle Tom choose to turn me out of course you can do so."

" I shall tell your uncle all about it," said Aunt Emme-line, angrily, " and then you will hear what he says." And so the conversation was ended.

At that moment Sir Thomas was, of course, in the City managing his millions, and as Lucy herself had suggested that Mr. Hamel might not improbably call on that very day, and as she was quite determined that Mr. Hamel should not enter the doors of the house in Queen's Gate, it was necessary that steps should be taken at once. Some hours afterwards Mr. Hamel did call and asked for Miss Dormer. The door was opened by a well-appointed footman, who, with lugubrious face,—with a face which spoke much more eloquently than his words,—declared that Miss Dormer was not at home. In answer to further inquiries he went on to express an opinion that Miss Dormer never would be at home ;—from all which it may be seen that Aunt Emmeline had taken strong measures to carry out her purpose. Hamel, when he heard his fate thus plainly spoken from the man's mouth, turned away, not doubting its meaning. He had seen Lucy's face in the park, and had seen also Lady Tringle's gesture after his greeting. That Lady Tringle should not be disposed to receive him at her house was not matter of surprise to him.

When Lucy went to bed that night she did not doubt that Mr. Hamel had called, and that he had been turned away from the door.

CHAPTER XVIII.

DOWN IN SCOTLAND.

When the time came, all the Tringles, together with the Honourable Mrs. Traffick, started for Glenbogie. Aunt Emmeline had told Sir Thomas all Lucy's sins, but Sir Thomas had not made so much of them as his wife had expected. " It wouldn't be a bad thing to have a husband for Lucy," said Sir Thomas.

" But the man hasn't g(»t a sixpence."

" He has a profession."

' I don't know that he makes anything. And then think of his father I He is—illegitimate ! " Sir Thomas seemed rather to sneer at this. "And if you knew the way the old man lives in Rome! He plays cards all Sunday! " Again Sir Thomas sneered. Sir Thomas was fairly submissive to the conventionalities himself, but did not think that they ought to stand in the way of a provision for a young lady who had no provision of her own. " You wouldn't wish to have him at Queen's Gate ? ' asked Lady Tringle.

" Certainly not, if he makes nothing by his profession. A good deal, I think, depends upon that." Then nothing further was said, but Lucy was not told her uncle's opinion

on the matter, as had been promised. When she went down to Glenbogie she only knew that Mr. Hamel was considered to be by far too black a sheep to be admitted into her aunt's presence, and that she must regard herself as separated from the man as far as any separation could be effected by her present protectors. But if he would be true to her, as to a girl whom he had a short time since so keenly rejoiced in "finding again," she was quite sure that she could be true to him.

On the day fixed, the 20th of August, Mr. Houston arrived at Glenbogie, with boots and stockings and ammunition, such as Tom had recommended when interrogated on those matters by his sister, Gertrude. " I travelled down with a man I think you know," he said to Lucy;— " at any rate your sister does, because I saw him with her at Rome." The man turned out to be Isadore Hamel. " I didn't like to ask him whether he was coming here," said Frank Houston.

" No ; he is not coming here," said Aunt Emmeline.

" Cerfainly not," said Gertrude, who was quite prepared to take up the cudgels on her mother's behalf against Mr. Hamel.

" He said something about another man he used to know at Rome, before you came. He was a nephew of that Marchesa Baldoni."

She was a lady we didn't like a bit too well," said Gertrude.

A very stuck-up sort of person, who did all she could to spoil Ayala," said Amit Emmeline.

" Ayala has just been staying with her," said Lucy. " She has been very kind to Ayala."

" We have nothing to do with that now," said Aunt EmmeHne. " Ayala can stay with whom she and her aunt pleases. Is this Mr. Hamel, whom you saw, a friend of the Marchesa's?"

'^ He seemed to be a fr'iend of the Marchesa's nephew," continued Houston ;—" one Colonel Stubbs. We used to see him at Rome, and a most curious man he is. His name is Jonathan, and I don't suppose that any man was ever seen so red before. He is shooting somewhere, and Hamel seems to be going to join him. I thought he might have been coming here afterwards, as you all were in Rome together."

" Certainly he is not coming here," said Aunt Emme-line. " And as for Colonel Stubbs, I never heard of him before."

A week of the time allotted to Frank Houston had gone before he had repeated a word of his suit to Sir Thomas. But with Gertrude every opportunity had been allowed him, and by the rest of the family they had been regarded as though they were engaged. Mr. Traffick, who was now at Glenbogie, in accordance with the compact made with him, did not at first approve of Frank Houston. He had insinuated to Lady Tringle, and had said very plainly to Augusta, that he regarded a young man, without any employment and without any income, as being quite unfit to marry. " If he had a seat in the House it would be quite a different thing," he had said to Augusta. But his wife had snubbed him; telling him, almost in so many words,

that if Gertrude was determined to have her way in opposition to her father she certainly would not be deterred by her brother-in-law. " It's nothing to me," Mr. Traffick had then said ; " the money won't come out of my pocket; but when a man has nothing else to do he is sure to spend all that he can lay his liands upon." After that, however, he withdrew his opposition, and allowed it to be supposed that he was ready to receive Frank Houston as his brother-in-law, should it be so decided.

The time was running by both with Houston, the expectant son-in-law, and with Mr. Traffick, who had achieved his position, and both were aware that no grace would be allowed to them beyond that which had been promised. Frank had fully considered the matter, and was quite resolved that it would be unmanly in him to run after his cousin Imogene, in the Tyrol, before he had performed his business. One day, therefore, after having returned from the daily allowance of slaughter, he contrived to find Sir Thomas in the solitude of his own room, and again began to act the part of Allan-a-Dale. " I thought, Mr. Houston," said Sir Thomas, " that we had settled that matter before."

Not quite," said Houston.

" I don't know why you should say so. I intended to be understood as expressing my mind."

But you have been good enough to ask me down here."

" I may ask a man to my house, I suppose, without intending to give him my daughter's hand." Then he

again asked the important question, to which AUan-a-Dale's answer was so unreasonable and so successful. '^ Have you an income on which to maintain my daughter ?"

"I cannot just say that I have, Sir Thomas," said Houston, apologetically.

" Then you mean to ask me to furnish you with an income."

" You can do as you please about that. Sir Thomas."

" You can hardly marry her without it."

" Well; no ; not altogether. No doubt it is true that T should not have proposed myself had I not thought that the young lady would have something of her own."

" But she has nothing of her own," said Sir Thomas. And then that interview was over.

^' You won't throw us over, Lady Tringle ?" Houston said to Gertrude's mother that evening.

" Sir Thomas likes to have his own way," said Lady Tringle.

" Somebody got round him about Septimus Traffick."

" That was different," said Lady Tringle. " Mr. Traffick is in Parliament, and that gives him an employment. He is a son of Lord Boardotrade, and some of these days he will be in office."

*' Of course, you know that if Gertrude sticks to it she will have her own way. When a girl sticks to it her father has to give way. What does it matter to him whether I have any business or not ? The money would be the same in one case as the other, only it does seem such an unnecessary trouble to have it put off."

All this Lady Tringle seemed to take in good part, and half acknowledged that if Frank Houston were constant in the matter he would succeed at last. Gertrude, when the time for his departure had come, expressed herself as thoroughly disgusted by her father's sternness. " It's all bosh," she said to her lover. " Who is Lord Boardotrade that that should make a difference ? I have as much right to please myself as Augusta." But there was the stern fact that the money had not been promised, and even Frank had not proposed to marry the girl of his heart without the concomitant thousands.

Before he left Glenbogie, on the evening of his departure, he wrote a second letter to Miss Docimer, as follows;—

" Dear cousin Im,

" Here I am at Glenbogie, and here I have been for a week, without doing a stroke of work. The father still asks ^ of his house and his home,' and does not seem to be at all affected by my reference to the romantic grandeur of my own peculiar residence. Perhaps I may boast so far as to say that I have laughed on the lass as successfully as did Allan-a-Dale. But what's the good of laughing on a lass when one has got nothing to eat. AUan-a-Dale could pick a pocket or cut a purse, accomplishments in which I am altogether deficient. I suppose I shall succeed sooner or later, but when I put my neck into the collar I had no idea that there would be so much up-hill work before me. It is all very well joking, but it is not nice to be asked * of

your house and your home' by a gentleman who knows very well youVe got none, and is conscious of inhabiting three or four palaces himself. Such treatment must be described as being decidedly vulgar. And then he must know that it can be of no possible permanent use. The ladies are all on my side, but I am told by Tringle mere that I am less acceptable than old Traffick, who married the other girl, because I'm not the son of Lord Boardo-trade ! Nothing astonishes me so much as the bad taste of some people. Now, it must all be put off till Christmas, and the cruel part is, that one doesn't see how I'm to go on living.

'^ In the meantime I have a little time in which to amuse myself, and I shall turn up in about three weeks at Merle Park, I wish chiefly to beg that you will not dissuade me from what I see clearty to be a duty. I know exactly your line of argument. Following a girl for her money is, you will say, mercenary. So, as far as I can see, is every transaction in the world by which men live. The judges, the bishops, the poets, the Eoyal academicians, and the Prime Ministers, are all mercenary;—as is also the man who breaks stones for 2s. 6d. a-day. How shall a man live without being mercenary unless he be born to fortune? Are not girls always mercenary? Will she marry me knowing that I have nothing ? Will you not marry some one whom you will probably like much less simply because he will have something for you to eat and drink? Of course I am mercenary, and I don't even pretend to old Tringle that I am not so. I feel a little tired of this special

effort;—but if I were to abandon it I should simply have to begin again elsewhere. I have sighted my stag, and I must go on following him, trying to get on the right side of the wind till I bring him down. It is not nice, but it is to me manifestly my duty,—and I shall do it. Therefore, do not let there be any blowing up. I hate to be scolded. " Yours always affectionately,

"F. H."

Grertrude, when he was gone, did not take the matter quite so quietly as he did, feeling that, as she had made up her mind, and as all her world would know that she had made up her mind, it behoved her to carry her purpose to its desired end. A girl who is known to be engaged, but whose engagement is not allowed, is always in a disagreeable plight.

" Mamma," she said, " I think that papa is not treating me well."

" My dear, your papa has always had his own way." " That is all very well;—but why am I to be worse used than Augusta ? It turns out now that Mr. Traffick has not got a shilling of his own."

" Your papa likes his being in Parliament." " All the girls can't marry Members of Parliament." ^' And he likes his being the son of Lord Boardotrade." '^ Lord Boardotrade! I call that very mean. Mr. Houston is a gentleman, and the Buncombe property has been for ever so many hundreds of years in the family. I think more of Frank as to birth and all that than I do of

Lord Boardotrade and his mushroom peerage. Can't you tell papa that I mean to marry Mr. Houston at last, and that he is making very little of me to let me be talked about as I shall be?"

" I don't think I can, Gertrude."

" Then I shall. What would he say if I were to run away with Frank?"

I don't think Frank Houston would do that."

" He would if I told him,—in a moment." There Miss Tringle was probably in error. " And unless papa consents I shall tell him. I am not going to be made miserable for ever."

This was at Glenbogie, in Inverness-shire, on the southeastern side of Loch Ness, where Sir Thomas Tringle possessed a beautiful mansion, with a deer-forest, and a waterfall of his own, and any amount of moors which the minds of sportmen could conceive. Nothing in Scotland could be more excellent, unless there might be some truth in the remarks of those who said that the grouse were scarce, and that the deer were almost non-existent. On the other side of the lake, four miles up from the gates, on the edge of a ravine, down which rushed a little stream called the Caller, was an inconvenient ricketty cottage, built piecemeal at two or three different times, called Drum-caller. From one room you went into another, and from that into a third. To get from the sitting-room, which was called the parlour, into another which was called the den, you had to pass through the kitchen, or else to make communication by a covered passage out of doors which

seemed to hang over the margin of the ravine. Pine-trees enveloped the place. Looking at the house from the outside any one would declai'e it to be wet through. It certainly could not with truth be described as a comfortable family residence. But you might, perhaps, travel through all Scotland without finding a more beautifully romantic spot in which to reside. From that passage, which seemed to totter suspended over the rocks, whence the tumbling rushing waters could always be heard like music close at hand, the view down over the little twisting river was such as filled the mind with a conviction of realised poetry. Behind the house across the little garden there was a high rock where a little path had been formed, from which could be seen the whole valley of the Caller and the broad shining expanse of the lake beyond. Those who knew the cottage of Drumcaller were apt to say that no man in Scotland had a more pictm-esque abode, or one more inconvenient. Even bread had to be carried up from Callerfoot, as was called the little village down on the lake side, and other provisions, such even as meat, had to be fetched twenty miles, from the town of Inverness.

A few days after the departure of Houston from Glen-bogie two men were seated with pipes in their mouths on the landing outside the room called the den to which the passage from the parlour ran. Here a square platform had been constructed capable of containing two arm-chairs, and here the owner of the cottage was accustomed to sit, when he was disposed, as he called it, to loaf away his time at Drumcaller. This man was Colonel Jonathan Stubbs,

VOL. I. Q

and his companion at the present moment was Isador© Hamel.

" I never knew them in Rome," said the Colonel. " I never even saw Ayala there, though she was so much at my aunt's house. I was in Sicily part of the time, and did not get back till they had all quarrelled. I did know the nephew, who was a good-natured but a vulgar young man. They are vulgar people, I should say."

" You could hardly have found Ayala vulgar ? " asked Hamel.

" Indeed, no. But uncles and aunts and nephews and nieces are not at all bound to run together. Ayala is the daintiest little darling I ever saw."

" I knew their father and mother, and certainly no one would have called them vulgar."

" Sisters when they marry of course go off according to their husbands, and the children follow. In this case one sister became Tringlish after Sir Tringle, and the other Dormerish, after that most improvident of human beings, your late friend the artist. I don't suppose any amount of experience will teach Ayala how many shillings there are in a pound. No doubt the Honourable Mrs. Traffick knows all about it."

I don't think a girl is much improved by knowing how many shillings there are in a pound," said Hamel.

" It is useful sometimes."

" So it might be to kill a sheep and skin it, or to milk a cow and make cheese; but here, as in other things, one acquirement will drive out others. A woman, if she cannot

be beautifiil, should at any rate be graceful, and if she cannot soar to poetry, should at least be soft and unworldly." " That's all very well in its way, but I go in for roasting, baking, and boiling.

I can bake and I can brew; I can make an Irish stew ; Wash a shirt and iron it too.

That's the sort of girl I mean to go in for if ever I marry; and when you've got six children and a small income it's apt to turn out better than grace and poetiy."

" A little of both perhaps," said Hamel.

" Well, yes; I don't mind a little Byron now and again, so there is no nonsense. As to Glenbogie, it's right over there across the lake. You can get a boat at Callerfoot, and a fellow to take you across and wait for you won't cost you more than three half-crowns. I suppose Glenbogie is as far from the lake on that side as my cottage is on this. How you'll get up except by walking I cannot say, unless you will write a note to Sir Thomas and ask him to send a horse down for you."

" Sir Tliomas would not accommodate me."

" You think he will frown if you come after his niece ?"

" I simply want to call on Miss Dormer," said Hamel, blushing, " because her father was always kind to me."

" I don't njean to ask any questions," said the Colonel.

"It is just so as I say. I do not like being in the neighbourhood without calling on Miss Dormer."

" I daresay not"

q2

"But I doubt whether Sir Thomas or Lady Trlngle would be at all inclined to make me welcome. As to the distance, I can walk that easily enough, and if the door is slammed in my face I can walk back again."

Thus it was resolved that early on the following morning after breakfast Isadore Hamel should go acro&s the lake and make his way up to Glenbogie,

CHAPTER XIX.

ISADORE HAMEL IS ASKED TO LUNCH.

On the following morning, the morning of Monday, 2nd September, Isadore Hamel started on his journey. He had thought much about the journey before he made it. No doubt the door had been slammed in his face in London. He felt quite conscious of that, and conscious also that a man should not renew his attempt to enter a door when it has been once slammed in his face. But he understood the circumstances nearly as they had happened, —except that he was not aware how far the door had been slammed by Lady Tringle without any concmTcnce on the part of Sir Thomas. But the door had, at any rate, not been slammed by Lucy. The only person he had really wished to see within that house had been Lucy Dormer ; and he had hitherto no reason for supposing that she would be unwilling to receive him. Her face had been sweet and gracious when she saw him in the Park. Was he to deny himself all hope of any future intercourse with her because Lady Tringle had chosen to despise him ? He must make some attempt. It was more than probable, no doubt, that this attempt would be futile. The servant at

Glenbogie would probably be as well instructed as the servant in Queen's Gate. But still a man has to go on and do something, if he means to do anything. There could be no good in sitting up at Drumcaller, at one side of the lake, and thinking of Lucy Dormer far away, at the other side. He had not at all made up his mind that he would ask Lucy to be his wife. His professional income was still poor, and she, as he was aware, had nothing. But he felt it to be incumbent upon him to get nearer to her if it were possible, and to say something to her if the privilege of speech should be accorded to him.

He walked down to Callerfoot, refusing the loan of the Colonel's pony carriage, and thence had himself carried across the lake in a hired boat to a place called Sandy's Quay. That, he was assured, was the spot on the other side from whence the nearest road would be found to Glenbogie. But nobody on the Callerfoot side could tell him what would be the distance. At

Sandy's Quay he was assured that it was twelve miles to Clenbogie House ; but he soon found that the man who told him had a pony for hire. " Ye'U nae get there under twalve mile,—or maybe saxteen, if ye attampt to walk up the glin." So said the owner of the pony. But milder information came to him speedily. A little boy would show him the way up the glen for sixpence, and engage to bring him to the house in an hour and a half. So he started with the little boy, and after a hot scramble for about two hours he found himself within the demesne. Poking their way up through thick bushes from a ravine, they showed their

two heads,—first the boy and then the sculptor,—close by the side of the private road,— just as Sir Thomas was passing, mounted on his cob. " It's his ain sell," said the boy, dropping his head again amongst the bushes.

Hamel, when he had made good his footing, had first to turn round so that the lad might not lose his wages. A dirty little hand came up for the sixpence, but the head never appeared again. It was well known in the neighbourhood,—especially at Sandy's Quay, where boats were used to land,—that Sir Thomas was not partial to visitors who made their way into Glenbogie by any but the authorised road. While Hamel was paying his debt, he stood still on his steed waiting to see who might be the trespasser. " That's not a high road," said Sir Thomas, as the young man approached him. As the last quarter of an hour from the bottom of the ravine had been occupied in very stiff climbing among the rocks the information conveyed appeared to Hamel to have been almost unnecessary. " Your way up to the house, if you are going there, would have been through the lodge down there."

" Perhaps you are Sir Thomas Tringle," said Hamel.

" That is my name."

Then I have to ask your pardon for my mode of ingress. I am going up to the house; but having crossed the lake from Callerfoot I did not know my way on this side, and so I have clambered up the ravine." Sir Thomas bowed, and then waited for further tidings. " I believe Miss Dormer is at the house ?"

My niece is there."

" My name is Hamel,—Isadore Hamel. I am a sculptor, and used to be acquainted with her father. I have had great kindness from the whole family, and so I was going to call upon her. If you do not object, I will go on to the house."

Sir Thomas sat upon his horse speechless for a minute. He had to consider whether he did not object or not. He was well aware that his wife objected,—aware also that he had declined to coincide with his wife's objection when it had been pressed upon him. Why should not his niece have the advantage of a lover, if a proper sort of a lover came in her way ? As to the father's morals or the son's birth, those matters to Sir Thomas were nothing. The young man, he was told, was good at making busts. Would any one buy the busts when they were made ? That was the question. His wife would certainly be prejudiced,—would think it necessary to reject for Lucy any suitor she would reject for her own girls. And then, as Sir Thomas felt, she had not shown great judgment in selecting suitors for her own girls. " Oh, Mr. Hamel, are you ?" he said at last. " Isadore Hamel."

'^ You called at Queen's Gate once, not long ago ?" " I did," said Hamel; " but saw no one." "No, you didn't; I heard that. Well, you can go on to the house if you like, but you had better ask for Lady Tringle. After coming over from Callerfoot you'll want some lunch. Stop a moment. I don't mind if I ride back with you." And so the two started towards the

house, and Hamel listened whilst Sir Thomas expatiated on the beauties of Glenbogie.

They had passed through one gate and were approaching another, when, away among the trees, there was a young lady seen walking alone. " There is Miss Dormer," said Hamel; " I suppose I may join her ?" Sir Thomas could not quite make up his mind whether the meeting was to be allowed or not, but he could not bring himself at the spur of the moment to refuse his sanction. So Hamel made his way across to Lucy, while Sir Thomas rode on alone to the house.

Lucy had seen her uncle on the cob, and, being accustomed to see him on the cob, knew of course who he was. She had also seen another man with him, but not in the least expecting that Hamel was in those parts, had never dreamt that he was her uncle's companion. It was not till Hamel was near to her that she understood that the man was coming to join herself; and then, when she did recognise the man, she was lost in amazement. " You hardly expected to see me here ?" said he.

*^ Indeed; no."

" Nor did I expect that I should find you in this way."

My uncle knows it is you ?" asked Lucy.

" Oh, yes. I met him as I came up from the ravine, and he has asked me to go on to the house to lunch." Then there was silence for a few moments as they walked on together. *^ I hope you do not think that I am persecuting you in making my way over here."

Oh, no ; not persecuting!" Lucy when she heard thg sound of what she herself had said, was angry with herself, feeling that she had almost declared him guilty of some wrong in having come thither. " Of course I am glad to see you," she added, " for papa's sake, but I'm afraid "

Afraid of what, Miss Dormer ?"

She looked him full in the face as she answered him, collecting her courage to make the declaration which seemed to be necessary. " My Aunt Emmeline does not want you to come."

" Why should she not want me ?"

" That I cannot tell. Perhaps if I did know I should not tell. But it is so. You called at Queen's Gate, and I know that you were not admitted, though I was at home. Of course, Aunt Emmeline has a right to choose who shall come. It is not as though I had a house of my own."

" But Sir Thomas asked me in."

" Then you had better go in. After what Aunt Emmeline said, I do not think that you ought to remain with me."

" Your uncle knows I am with you," said Hamel. Then they walked on towards the house together in silence for a while. " Do you mean to say," he continued, that because your aunt objects you are never to see me again?"

" I hope I shall see you again. You were papa's friend, and I should be so very sorry not to see you again."

" I suppose," he said, slowly, " I can never be more than your papa's friend."

" You are mine also."

^ I would be more than that." Then he paused as if waiting for a reply, but she of course had none to make. ' I would be so much more than that, Lucy." Still she had no answer to give him. But there comes a tijne when no answer is as excellent eloquence as any words that can be spoken. Hamel, who had probably not thought much of this, was nevertheless at once informed by his instincts that it was so. "Oh, Lucy," he said, "if you can love me say so."

" Mr. Hamel," she whispered.

"Lucy."

" Mr. Hamel, 1 told you about Aunt Emmeline. She will not allow it. I ought not to have let you speak to me like this, while I am staying here."

" But your uncle knows I am with you."

" My aunt does not know. We must go to the house. She expressly desired that I would not speak to you."

" And you will obey her—always ?"

" No; not always. I did not say that I should obey her always. Some day, perhaps, I shall do as I think fit myself."

" And then you will speak to me?"

" Then 1 will speak to you," she said.

" And love me ?"

" And love you," she answered, again looking him full in the face. " But now pray, pray let us go on." For he had stopped her awhile amidst the trees, and had put out his hand as though to take hers, and had opened his arms as though he would embrace her. But she passed on

quickly, and hardly answered his further questions till they found themselves together in the hall of the house.

Then they met Lady Tringle, who was just passing into the room where the lunch was laid, and following her were Augusta, Gertrude, and the Honourable Septimus Traffick. For, though Frank Houston had found himself compelled to go at the day named, the Honourable Septimus had contrived to squeeze out another week. Augusta was indeed still not without hope that the paternal hospitality of Glen-bogie might be prolonged till dear Merle Park should once again open her portals. Sir Thomas had already passed into the dining-room, having in gruff voice informed his wife that he had invited Mr. Hamel to come in to lunch. ^' Mr. Hamel!" she had exclaimed. " Yes, Mr. Hamel. I could not see the man starving when he had come all this way. I don't know anything against him." Then he had turned away, and had gone into the dining-room, and was now standing with his back to the empty fire-place, determined to take Mr. Hamel's part if any want of courtesy were shown to him.

It certainly was hard upon Lady Tringle. She frowned and was going to walk on without any acknowledgment, when Lucy timidly went through a form of introduction. '^ Aunt Emmeline, this is Mr. Hamel. Uncle Tom met him somewhere in the grounds and has asked him to come to luncheon.'- Then Lady Tringle curtseyed and made a bow. The curtsey and the bow together were sufficient to have crushed the heart of any young man who had not been comforted and exalted by such words as Isadore had

heard from Lucy's lips not five minutes since. "And love you," she had said. After that Lady Tringle might curtsey and bow as she would, and he could still live uncrushed. After the curtsey and the bow Lady Tringle passed on. Lucy fell into the rank behind Gertrude; and then Hamel afterwards took his place behind the Honourable Septimus, "If you will sit there, Mr. Hamel," said Lady Tringle, pointing to a chair, across the table, obliquely, at the greatest possible distance from that occupied by Lucy. There he was stationed between Mr. Traffick and Sir Thomas. But now, in his present frame of mind, his position at the table made very little difference to him.

The lunch was eaten in grim silence. Sir Thomas was not a man profuse with conversation at his meals, and at this moment was ill-inclined for any words except what he might use in scolding his wife for being uncivil to his guest. Lady Tringle sat with her head erect, hardly opening her mouth sufficiently to allow the food to enter it. It was her purpose to show her displeasure at Mr. Hamel, and she showed it. Augusta took her mother's part, thoroughly despising the two Dormer girls and any lover that they might have. Poor Gertrude had on that morning been violently persecuted by a lecture as to Frank Houston's impecuniosity. Lucy of course would not speak. The Honourable Septimus was anxious chiefly about his lunch,— somewhat anxious also to ofiend neither the master nor the mistress of Merle Park. Hamel made one or two little efforts to extract answers from Sir Thomas, but soon found that Sir Thomas would prefer to be left in silence.

What did it signify to him ? He had done all that he wanted, and much more than he had expected.

The rising and getting away from luncheon is always a difficulty,^so great a difficulty when there are guests that lunch should never be much a company festival. There is no provision for leaving the table as there is at dinner. But on this occasion Lady Tringle extemporised provision the first moment in which they had all ceased to eat. " Mr. Hamel," she said very loudly, " would you like some cheese ?" Mr. Hamel, with a little start, declared that he wanted no cheese'. " Then, my dears, I think we will go into my room. Lucy, will you come with me ?" Upon this the four ladies all went out in procession, but her ladyship was careful that Lucy should go first so that there might be no possibility of escape. Augusta and Gertrude followed her. The minds of all the four were somewhat perturbed; but among the four Lucy's heart was by far the lightest.

" Are you staying over with Stubbs at that cottage?" asked the Honourable Septimus. A very queer fellow is Stubbs."

" A very good fellow," said Hamel.

" I dare say. He hasn't got any shooting?"

" I think not."

" Not a head. Glentower wouldn't let an acre of shooting over there for any money." This was the Earl of Glentower, to whom belonged an enormous tract of country on the other side of the lake. " What on earth does ho do with himself stuck up on the top of those rocks ?"

He does shoot sometimes, I believe, when Lord Glen-tower is there."

"That's a poor kind of fun, waiting to be asked for a day," said the Honourable Septimus, who rarely waited for anything till he was asked. " Does he get any fish-ing?"

" He catches a few trout sometimes in thq tarns above. But I fancy that Stubbs isn't much devoted to shooting and fishing."

" Then what the d does he do with himself in such

a country as this ?" Hamel shrugged his shoulders, not caring to say that what with walking, what with reading and writing, his friend could be as happy as the day was long in such a place as Drumcaller.

"Is he a Liberal?"

"A what?" asked Hamel. "Oh, a Liberal? Upon my word I don't know what he is. He is chiefly given to poetry, tobacco, and military matters." Then the Honourable Septimus turned up his nose in disgust, and ceased his cross-examination as to the character and pursuits of Colonel Jonathan Stubbs.

" Sir Thomas, I am very much obliged to you for your kindness," said Hamel, getting up suddenly. " As it is a long way over to Drumcaller I think I will make a start. 1 know my way down the Glen and should be sure to miss it by any other route. Perhaps you'll let me go back as I came." Sir Thomas offered him the loan of a horse, but this was refused, and Hamel started on his return journey across the lake.

When he had gone a few steps from the portal he turned to look at the house which contained one whom he now regarded as belonging exclusively to himself; perhaps he thought that he might catch some final view of Lucy; or, not quite thinking it, fancied that some such chance might at least be possible ; but he saw nothing but the uninteresting fa9ade of the grand mansion. Lucy was employed quite otherwise. She was listening to a lecture in which her aunt was describing to her how very badly Mr. Hamel had behaved in obtruding himself on the shades of Glen-bogie. The lecture was somewhat long, as Aunt Emme-line found it necessary to repeat all the arguments which she had before used as to the miscreant's birth, as to his want of adequate means, and as to the general iniquities of the miscreant's father. All this she repeated more than once with an energy that was quite unusual to her. The flood of her eloquence was so great that Lucy found no moment for an interposing word till all these evils had been denunciated twice and thrice. But then she spoke. " Aunt Emmeline," she said, " I am engaged to Mr. Hamel now."

"What I"

" He has asked me to be his wife and I have promised." " And that after all that I had said to you !" " Aunt Emmeline, I told you that I should not drop him. 1 did not bid him come here. Uncle Tom brought him. When I saw him I would have avoided him if I could. I told him he ought not to be here because you did not wish it; and then he answered that my uncle knew

that he was with me. Of course when he told me that he —loved me, I could not make him any other answer." Then Aunt Emmeline expressed the magnitude of her indignation simply by silence, and Lucy was left to think of her lover in solitude.

" And how have you fared on your day's journey ?" said the Colonel, when Hamel found him still seated on the platform with a book in his hand.

" Much better than I thought. Sir Thomas gave me luncheon."

-And the young lady ?"

" The young lady was gracious also; but I am afraid that 1 cannot carry my praises of the family at Glenbogie any further. The three Tringle ladies looked at me as I was sitting at table as though I certainly had no business in their august society."

VOL. I.

CHAPTER XX.

STUBBS UPON MATRIMONY.

Before that evening was over, —or in the course of the* night, it might be better said, as the two men sat up late* with their pipes,—Hamel told his friend the Colonel exactly what had taken place that morning over at Glen-bogio. " You went for the purpose, of course ?" asked the ColoneL

"For an off chance?"

" I know that well enough. I never heard of a man's walking twelve miles to call upon a yoimg lady merely because he knew her father; and when there was to be a second call within a few weeks, the first having not been taken in very good part by the young lady's friends, my inquiring mind told mo that there was something more than old family friendship."

" Your inquiring mind saw into the truth.'^'

" And now looks forward to further events. Can she bake and can she brew ?"

" I do not d^ubt that she could if she tried."

" And can she wash a shirt for a man ? Don^t suppose, my dear fellow, that I intend to say that your wife will have to wash yours. Washing a shirt, as read in thc'

poem from which I am quoting, is presumed to be simply emblematic of household duties in general."

" I take all you say in good part,—as coming from a friend."

" I regard matrimony," said the Colonel, " as being altogether the happiest state of life for a man,—unless- to be engaged to some lovely creature, in whom one can have perfect confidence, may be a thought happier. One can enjoy all the ecstatic mental reflection, all the delights of conceit which come from being loved, that feeling of superiority to all the world around which illumines the bosom of the favoured lover, without having to put one's hand into one's pocket, or having one's pipe put out either morally or physically. The next to this is matrimony itself, which is the only remedy for that consciousness of disreputable debauchery, a savour of which always clings, more or less strongly, to unmarried men in our rank of life. The chimes must be heard at midnight, let a young man be ever so well given to the proprieties, and he must have just a touch of the swingebuckler about him, or he will seem to himself to be deficient in virility. There is no getting out of it until a man marry. But then "

^'WeU; then?"

'^ Do you know the man whose long-preserved hat is always brushed carefully, whose coat is the pattern of neatness, but still a little threadbare when you look at it, —in the colour of whose cheek there is still some touch of juvenility, but whose step is ever heavy and whose brow is always sad ? The seriousness of life has pressed the smiles

r2

out of him. He has learned hardly to want anything for himself but outward decency and the common necessaries of life. Such little personal indulgences as are common to you and to me are as strange to him as ortolans or diamonds."

I do not think I do know him."

" I do ;—well. I have seen him in the regiment, I have met him on the steps of a public office, I have watched him as he entered his parsonage house. You shall find him coming out of a lawyer's office, where he has sat for the last nine hours, having supported nature with two penny biscuits. He has always those few thin hairs over his forehead, he has always that well-brushed hat, he has always that load of care on his brow. He is generally thinking whether he shall endeavour to extend his credit with the butcher, or resolve that the supply of meat may be again curtailed without injury to the health of his five daughters."

" That is an ugly picture."

" But is it true ?"

" In some cases, of course, it is

"And yet not ugly all round," said the meditative Colonel, who had just replenished his pipe. " There are^ on the other side, the five daughters, and the partner of this load of cares. He knows it is well to have the five daughters, rather than to live with plenty of beef and mutton,—even with the ortolans if you will,—and with na one to care whether his body may be racked in this world or his spirit in the next. I do not say whether the balance

of good or evil be on one side or the other; but when a man is going to do a thing he should J:now what it is he is going to do."

" The reading of all this said Hamel, " is, that if I succeed in marrying Miss Dormer I must have thin locks, and a bad hat, and a butcher's bill."

" Other men do."

" Some, instead, have balances at their bankers, and die worth thirty, forty, or fifty thousand pounds, to the great consolation of the five daughters."

" Or a hundred thousand pounds ! There is, of course, no end to the amount of thousands which a successful professional man may accumulate. You may be the man ; but the question is, whether you should not have reasonable ground to suppose yourself the man, before you encumber yourself with the five daughters."

" It seems to me," said Hamel, " that the need of such assurance is cowardly."

" That is just the question which I am alw^ays debating with myself. I also want to rid myself of that swinge-buckler flavour. I feel that for me, like Adam, it is not Sfood that I should be alone. I would fain ask the first girl, that I could love well enough to wish to make myself one with her, to be my wife, regardless of hats, butchers, and daughters. It is a plucky and a fine thing for a man to feel that he can make his back broad enough for all burdens. But yet what is the good of thinking that you can carry a sack of wheat when you are sure that you have not, in truth, strength to raise it from the ground ?"

'^ Strength will come," said Hamel.

" Yes, and the bad hat. And, worse than the bad hat, the soiled gown; iand perhaps with the soiled gown the altered heart;—and perhaps with the altered heart an absence of all that tenderness which it is a woman*s special right to expect from a man."

" I should have thought you would have been the last to be so self-diffident."

To be so thoughtful, you mean," said the Colonel. I am unattached now, and having had no special duty for the last three months I have given myself over to thinking in a nasty morbid manner. It comes, I daresay, partly from tobacco. But there is comfort in this,—that no such reflections falling out of one man's mouth ever had the slightest effect in influencing another man's conduct."

Hamel had told his friend with great triumph of his engagement with Lucy Dormer, but the friend did not return the confidence by informing the sculptor that during the whole of this conversation, and for many days previous to it, his mind had been concerned with the image of Lucy's sister. He was aware that Ayala had been, as it were, turned out from her rich uncle's house, and given over to the comparative poverty of Kingsbury Crescent. He himself, at the present moment, was possessed of what might be considered a comfortable income for a bachelor. He had been accustomed to live almost more than comfortably; but, having so lived, was aware of himself that he had not adapted himself for straitened circumstances. In spite of that advice of his as to the brewing, baking, and washing

capabilities of a female candidate for marriage, he knew himself well enough to be aware that a wife red with a face from a kitchen fire would be distasteful to him. » He had often told himself that to look for a woman with money-would be still more distasteful. Therefore he had thought that for the present, at least, it would be well for him to remain as he was. But now he had come across Ayala, and though in the pursuance of his philosophy he had assured himself that Ayala should be nothing to him, still he found himself so often reverting to this resolution that Ayala, instead of being nothing, was very much indeed to him.

Three days afber this Hamel was preparing himself for his departure immediately after breakfast. ^* What a beast you are to go," said the Colonel, " when there can be no possible reason for your going."

" The five daughters and the bad hat make it necessary that a fellow should do a little work sometimes."

" Why can't you make your images down here ?"

" With you for a model, and mud out of the Caller for clay."

"I shouldn't have the slightest objection. In your art you cannot perpetuate the atrocity of my colour, as the fellow did who painted my portrait last winter. If you will go, go, and make busts at unheard-of prices, so that the ^ve daughters may live for ever on the fat of the land. Can I do any good for you by going over to Glenbogie ?"

" If you could snub that Mr. Traffick, who is of all men the most atrocious."

" The power doesn't exist," said the Colonel, '^ which could snub the Honourable Septimus. That man is possessed of a strength which I thoroughly envy,—which is perhaps more enviable than any other gift the gods can give. Words cannot penetrate that skin of his. Satire flows off him like water from a duck. Ridicule does not touch him. The fellest abuse does not succeed in inflicting the slightest wound. He has learnt the great secret that a man cannot be cut who will not be cut. As it is worth no man's while to protract an enmity with such a one as he, he suffers from no prolonged enmities. He walks unassailable by any darts, and is, I should say, the happiest man in London."

" Then I fear you can do nothing for me at Glenbogie. To mollify Aunt Emmeline would, I fear, be beyond your power. Sir Thomas, as far as I can see, does not require much mollifying."

^' Sir Thomas might give the young woman a thousand or two."

" That is not the way in which I desire to keep a good hat on my head," said Hamel, as he seated himself in the little carriage which was to take him down to Callerfoot.

The Colonel remained at Drumcaller till the end of September, when his presence was required at Aldershot,— during which time he shot a good deal, in obedience to the good-natured behests of Lord Glentower, and in spite of the up-turned nose of Mr. Traflick. He read much, and smoked much,—so that as to the passing of his time there was not need to pity him, and he consumed a portion of

his spare hours in a correspondence with his aunt, the Marchesa, and with his cousin Nina. One of his letters from each shall be given,—and also one of the letters written to each in reply.

Nina to her cousin the Colonel.

My DEA.R Jonathan,

Lady Albury says that you ought to be here, and so you ought. It is ever so nice. There is a Mr. Ponsonby here, and he and I can beat any other couple at lawn tennis. There is an awning over the ground, which is such a lounge. Playing lawn tennis with a parasol as those Melcombe girls did is stupid. They were here, but hae gone. One I am quite sure was over head and ears in love with Mr. Ponsonby. These sort of things are always all on one side, you know. He isn't very much of a man, but he does play lawn tennis divinely. Take it altogether, I don't think there is anything out to beat lawn tennis. I don't know about hunting,—and I don't suppose I ever shall.

We tried to have Ayala here, but I fear it will not come off. Lady Albury was good-natured, but at last she did not quite like writing to Mrs. Dosett. So mamma wrote, but the lady's answer was very stiff. She thought it better for Ayala to remain among her own friends. Poor Ayala! It is clear that a knight will be wanted to go in armour, and get her out of prison. I will leave it to you to say who must be the knight.

" I hope you will come for a day or two before you go

to Aldershot. We stay till the 1st of October. You will be a beast if you don't. Lady Albury says she never means to ask you again. ' Oh, Stubbs !' said Sir Harry ; ' Stubbs is one of those fellows who never come if they're asked.' Of course we all sat upon him. Then he declared that you were the dearest friend he had in the world, but that he never dared to dream that you would ever come to Stalham again. Perhaps if we can hit it off at last with Ayala, then you would come. Mamma means to try again.—Your affectionate cousin, " Nina."

The Marchesa Baldoni to her nephew. Colonel Stubbs.

" My dear Jonathan,

" I did my best for my protege, but I am afraid it will not succeed. Her aunt Mrs. Dosett seems to think that, as Ayala is fated to live with her, Ayala had better take her fate as she finds it. The meaning of that is, that if a girl is doomed to have a dull life she had better not begin it with a little pleasure. There is a good deal to be said for the argument, but if I werp the girl I should like to begin with the pleasure and take my chance for the reaction. I should perhaps be vain enough to think that during the preliminary course I might solve all the difficulty by my beaux yeux. I saw Mrs. Dosett once, and now I have had a letter from her. Upon the whole, I am inclined to pity poor Ayala.

We are very happy here. The Marchese has gone to Como to look after some property he has there. Do not

be ill-natured enough to say that the two things go together;—but in truth he is never comfortable out of Italy. He had a slice of red meat put before him the other day, and that decided him to start at once.

" On the first of October we go back to London, and shall remain till the end of November. They have asked Nina to come again in November in order that she may see a hunt. I know that means that she will try to jump over something, and have her leg broken. You must be here and not allow it. If she does come here I shall perhaps go down to Brighton for a fortnight.

" Yes;—I do think Ayala Dormer is a very pretty girl, and I do think, also, that she is clever. I quite agree that she is ladylike. But I do not therefore think that she is just such a girl as such a man as Colonel Jonathan Stubbs ought to marry. She is one of those human beings who seem to have been removed out of this world and brought up in another. Though she knows ever so much that nobody else knows, she is ignorant of ever so much that everybody ought to know. Wandering through a grove, or seated by a brook, or shivering with you on the top of a mountain, she would be charming. I doubt whether she "would be equally good at the top of your table, or looking after your children, or keeping the week's accounts. She would tease you with poetry, and not even pretend to be instructed when you told her how an army ought to be moved. I say nothing as to the fact that she hasn't got a penny, though you are just in that position which makes it necessary for a man to get some money with his wife. I

therefore am altogether indisposed to any matrimonial outlook in that direction.—Your aifectionate aunt,

Beatrice Baldoni."

Colonel Stubbs to his cousin Nina.

" Dear Nina,

" Lady Albury is wrong ; I ought not to be at Stalham. What should I do at Stalham at this time of year, who never shoot partridges, and what would be the use of attempting lawn tennis when I know I should be cut out by Mr. Ponsonby ? If that day in November is to come off then I'll come and coach you across the country. You tell Sir Harry that I say so, and that I will bring three horses for one week. I think it very hard about poor Ayala Dormer, but what can any knight do in such a case ? When a young lady is handed over to the custody of an uncle or an aunt, she becomes that uncle's and aunt's individual property. Mrs. Dosett may be the most noxious dragon that ever was created for the mortification and general misery of an imprisoned damsel, but still she is omnipotent. The only knight who can be of any service is one who will go with a ring in his hand, and absolutely carry the prisoner away by force of the marriage service. Your unfortunate cousin is so exclusively devoted to the duty of fighting his country's battles that he has not even time to think of a step so momentous as that.

" Poor Ayala ! Do not be stupid enough to accuse me of pitying her because I cannot be the knight to release

her; but I cannot but think how happy she would be at Stalham, struggling to beat you and Mr. Ponsonby at lawn tennis, and then risking a cropper when the happy days of November should come round.—Your loving cousin,

"J. S."

Colonel Stubbs to the Marchesa Baldoni.

" My dear Aunt,

" Your letter is worthy of the Queen of Sheba, if, as was no doubt the case, she corresponded with King Solomon. As for Ayala's fate, if it be her fate to live with Mrs. Dosett, she can only submit to it. You cannot carry her over to Italy, nor would the Marcheso allow her to divide his Italian good things with Nina. Poor little bird I She had her chance of living amidst diamonds and banknotes, with the Tringle millionaires, but threw it away after some fashion that I do not understand. No doubt she was a fool, but I cannot but like her the better for it. I hardly think that a fortnight at Stalham, with all Sir Harry's luxuries around her, would do her much service.

" As for myself and the top of my table, and the future companion who is to be doomed to listen to my military lucubrations, I am altogether inclined to agree with you, seeing that you write in a pure spirit of worldly good sense. No doubt the Queen of Sheba gave advice of the same sort to King Solomon. I never knew a woman to speak confidentially of matrimony otherwise than as a matter of pounds, shillings, and pence. In counsels so given, no word of love has ever been known to creep in. Why should

it, seeing that love cannot put a leg of mutton into the pot ? Don't imagine that I say this in a spirit either of censure or satire. Your ideas are my own, and should I ever marry I shall dp so in strict accordance with your tenets, thinking altogether of the weekly accounts, and determined to eschew any sitting by the sides of brooks.

" I have told Nina about my plans. I will be at Stal-ham in November to see that she does not break her neck.—Yours always, J. S."

255

CHAPTEH XXL ayala's indignation*

pElifiAPS Mrs. Dosett had some just cause for refusing her sanction for the proposed visit to Albury. If Fate did require that Ayala should live permanently in Kingsbury Crescent, the gaiety of a very gay house, and the wealth of a very wealthy house, would hardly be good preparation for such a life. Up to the time of her going to the Marchesa in Brook Street, Ayala had certainly done her best to suit herself to her aunt's manners,—though she had done it with pain and suffering* She had hemmed the towels and mended the sheets, and had made the rounds to the shops. She had endeavoured to attend to the pounds of meat and to sympathise with her aunt in the interest taken in the relics of the joints as they escaped from the hungry treatment of the two maidens in the kitchen. Ayala had been clever enough to understand that her aunt had been wounded by Lucy's indifference, not so much because she had desired to avail herself of Lucy's labours as from a feeling that that indifference had seemed to declare that her own pursuits were mean and vulgar. Understanding this she had

struggled to make those pursuits her own,—and had in part succeeded. Her aunt could talk to her about the butter and the washing, matters as to which her lips had been closed in any conversation with Lucy. That Ayala was struggling Mrs. Dosett had been aware;—but she had thought that such struggles were good and had not been hopeless. Then came the visit to Brook Street, and Ayala returned quite an altered young woman. It seemed as though she neither could nor would struggle any longer. *' I hate mutton-bones," she said to her aunt one morning soon after her return.

" No doubt wa would all like meat joints the best," said her aunt, frowning.

" I hate joints too,"

" You have, I dare say, been cockered up at the Mar-chesa's with made dishes."

" I hate dishes," said Ayala, petulantly.

" You don't hate eating?"

" Yes, I do. It is ignoble. Nature should have managed it differently. We ought to have sucked it in from the atmosphere through our fingers and hairs, as the trees do by their leaves. There should have been no butchers, and no grease, and no nasty smells from the kitchen,—and no gin."

This was worse than all,—this allusion to the mild but unfashionable stimulant to which Mr. Dosett had been reduced by his good nature. " You are flying in the face of the Creator, Miss," said Aunt Margaret, in her most angry voice,—" in the face of the Creator who made every-

thing, and ordained what his creatures should eat and drink by His infinite wisdom."

" Nevertheless," said Ayala, " I think we might have done without boiled mutton." Then she turned to some articles of domestic needlework which were in her lap so as to show that in spite of the wickedness of her opinions she did not mean to be idle. But Mrs. Dosett, in her wrath, snatched the work from her niece's hands and carried it out of the room, thus declaring that not even a pillow-case in her house should owe a stitch to the hands of a girl so ungrateful and so blasphemous.

The wrath wore off soon. Ayala, though not contrite was meek, and walked home with her aunt on the following morning, patiently carrying a pound of butter, six eggs, and a small lump of bacon in a basket. After that the pillow-case was recommitted to her. But there still was left evidence enough that the girl's mind had been upset by the luxuries of Brook Street,—evidence to which Aunt Margaret paid very much attention, insisting upon it in her colloquies with her husband. " I think that a little amusement is good for young people," said Uncle Reginald, weakly.

" And for old people too. No doubt about it, if they can get it so as not to do them any harm at the same time. Nothing can be good for a young woman which unfits her for that state of life to which it has pleased God to call her, Ayala has to live with us. No doubt there was a struggle when she first came from your sister, Lady Tringle, but she made it gallantly, and I gave her great credit She

VOL. I. s

was just falling into a quiet mode of life when there came this invitation from the Marchesa Baldoni. Now she has come back quite an altered person, and the struggle has to be made all over again/' Uncle Reginald again expressed his opinion that young people ought to have a little amusement, but he was not strong enough to insist very much upon his theory. It certainly^ however, was true that Ayala, though she still struggled, had been very much disturbed by the visit.

Then came the invitation to Stalham. There was a very pretty note from Lady Albury to Ayala herself, saying how much pleasure she would have in seeing Mis» Dormer at her house, where Ayala's old friends the Marchesa and Nina were then staying. This was accompanied by a long letter from Nina herself, in which all the charms-of Stalham, including Mr. Ponsonby and lawn tennis, were set forth at full length. Ayala had already heard much about Stalham and the Alburys from her friend Nina, wha had hinted in a whisper that such an invitation as this might perhaps be forthcoming. She was ready enough for the visit, having loo-ked through her wardrobe, and resolved that things which had been good enough for Brook Street would still be good enough for Stalham. But the same post had brought a letter for Mrs. Dasett, and Ayala could see, that, as the letter was read, a frown can>e upon her aunt's brow, and that the lock on her aunt's face was-decidedly averse to Stalham. This took place soon after breakfast, when Uncle Reginald had just started for his office, and neither of th«m for awhile said a word to the

other of the letter that had been received. It was not till after lunch that Ayala spoke. " Aunt," she said, " you have had a letter from Lady Albury ?"

" Yes," said Mrs. Dosett, grimly, I have had a letter from Lady Albury."

Then there was another silence, till Ayala, whose mind was full of promised delights, could not refrain herself longer. " Aunt Margaret," she said, ^* I hope you mean to let me go." For a minute or two there was no reply, and Ayala again pressed her question. " Lady Albury wants me to go to Stalham."

" She has written to me to say that she would receive you."

"And I may go?"

" I am strongly of opinion that you had better not," said Mrs. Dosett, confirming her decree by a nod which might have suited Jupiter.

'^ Oh, Aunt Margaret, why not ?"

^' I think it would be most prudent to decline."

" But why,—why,—why. Aunt Margaret ?"

" There must be expense."

" I have money enough for the journey left of my own from what Uncle Tom gave me," said Ayala, pleading her cause with all her eloquence*

" It is not only the money. There are other reasons,— very strong reasons."

" What reasons. Aunt Margaret?"

" My dear, it is your lot to have to live with us, and not with such people as the Marchesa Baldoniand Lady Albury."

s2

" I am sure I do not complain."

" But you would complain after having for a time been used to the luxuries of Albury Park. I do not say that as finding fault, Ayala. It is human nature that it should be so."

*' But I won't complain. Have I ever complained ?"

" Yes, my dear. You told me the other day that you did not like bonea of mutton, and you were disgusted because things were greasy. I do not say this by way of f^colding you, Ayala, but only that you may understand what must be the effect of your going from such a house as this to such a house as Stalham, and then returning back from Stalham to such a house as this. You had better be contented with your position."

" I am contented with my position," sobbed Ayala.

"And allow me to write to Lady Albury refusing the invitation."

But Ayala «ould not be brought to look at the matter with her aunt's eyes. When her aunt pressed her for an answer which should convey her consent she would give none, and at last left the room bitterly sobbing. Turning the matter over in her own bosom upstairs she determined to be mutinous. No doubt she owed a certain amount of obedience to her aunt; but had she not been obedient, had she not worked hard and lugged about that basket of provisions, and endeavoured to take an interest in all her aunt's concerns ? Was she so absolutely the property of her aunt that she was bound to do everything her aunt; desired to the utter annihilation of all her hopes, to the

extermination of her promised joys ? She felt that she had succeeded in Brook Street. She had met no Angel of Light, but she was associated with people whom she had liked, and had been talked to by those to whom it had been a pleasure to listen. That colonel with the quaint name and the ugly face was still present to her memory as he had leaned over her shoulder at the theatre, making her now laugh by his drollery, and now filling her mind with interest by his description of the scenes which she was seeing. She was sure that all this, or something of the same nature, would be renewed for her delight at Stalham. And was she to be robbed of this,— the only pleasure which seemed to remain to her in this world,—merely because her aunt chose to entertain severe notions as to duty and pleasure ? Other girls went out when they were asked. At Rome, when that question of the dance at the Mar-chesa's had been discussed, she had had her own way in opposition to her Aunt Emmeline and her cousin Augusta. No doubt she had, in consequence partly of her conduct on that occasion, been turned out of her Uncle Tom's house ; but of that she did not think at the present moment. She would be mutinous, and would appeal to her Uncle Reginald for assistance.

But the letter which contained the real invitation had been addressed to her aunt, and her aunt could in truth answer it as she pleased. The answer might at this moment be in the act of being written, and should it be averse Ayala knew very well that she could not go in opposition to it. And yet her aunt came to her in the after-

noon consulting her again, quite unconquered as to her own opinion, but still evidently unwilling to write the fatal letter without Ayala's permission. Then Ayala assured herself that she had rights of her own, which her aunt did not care to contravene. " I think I ought to be allowed to go," she said, when her aunt came to her during the afternoon.

" When I think it will be bad for you ?"

'^ It won't be bad. They are very good people. I think that I ought to be allowed to go."

" Have you no reliance on those who are your natural guardians ?"

' Uncle Reginald is my natural guardian,' said Ayala, through her tears.

^' Very well I If you refuse to be guided by me as though I were not your aunt, and as you will pay no attention to what I tell you is proper for you and best, the question must be left till your uncle comes home. I cannot but be very much hurt that you should think so little of me. I have always endeavoured to do the best I could for you, just as though I were your mother."

" I think that I ought to be allowed to go," repeated Ayala.

As the first consequence of this, the replies to all the three letters were delayed for the next day's post. Ayala had considered much with what pretty words she might best answer Lady Albury's kind note, and she had settled upon a form of words which she had felt to be very pretty. Unless her uncle would support her, that would be of no

avail, and another form must be chosen. To Nina she would tell the whole truth, either how full of joy she was, —or else how cruelly used and how thoroughly brokenhearted. But she could not think that her uncle would be unkind to her. Her uncle had been uniformly gentle. Her uncle, when he should know how much her heart was set upon it, would surely let her go.

The poor girl, when she tacitly agreed that her uncle should be the arbiter in the matter, thus pledging herself to abide by her uncle's decision, let it be what it might, did not think what great advantage her aunt would have over her in that discussion which would be held upstairs while the master of the house was washing his hands before dinner. Nor did she know of how much stronger will was her Aunt Margaret than her Uncle Keginald, While he was washing his hands and putting on his slippers, the matter was settled in a manner quite destructive of poor Ayala's hopes. *^ I won't have it," said Mrs. Dosett, in reply to the old argument that young people ought to have some amusement. ** If I am to be responsible for the girl I must be allowed my own way with her. It is trouble enough, and veiy little thanks I get for it. Of course she hates mo. Nevertheless, I can endeavour to do my duty, and I will. It is not thanks, nor love, nor even gratitude, that I look for. I am bound to do the best I can by her because she is your niece, and because she has no other real friends. I knew what would come of it when she went to that house in Brook Street. I was soft then and gave way. The girl has moped about like a miserable

creature ever since. If I am not to have my way now I will have done with her altogether." Having heard this very powerful speech, Uncle Reginald was obliged to give way, and it was settled that after dinner he should convey to Ayala the decision to which they had come.

Ayala, as she sat at the dinner-table, was all expectation, but she asked no question. She asked no question after dinner, while her uncle slowly, solemnly, and sadly sipped his one beaker of cold gin-and-water. He sipped it very slowly, no doubt because he was anxious to postpone the evil moment in which he must communicate her fate to his niece. But at last the melancholy glass was drained, and then, according to the custom of the family, Mrs. Dosett led the way up into the drawing-room, followed by Ayala and her husband. He, when he was on the stairs, and when the eyes of his wife were not upon him, tremulously put out his hand and laid it on Ayala's shoulder, as though to embrace her. The poor girl knew well that mark of affection. There would have been no need for such embracing had the offered joys of Stalham been in store for her. The tears were already in her eyes when she §eated herself in the drawing-room, as far removed as possible from the arm-chair which was occupied by her aunt.

Then her uncle pronounced his judgment in a vacillating voice,—with a vacillation which was ineffectual of any good to Ayala. ^'Ayala," he said, "your aunt and I have been talking over this invitation to Stalham, and we are of opinion, my dear, that you .had better not accept it."

" Why not, Uncle Reginald ?"

" There would be expense."

" I can pay for my own ticket."

^* There would be many expenses, which I need not explain to you more fully. The truth is, my dear, that poor people cannot afiPord to live with rich people, and had better not attempt it."

" I don't want to live with them."

" Visiting them is living with them for a time. I am sorry, Ayala, that we are not able to put you in a position in which you might enjoy more of the pleasures incidental to your age; but you must take the things as they are. Looking at the matter all round, I am sure that your aunt is right in advising that you should stay at home."

" It isn't advice at all," said Ayala.

Ayala I" exclaimed her aunt, in a tone of indignation.

" It isn't advice," repeated Ayala. " Of course, if you won't let me go, I can't."

You are a very wicked girl," said Mrs. Dosett, " to speak to your uncle like that, after all that he has done for you."

Not wicked," said the uncle.

" I say, wicked. But it doesn't matter. I shall at once write to Lady Albury, as you desire, and of course there will be no further question as to her going." Soon after that Mrs. Dosett sat down to her desk, and wrote that letter to which the Marchesa had alluded in hers to her nephew. No doubt it was stern and hard, and of a nature to make such a woman as the Marchesa feel that Mrs.

Dosett would not be a pleasant companion for a girl like Ayala. But it was written with a full conviction that duty-required it; and the words, though hard and stiff, had been chosen with the purpose of showing that the doing of this disagreeable duty had been felt to be imperative.

When the matter had been thus decided, Ayala soon retreated to her own room. Her very soul was burning with indignation at the tyranny to which she thought herself subjected. The use of that weak word, advice, had angered her more than anything. It had not been advice. It had not been given as advice. A command had been laid upon her, a most cruel and unjust command, which she was forced to obey, because she lacked the power of escaping from her condition of slavery. Advice, indeed ! Advice is a thing with which the advised one may or may not comply, as that advised one may choose. A slave must obey an order ! Her own papa and her own mamma had always advised her, and the advice had always been followed, even when read only in the glance of an eye, in a smile, or a nod. Then she had known what it was to be advised. Now she was ordered,—as slaves are ordered; and there was no escape from her slavery!

She, too, must write her letter, but there was no need now of that pretty studied phrase, in which she had hoped to thank Lady Albury fitly for her great kindness. She found, after a vain attempt or two, that it was hopeless to endeavour to write to Lady Albury. The words would not come to her pen. But she did write to Nina;—

"Dear, dearest Nina,

" They won't let me go! Oh, my darling, I am so miserable ! Why should they not let me go, when people are so kind, so very kind, as Lady Albury and your dear mamma ? I feel as though I should like to run from the house, and never come back, even though I had to die in the streets. I was so happy when I got your letter and Lady Albury's, and now I am so wretched! I cannot write to Lady Albury. You must just tell her, with many thanks from me, that they will not let me go !

" Your unhappy but affectionate friend,

" Ayala."

CHAPTER XXII.

ayala's gratitude.

There was much pity felt for Ayala among the folk at Stalham. The sympathies of them all should have been with Mrs. Dosett. They ought to have felt that the poor aunt was simply performing an unpleasant duty, and that the girl was impracticable if not disobedient. But Ayala was known to be very pretty, and Mrs. Dosett was supposed to be plain. Ayala was interesting, while Mrs. Dosett, from the nature of her circumstances, was most uninteresting. It was agreed on all sides, at Stalham, that so pretty a bird as Ayala should not be imprisoned for ever in so ugly a cage. Such a bird ought, at least, to be allowed its chance of captivating some fitting mate by its song and its plumage. That was Lady Albury's argument,—a woman very good-natured, a little given to match-making, a great friend to pretty girls,—and whose eldest son was as yet only nine, so that there could be no danger to herself or her own flock. There was much ridicule thrown on Mrs. Dosett at Stalham, and many pretty things said of the bird who was so unworthily imprisoned in Kingsbury Crescent. At last there was something like u conspiracy, the purport of which was to get the bird out of its cage in November.

In this conspiracy it can hardly be said that the Mar-

chesa took an active part. Much as she liked Ayala, she was less prone than Lady Albury to think that the girl was ill-used. She was more keenly alive than her cousin,—or rather her cousin's wife,—to the hard necessities of the world. Ayala must be said to have made her own bed. At any rate there was the bed and she must lie on it* It was not the Dosetts' fatdt that they were poor. According to their means they were doing the best they could for their niece, and were entitled to praise rather than abuse. And then the Marchesa was afraid for her nephew. Colonel Stubbs, in his letter to her, had declared that he quite agreed with her views as to matrimony; but she was quite alive to her nephew's sarcasm. Her nephew, though he might in truth agree with her, nevertheless was sarcastic. Though he was sarcastic, still he might be made to accede to her views, because he did, in truth, agree with her* She was eminently an intelligent woman, seeing far into character, and she knew pretty well the real condition of her nephew's mind, and could foresee his conduct. He would marry before long, and might not improbably marry a girl with some money if one could be made to come in his way, who would at the same time suit his somewhat fastidious taste. But Ayala suited his taste, Ayala who had not a shilling, and the Marchesa thought it only too likely that if Ayala were released from her cage, and brought to Albury, Ayala might become Mrs. Jonathan Stubbs. That Ayala should refuse to become Mrs. Jonathan Stubbs did not present itself as a possibility to the Marchesa.

So the matters were when the Marchesa and Nina returned from Stalham to London, a promise having been given that Nina should go back to Stalham in November, and be allowed to see the glories of a hunt» She was not to ride to hounds. That was a matter of course, but she was to be permitted to see what a pack of hounds was like, and of what like were the men in their scarlet coats, and how the huntsman's horn would sound when it should be heard among the woods and fields* It was already decided that the Colonel should be there to meet her, and the conspiracy was formed with the object of getting Ayala out of her cage at the same time. Stalham was a handsome country seat, in the county of Rufford, and Sir Harry Albury had lately taken upon himself the duties of Master of the Rufford and Ufford United Pack. Colonel Stubbs was to be there with his horses in November, but had, in the meantime, been seen by Lady Albury, and had been instigated to do something for the release of Ayala. But what could he do ? It was at first suggested that he should call at Kingsbury Crescent, and endeavour to mollify the stony heart of Aunt Dosett. But, as he had said himself, he would be the w^orst person in the world to perform such an embassy. " I am not an Adonis, I know," he said, " nor do I look like a Lothario, but still I am in some sort a young man, and therefore certain to be regarded as pernicious, as dangerous and damnable, by such a dragon of virtue as Aunt Dosett. I don't see how I could expect to have a chance." This interview took place in London during the latter end of October, and it was at last decided

that the mission should be made by Lady Albury herself, and made, not to Mrs. Dosett, at Kingsbury Crescent, but to Mr» Dosett at his office in Somerset House. *^I don't think I could stand Mrs. D.," said Lady Albury.

Lady Albury was a handsome fashionable woman, rather tall, always excellently dressed, and possessed of a personal assurance which nothing could daunt. She had the reputation of an affectionate wife and a good mother, but was nevertheless declared by some of her friends to be "a little fast." She certainly was fond of comedy,—those who did not like her were apt to say that her comedy was only fun, —and was much disposed to have her own way when she could get it. She was now bent upon liberating Ayala from her cage, and for this purpose had herself driven into the huge court belonging to Somerset House.

Mr. Dosett was dignified at his office with the use of a room to himself, a small room looking out upon the river, in which he spent six hours on six days of the week in arranging the indexes of a voluminous library of manuscript letter-books. It was rarely indeed that he was disturbed by the presence of any visitor. When, therefore, his door was opened by one of the messengers, and he was informed that Lady Albury desired to see him, he was for the moment a good deal disturbed. No option, however, was given to him as to refusing admission to Lady

Albury. She was in the room before the messenger had completed his announcement, and had seated herself in one of the two spare chairs which the room afforded as soon as the door was closed. " Mr. Dosett," she said, " I

have taken the great liberty of calling to say a few words about your niece, Miss Ayala Dormer."

When the lady was first announced, Mr. Dosett, in his confusion, had failed to connect the name which he had heard with that of the lady who had invited Ayala to her house. But now he recognised it, and knew who it was that had come to him. ** You were kind enough,*' he said, "to invite my little girl to your house some weeks

" And now I have come to invite her again."

Mr. Dosett was now more disturbed than ever. With what words was he to refuse the request which this kind but very grand lady was about to make ? How could he explain to her all those details as to his own poverty, and as to Ayala's fate in having to share that poverty with him ? How could he explain the unfitness of Ayala's temporary sojourn with people so wealthy and luxurious? And yet were he to yield in the least how could he face his wife on his return home to the Crescent ? " You are very kind. Lady Albury," he said.

" We particularly wish to have her about the end of the first week in November," said the lady. " Her friend Nina Baldoni will be there, and one or two others whom she knows. We shall try to be a little gay for a week or two."

" I have no doubt it would be gay, and we at home are very dull."

" Do you not think a little gaiety good for young people?" said her ladyship, using the very argument

which poor Mr. Dosett had so often attempted to employ on Ayala's behalf.

" Yes; a little gaiety," he said, as though deprecating the excessive amount of hilarity which he imagined to prevail at Stalham.

"Of course you do," said Lady Albury. " Poor little girl I I have heard so much about her, and of all your goodness to her. Mrs. Dosett I know is another mother to her; but still a little country air could not but be beneficial. Do say that she shall come to us, Mr. Dosett."

Then Mr. Dosett felt that, disagreeable as it was, he must preach the sermon which his wife had preached to him, and he did preach it. He spoke timidly of his own poverty, and the need which there was that Ayala should share it. He spoke a word of the danger which might come from luxury, and of the discontent which would be felt when the girl returned to her own home. Something he added of the propriety of like living with like, and ended by praying that Ayala might be excused. The words came from bim with none of that energy which his wife would have used,—were uttered in a low melancholy drone; but still they were words hard to answer, and called upon Lady Albury for all her ingenuity in finding an argument against them.

But Lady Albury was strong-minded, and did find an argument. " You musn't be angry with me," she said, " if I don't quite agree with you. Of course you wish to do. the best you can for this dear child."

" Indeed I do, Lady Albury."

VOL. I. T

" How is anything then to be done for her if she remains shut up in your house ? You do not, if I understand, see much company yourselves."

" None at all."

" You won't be angry with me for my impertinence in alluding to it."

'* Not in the least. It is the fact that we live altogether to ourselves."

" And the happiest kind of life too for married people," said Lady Albury, who was accustomed to fill her house in the country with a constant succession of visitors, and to have engagements for every night of the week in town. " But for young people it is not quite so good. How is a young lady to get herself settled in life ? "

" Settled?" asked Mr. Dosett, vaguely.

" Married," suggested Lady Albury, more plainly. Mr, Dosett shook his head. No idea on the subject had ever flashed across his mind. To provide bread and meat, a bed and clothes, for his sister's child he had felt to be a duty,—but not a husband. Husbands came, or did not,— as the heavens might be propitious. That Ayala should go to Stalham for the sake of finding a husband was certainly beyond the extent of his providing care. ^^ In fact how is-a girl to have a chance at all unless she is allowed to see some one ? Of course I don't say this with reference to-our house. There will be no young men there, or anything of that kind. But, taking a broad view, unless you let a girl like that have what chances come in her way howls she to get on? I think you have hardly a right to do it,'^

 We have done it for the best."

" I am sure of that, Mr. Dosett. And I hope you will tell Mrs. Dosett, with my compliments, how thoroughly I appreciate her goodness. I should have called upon her instead of coming here, only that I cannot very well get into that part of the town."

" I will tell her what you are good enough to say.*'

"•Poor Ayala! I am afraid that her other aunt. Aunt Tringle, was not as good to her as your wife. I have heard about how all that occurred in Rome. She was very much admired there. I am told that she is perfectly lovely."

" Pretty well."

" A sort of beauty that we hardly ever see now,—and very, very clever."

" Ayala is clever, I think."

" She ought to have her chance. She ought indeed. I don't think you quite do your duty by such a girl as that unless you let her have a chance. She is sure to get to know people, and to be asked from one house to another. I speak plainly, for I really think you ought to let her come."

All this sank deeply into the heart of Uncle Reginald. Whether it was for good or evil it seemed to him at the moment to be unanswerable. If there was a chance of any good thing for Ayala, surely it could not be his duty to bar her from that chance. A whole vista of new views in reference to the treatment of young ladies was opened to him by the words of his visitor. Ayala certainly was pretty. Certainly she was clever. A husband with an

income would certainly be a good thing. Embryo husbands with incomes do occasionally fall in love with pretty girls. But how can any pretty girl be fallen in love with unless some one be permitted to see her ? At Kingsbury Crescent there was not a man to be seen from one end of the year to another. It occurred to him now, for the first time, that Ayala by her present life was shut out from any chance of marriage. It was manifestly true that he had no right to seclude her in that fashion. At last ho made a promise, rashly, as he felt at the very moment of making it, that he would ask his wife to allow Ayala to go to Stalham. Lady Albury of course accepted this as an undertaking that Ayala should come, and went away triumphant.

Mr. Dosett walked home across the parks with a troubled mind, thinking much of all that had passed between him and the lady of fashion. It was with great difficulty that he could quite make up his mind which was right,— the lady of fashion or his wife. If Ayala was to live always as they lived at Kingsbury Crescent, if it should in process of time be her fate to marry some man in the same class as themselves, if continued care as to small pecuniary needs was to be her future lot, then certainly her comfort would only be disturbed by such a visit as that now proposed. And was it not probable that such would be the destiny in store for her ? Mr. Dosett knew the world well enough to be aware that all pretty girls such as Ayala cannot find rich husbands merely by exhibiting their prettiness. Kingsbury Crescent, unalloyed by the dangers

of Stalham, would certainly be the most secure. But then he had been told that Ayala now had special chances offered to her, and that he had no right to rob her of those chances. He felt this the more strongly, because she was not his daughter,—only his niece. With a daughter he and his wife might have used their own judgment without check. But now he had been told that he had no right to rob Ayala of her chances, and he felt that he had not the right. By the time that he reached Kingsbury Crescent he had, with many misgivings, decided in favour of Stal-ham«

It was now some weeks since the first invitation had been refused, and during those weeks life had not been pleasant at the Crescent. Ayala moped and pined as though some great misfortune had fallen upon her. When she had first come to the Crescent she had borne herself bravely, as a man bears a trouble when he is conscious that he has brought it on himself by his own act, and is proud of the act which has done it. But when that excitement has gone, and the trouble still remains, the pride wears off, and the man is simply alive to his suffering. So it had been with Ayala. Then had come the visit to Brook Street. When, soon after that, she was invited to Stalham, it seemed as though a new world was being opened to her. There came a moment when she could again rejoice that she had quarrelled with her Aunt Emmeline. This new world would be a much better world than the Tringle world. Then had come the great blow, and it had seemed to her as though there was

nothing but Kingsbury Crescent before her for the rest of her wretched life.

There was not a detail of all this hidden from the eyes of Aunt Margaret. Stalham had decided that Aunt Margaret was ugly and uninteresting. Stalham, according to its own views, was right. Nevertheless the lady in Kingsbury Crescent had both eyes to see and a heart to feel. She was hot of temper, but she was forgiving. She liked her own way, but she was aflPectionate. She considered it right to teach her niece the unsavoury mysteries of economy, but she was aware that such mysteries must be distasteful to one brought up as Ayala. Even when she had been loudest in denouncing Ayala's mutiny, her heart had melted in ruth because Ayala had been so unhappy. She, too, had questioned herself again and again as to the justness of her decision. Was she entitled to rob Ayala of her chances ? In her frequent discussions with her husband she still persisted in declaring that Kingsbury Crescent was safe, and that Stalham would bo dangerous. But, nevertheless, in her own bosom she had misgivings. As she saw the poor girl mope and weary through one day after another, she could not but have misgivings.

^^ I have had that Lady Albury with me at the office today, and have almost promised that Ayala shall go to her on the 8th of November." It was thus that Mr. Dosett rushed at once into his difficulty as soon as he found himself up-stuirs with his wife.

"You have?"

*' Well, my dear, I almost did. She said a great deal, and I could not but agree with much of it. Ayala ought to have her chances."

" What chances ?" demanded Mrs. Dosett, who did not at all like the expression.

" Well; seeing people. She never sees anybody here."

" Nobody is better than some people," said Mrs. Dosett, meaning to be severe on Lady Albury's probable guests.

" But if a girl sees nobody," said Mr. Dosett, ^' she can have no,—no,—no chances."

" She has the chance of wholesome victuals," said Mrs. Dosett, " and I don't know what other chances you or I can give her."

" She might see—a young man." This Mr. Dosett said very timidly.

" A young fiddlestick I A young man ! Young men should be waited for till they come naturally, and never thought about if they don't come at all. I hate this looking after young men. If there wasn't a young man for the next dozen years we should do better,—so as just to get out of the way of thinking about them for a time." This was Mrs. Dosett's philosophy; but in spite of her philosophy she did yield, and on that night it was decided that Ayala after all was to be allowed to go to Stalham.

To Mr. Dosett was deputed the agreeable task of telling Ayala on the next evening what was to befall her. If any-

thing agreeable was to be done in that sombre house it was always deputed to the master.

" What I" said Ayala, jumping from her chair.

" On the eighth of November," said Mr. Dosett.

"ToStalham?"

" Lady Albury was with me yesterday at the office, and your aunt has consented."

" Oh, Uncle Eeginald !" said Ayala, falling on her knees, and hiding her face on his lap. Heaven bad been once more opened to her.

" I'll never forget it," said Ayala, when she went to thank her aunt, never."

 I only hope it may not do you a mischief"

" And I beg your pardon. Aunt Margaret, because I

was,—I was,—because I was " She could not find

the word which would express her own delinquency, without admitting more than she intended to admit,—"too self-asserting, considering that I am only a young girl." That would have been her meaning could she have found appropriate words.

" We need not go back to that now^," said Aunt Margaret.

END OF VOL. I.

CPSIA information can be obtained
at www.ICGtesting.com
Printed in the USA
LVHW060239241218
601573LV00003B/226/P

9 781542 895682